JACK A. ORI

IMPACTFUL WORDS BOOKS * NEW YORK

Paperback edition: September 15, 2025

This book was previously published as Open Secrets

ISBN: 979-8-9901436-3-0

fyi...

I hope you have fun solving the mystery along with CJ and their friends! But it's not fun if you're a trauma survivor like CJ is and get triggered, so you should be aware that this novel contains references to:

- Kidnapping
- Sexual misconduct
- Abusive relationships (including child abuse)

None of this is graphic. This is a murder mystery, so it will also contain a dead body, and the description of that body might bother some readers.

one

"ELLIE'S MISSING."

The caller's young—I'd reckon no more than ten, eleven at the outset—and speaking so low I can barely hear them. I sit up straighter in my chair at the college podcast studio, suddenly more alert than I've been the whole call-in section of tonight's episode.

"Who now?" My cheeks get hot; if I looked in a mirror, which you'll never catch me doing, I'd be as red as a freshly-picked tomato. My Southern accent already flags me as stupid to too many people up here without me slipping into the way people talk back home. "I mean to say, who's Ellie, sweetheart? And speak up a little so we can all hear you, all right?"

"Sorry. This is Bobby. Ellie's my big sister and she's missing. My daddy didn't want me to call the police so I called you instead."

"Brave boy." I bite my lip, unsure if that's an appropriate way to talk to a child on the air. "Let's begin at the beginning, all right? What makes you think Ellie's missing?"

"She didn't call to say goodnight and she always—"

Static overtakes him, followed by:

"Daddy, no! We have to—"

"I told you not to bother anyone with this nonsense, didn't I?"

"Hello?" I raise my voice.

More static, and then the daddy's voice, deeper and more sure of itself than the boy could ever dream of being, says, "Wrong number, sorry."

The line goes dead.

I take a deep breath as I switch to commercial, knowing there's space for one more caller after the break. I don't have a whole lot of patience for people calling in to tell me they think their neighbor's having an affair and whatnot.

Before tonight, that's all I got. And that's people's idea of a mystery? This nonsense that doesn't do anything positive for anyone? Before I started up this podcast, I'd thought I'd be doing big, important things, but it had become little more than a live version of the gossip page in the paper back home.

Sure enough, the next caller is some lady speaking so low she might as well be dead air while she tells me that she thinks her friend's boyfriend is sleeping with someone else.

I rub the bridge of my nose, feeling a headache coming on. "Ma'am, you'll have to speak up so everyone can hear."

"Sorry," the lady says. She sounds like she's an older woman, but something's off about that, almost like she's a kid playing at something. "I'm just so upset, but after hearing that last call..." My head jerks up and she says, "The girl who's stealing my friend's boyfriend... her name is Ellie too. I hope it's not the same one as the last caller."

"That sure would be a coincidence. What's her full name?"

Footsteps echo in the background, "Sorry, have to go. I hope you look into this." She hangs up.

My throat tightens with anger; I'm pretty sure I've just been pranked.

When my show ends a few minutes later, I have to set up the prerecorded shows that play overnight before I can get to that call log and see what's what. I hurry through my responsibilities so I can check the computer in the production booth.

The second caller's phone says it's registered to an Ellie Armstrong, convincing me even more that it was a prank. I stab at the touchscreen to cycle through to the previous call and check out the little boy's phone. It's registered to a Robert Bishop, Senior.

I stare at the name, willing it to mean something, but it doesn't. I don't know any more about who these people are than I did before, other than inferring that this man must be the daddy who didn't want his phone used for this purpose.

I take a photo of the call log and hurry out into the lobby to meet my friend Ken. Ken's what folks up here call my ride-or-die, I reckon literally since he insists on taking me from the studio to my dorm after my show every other Tuesday even though it's close enough to walk. It's overkill if you ask me, but it comes from a good place, so I'm not about to be ungrateful.

I blink hard, trying to adjust to the brighter lights. When I can focus again, I shiver involuntarily. The navy blue winter coat Ken's bundled himself into makes him even more attractive than usual. The matching hat contrasts with his dark brown skin and the sleeves show off his muscles. It makes me unable to stop wishing for something I can never have, not when Ken's straight and I ain't a woman. He knows the baggy men's sweatshirts I live in don't mean I'm not attracted to men, but he's never asked me what they do mean. And if I told him, that'd be a dealbreaker—wouldn't it?

"Finally!" Ken says. "That took forever tonight, Ceej."

"Sorry. I had to do something." I hug myself. "Where's

Vicki?" Vicki is Ken's baby sister. She's caught between two worlds; she can read above her grade level and schoolwork comes to her without much effort, but she's just as much a kid as any other middle schooler, and small for her age to boot.

"Car," Ken rolls his eyes as he holds the heavy studio door open for me. "She insisted she wasn't going out into the dark and there was nothing I could do to move her."

"Even though they've got streetlights on?"

"You ever met my sister before?" Ken shoves his hands in his pockets. "Look, we only got about 15 seconds without her trying to get in our business. So spill. What happened on your show that's got you looking like you've seen a ghost?"

I look away, my cheeks heating up for the second time this hour. Last thing I want is for Ken to get the idea I'm a coward. I give him the shortest version I can of the call, wrapping up with, "I don't have any idea who this Ellie is, but I got a feeling something's happened that needs looking into."

"If anyone can figure out who and what, it's you." Ken's voice is soft enough that if I didn't know better, I'd think he does like me that way. "Don't know how you're going to pull this one off, though."

"I've already looked at the call-in log. Now I need to—"

I reach into my pocket for my phone, but Ken brushes my wrist with his fingertips, making electricity shoot through me even though I also want to pull away cause I don't like being touched without warning. "Not here," he says. "Too tempting for muggers."

If you ask me, he's paranoid, but what do I know? Where I come from, people don't always lock their doors at night, but it being the kind of place everyone thinks is safe didn't stop what happened to me when I was fourteen. And I'm in a different world, now, one far closer to New York City, and they say there's a lot more crime up here.

"Fine." I shove my phone back into my front pocket.

Ken presses the button to unlock his car doors. "We're back, Vic. Did you survive?" There's no answer. "Vicki?"

I turn toward the back seat too. It's too dark to see much, but one thing's clear: the safety straps are hanging off Vicki's car seat and it's empty.

two

KEN GASPS. "VICKI?" he says again, uncertainly.

"Ken?" Vicki says, her voice shaking. "Is that you?" The sound's coming from behind the passenger seat and now that I'm not trying to calm down about where Vicki's gone, I see a silhouette of a small girl with two exactly even pigtails crouched behind it, holding a paperback book tightly in her hands.

"Course it's me," Ken says. "And CJ. You wanna get up and tell me why you're hiding back there and almost giving me a heart attack?"

"Cause of the man," Vicki says. "He was looking in the window so I had to hide."

Ken's eyes widen and he almost drops his keys, but he says, "I don't know what you're talking about, but get back in your seat before you tell me."

Vicki throws herself in her seat, leaving her copy of *10 Wacky Ways Science Solved Crimes* open facedown on the floor. I pick it up and put it on the seat next to her so she won't lose it.

"I heard his footsteps crunching on the gravel," Vicki says. "It interfered with my concentration." She tugs at one of her pigtails. "I was reading the most interesting story in the whole book, too. Did you know that —"

I put my hand on her shoulder. "Stay focused on what happened, okay? You heard someone running and then what?"

Vicki swallows hard. "I felt like there were two little lasers aimed right at me. So I turned real slow and looked out the window and I saw him standing there breathing heavy like a wolf who wanted to eat me for dinner. So I unbuckled myself fast as could be and slid down behind the seat where he couldn't see me anymore. I didn't even turn my book light on in case he was watching."

Ken rolls his eyes. "Didn't it ever occur to you that he was out jogging and stopped to rest?" He climbs over the console into the driver's seat.

"He was not! He wanted to do something bad to me." Vicki slams the strap into its buckle while a smile spreads slowly across her face. That's Vicki-language for leave her alone or pay the price.

As Ken starts the car, I lower my voice. "I believe you."

Vicki nods. It's too dark to tell, but I'm pretty sure she's got tears in her eyes.

"Any luck?" Ken asks me when we pull up to my dorm. It's only been a five-minute drive, which I have to admit beats the 20 minutes it would have taken me to bike up a bunch of hills.

"With what?" Vicki asks, her eyes sparkling. Her face matches what I think she's feeling this time, her lips slightly parted and her head jutted forward to look over my shoulder.

"With nunya," Ken tells her.

I don't like that, but it ain't my baby sister so there's nothing I can say. I shield the screen with my hand so Vicki can't see it. "The caller's phone was registered to a Robert Bishop, Senior, so I reckon the boy was his son."

"That's my friend Bobby," Vicki says. "It has to be, it would be an awfully big coincidence if there were two Robert Bishop, Juniors running around Cedarwood Middle School."

"Maybe, maybe not. Does your Bobby have a big sister named Ellie?"

"How should I know? We only ever talk on the bus." Vicki's mouth is a thin line, but her voice is soft. She looks away. "So far, anyway."

I can tell she likes him, but I don't want to ask and humiliate her in front of Ken. "Let's see if we can find out, okay?"

I Google: *Ellie Bishop Cedarwood*

Pay dirt. Here's an Instagram page for a graduate student right here at Cedarwood University. According to her bio, she's the youngest-ever team leader in the school's Neuroscientific Research Lab run by someone with the handle @brainchemprofJA.

I'm tempted to click through to see who that is, but I ain't 100% sure I got the right Ellie and don't want to waste time. I move onto examining her profile photo.

She's gorgeous, with long, dark hair that contrasts perfectly with her peach skin, an oval face, and the widest smile I've ever seen. My heart beats in my throat, making it hard to breathe, and I have to remind myself to focus.

In the photo, Ellie's got her arm around a little boy. They look just alike only Bobby's got a crew cut instead of long hair and he's what my mama would call big-boned—he's got short legs and a round face, and more than a little stomach on him. He's smiling, but it feels fake, and there's no light in his eyes. There ain't much in Ellie's, either.

What is going on in this family?

"Is this Bobby?" I ask Vicki.

Vicki glances at the page. "Yep."

"Take a good look before you answer," Ken says. "Don't do that two-second glance and think that's good enough."

"I am too sure," Vicki says. "I could never forget Bobby's face."

"Can you do me a favor, then?" I ask. "Tell Bobby tomorrow—"

"We'd better go, Vic," Ken interrupts. "Mom'll text in a minute wanting to know where we're at. I'll walk you to the door, CJ."

I lean over and drop my voice. "Reckon you can remember to tell Bobby I want to talk to him more about what he called me about?"

Vicki nods.

Ken opens the back door and I hurry out of the car, hoping my annoyance doesn't show. I can't help but notice the scratches on the door as I slam it closed. The trunk too—a bunch around the lock spiral out like a flower.

"Someone must have tried to get into your trunk," I say.

Ken shrugs. "They suck at being a thief, then. Nothing in there but junk." Lowering his voice, he adds, "Listen, my sister can't be involved in this thing. If this Ellie person's really missing, that's the kind of dangerous situation you can't throw Vicki into the middle of."

"I ain't gonna involve her in any way but asking Bobby to call me."

"It won't end there. Trust me on this. She likes this boy, she's gonna do whatever pops into her head to impress him. Please, CJ, I'm begging you ... find another way before my sister ends up smack in the middle of something she can't handle."

"Okay, fine." I already got the ball rolling with Vicki, so there's no use fighting about it now. Still, I can't help the sinking feeling in my stomach when Ken thanks me. It's a good thing he isn't into me. I don't deserve a guy like him, not when he's got no idea that I broke my word before he even made me give it. "But will you help me, then? Please?"

Ken sighs. "I don't know the first thing about how to find a missing person, but I'll do what I can to help, long as you leave my sister out of it." He holds out his arms to hug me good night and I want to crawl into them forever even though I know I don't deserve to.

three

AFTER TALKING TO KEN, I reckon I'd better let this whole thing go. I don't want to, not when Ellie could be in trouble, but what choice do I have? Ken's right that it could be dangerous; I don't believe for a second that Vicki would go running after a kidnapper herself, but what about me? I was lucky to escape with my life when someone forced me into the back of a car once; do I really want to risk it happening again?

But when I get in and my roommate, Dani, asks me what's up, I can't help opening my phone and showing her Ellie's IG photo. "I don't suppose you've seen this girl anywhere, have you?"

Dani takes a look as she ties her thick, brown hair back into a high ponytail. "I wish. She's drop-dead gorgeous. Why?"

As I sink into Dani's mattress, I can't help thinking she should have taken the side of the room that's visible when you walk in. Her bed's perfectly made and there's not a thing out of place on her desk, whereas my blanket's always on the floor cause I don't have time to put it up properly and there's a sea of papers everywhere. "I reckon you didn't hear tonight's show."

"God, I'm such a shitty friend." Dani sighs. "I was drowning in homework and then my mom called. I totally forgot today's Tuesday. I'm sorry. So who is this mystery lady, exactly?"

I lean forward, cupping my head in my hands, as I explain Ellie's a graduate student whose little brother claims she's missing. "But chances are it's as inconsequential as anything else I ever end up covering on that stupid podcast. I really need to just forget it."

"Yeah, right. You don't believe that or you wouldn't have brought it up." Dani sits down next to me on the bed. "Let's try to work this out logically, okay? We know she disappeared before her kid brother called, but we don't know how soon before. But it should be easy to work out since you have her Instagram page up." Dani holds out her hand for my phone and I give it to her, feeling stupid.

Dani scrolls down. "Wow," she says. "She looked amazing." She shows me the phone and I see a low-cut red dress out of the corner of my eye, but Dani pulls it away before it registers fully. "Concentate, Dani," she tells herself. "Timestamp 7:28 PM. So she disappeared sometime within the next hour." She hands me back my phone.

"Wow," I say. "It's so freakin' obvious now that you've showed me."

"Yeah, well, you can check her out while I'm gone," Dani says. She stands. "I have to get dressed and get out of here. There's a party on the quad tonight. I'd invite you, but I know you don't do parties."

"It ain't my idea of a good time, thanks." I rub my temples, trying to think. "But you think it might have been Ellie's? Maybe she went to one and walked off with someone she shouldn't have."

Dani frowns. "This early in the evening? Doubtful. But maybe someone who knows what happened to her will be at the one I'm off to. You never know who's a friend of a friend, and once alcohol hits their brain, they might think it's a good idea to start talking." She grins.

I raise my eyebrows. "You're gonna stay clearheaded enough to pull this off?" Dani tends to get out of control when she's around freely-poured alcohol. It seems like most people here do, so I don't judge her for it, but she ain't trustworthy at a party either.

Dani hesitates. "I won't drink a lot. It'll feel weird, but I'll do it just because it's important to you." She brushes my fingertips with hers. "Please let me do this. I feel so shitty about missing your podcast, but at least I can help you search for this girl."

"You think you can help me put together a flyer first? I reckon if I put something up on social media, I might get some hits."

Dani's eyes light up, but she says, "I'll show you how to use AI. It's ten times faster than me and that way you can do it on your own while I'm undercover on the quad."

My stomach sinks. "I don't want AI, not for this. This is a real person who needs help, and I'd rather someone like you who knows what they're doing than an app that doesn't understand the stakes."

Dani bites her lip. "I appreciate your confidence in me. Let me get changed and I'll see what I can do."

I don't want to waste time, but there's no sense arguing about it so I go back to my side of the room and busy myself making the bed that I should have made this morning.

Dani comes out a few minutes later, wearing a purple crop top that shows off way too much of her belly and a too-tight pair of jeans. "Do me a favor and upload that photo to Canva, 'k?"

Dani sits down at my computer even though she could just as easily bring hers over from the other side of the room.

She grabs a bunch of papers and puts them in a stack behind the computer. Within two minutes, she's got something workable: a poster that says MISSING in big, white letters on a black stripe on the top, Ellie's photo in the center, and another stripe underneath that has the podcast's email and phone number in case anyone's seen her.

Dani barely waits for me to nod my approval before she gets up. "God, I'm looking forward to this." She takes her lip gloss out of her pocketbook and redoes her lips, making them purple, before checking for her keys and slipping out the door.

After Dani leaves, I sit on my bed, tapping my phone against the palm of my hand. She made it look so effortless to get info that I reckon it's possible we could actually get answers to what happened to this girl. But somehow, I can't make myself look at Ellie's Instagram and see if it has any more to tell me about what happened to her. It's almost like I don't want to know.

I'm being selfish as hell and I know it. Where would I be if a stranger had looked the other way after she saw me kick open the door of that car and slide out, desperate to escape a place I wasn't supposed to be? Yet I can't shake the dread whenever I contemplate looking deeper into this, or Ken's voice in my head saying that if there's a killer loose on campus, things could get dangerous fast.

I make myself sit down at my desk and upload the flyer to the student group on Social Strands instead of dwelling on how I'm letting Dani do all the legwork and won't as much as look at Ellie's posts to get answers.

There. I've done something. But is it enough? Every minute counts in a case like this. Ellie could be fighting to get to safety right now, and she shouldn't be fighting alone.

I throw myself onto the bed and close my eyes, but I keep

hearing Bobby's scared little voice. What if his big sister never comes home? Can I live with knowing it's partially my fault cause I didn't do anything but throw a flyer up online?

I press my head into the pillow, begging sleep to come quickly even though I know it won't.

My phone rings again. I reach for it. Maybe that's someone with news about Ellie's disappearance.

I have a new text from an unknown number:

> Ellie doesn't need your help. After all, you wouldn't want anyone else to disappear, would you?

My phone buzzes a second time and a photo comes through: a bunch of grainy people partying on the quad.

I can't quite make them out, but one of them just might be Dani.

four

I STARE AT THE PHONE, breathing heavily. Ken had been right, more right than he knew. Now Dani's got a target on her back, all cause of me.

I start to dial 911 but don't hit the SEND button. What for? I reckon 911 will send me to Campus Police, and maybe they should, but odds are Campus Police'll just pass the buck right back to Cedarwood PD, and while I'm fighting for someone to do something, whoever took Ellie could be making Dani disappear too.

I call Dani instead, but that's the complete wrong move. Her voice is slurred and she repeats herself ten times about how Ellie's not at the party. "You need to lighten up," she says. "I'm having fun, you should too." She won't let me get off the phone til I promise I'll stop being so serious. I say the words even though I mean them about as much as she did about not drinking tonight.

I flop back on my pillow after I hang up. I shouldn't have trusted Dani to stay sober, not when she's a party girl through and through. No one's responded to my post about Ellie, either, so I suppose no one cares.

Might as well try to get some sleep.

The next morning, I jerk awake, wondering if Dani ever made it home. I slide quietly through the space in the wall dividing our room, only to find her fast asleep, her arm draped around her friend Hailey, a pretty girl with light brown skin and curly hair. I can't help wondering if they did more than sleep in that tiny bed as I stare at them. Hailey's pressed against Dani and I feel like they're the only thing stopping each other from falling out.

I can't help thinking Dani would deserve it if she did.

I hurry back to my side of the room. Ugly thoughts like that bring bad karma and I don't need any more of that in my life.

Instead, I stab at the power button on my Mac to wake it up and log on to see if anyone reached out about Ellie. As the computer chimes to tell me it's cutting on, a chill goes through me.

LOCAL MAN ARRESTED AFTER SECOND KIDNAPPING ATTEMPT. POLICE SAY HE HAD A MATTRESS AND RESTRAINTS BEHIND FALSE WALL.

I shudder at the unwanted memory of the headlines after the man who tried to take me got caught with his next victim. That was a few years ago, so there ain't any reason to be thinking about it now.

Except one. It could have happened to Dani last night if Hailey hadn't been there and with it enough to get her home.

Could be we got a serial kidnapper hanging around campus, one who could have easily convinced Dani last night to get in a car and get whisked off somewhere, never to be seen again.

I'd thought the best way to keep us all safe was to give this up, but now I know the opposite's true: it's up to me to find

Ellie and whoever took her before someone else gets hurt, cause next time it could be my best friend.

My computer comes to life. I click onto my Social Strands account to see if anyone's left me any tips on Ellie's disappearance, but all I get is more bad news:

A message from a girl named Sarah Buchanan, who apparently administers the school page, informing me she's removed my post:

> Sorry, but I had to remove this post. I can't let you or anyone else spread unverified rumors. After all, we don't want to cause a panic, do we? Dean Northrop said I also have to suspend your posting privileges for seven days. Sorry again.

I stare at it, unable to believe I'm being punished for trying to help find Ellie. Now no one can tell me what they know. The longer Ellie's missing, the more likely it is she'll never be found, and the school apparently doesn't care.

Who is this Sarah anyway?

I click on her profile. She has it mostly locked down, though I can see her profile picture and bio. She's got curly black hair, brown eyes, and understated makeup -- just eyeliner and soft pink on her lips that doesn't make her stand out any. She's also got one mutual follower and that's Hailey.

I stare at that for a minute before glancing at her bio to see if she's really associated with the Dean or what. She's a junior researcher working with Joshua Armstrong. That name's vaguely familiar—does my friend Alicia, who's already declared a pre-med major, have a class with him? Anyway, this girl's also an admin on the school group, so she's got the power to do what she did and there's nothing I can do about it.

I slam my computer closed, aggravated.

Dani's bed creaks, which I ignore, along with the whispered conversation coming from the other side of the room. A minute later, Hailey comes out fully dressed, including her glasses. She's also wearing a t-shirt and jeans that are a lot less revealing than what Dani was wearing last night.

"I didn't wake you, did I?" I say nervously.

Hailey smiles slightly. "Look at you apologizing when it's your space and we should have asked before I stayed over." Her expression gets serious and she lowers her voice. "I needed to make sure Dani was okay. Before she started drinking she told me something about this girl that disappeared and I just thought..."

I nod. "Me too. Um, there wasn't anyone hanging around at the party that gave you a bad feeling, was there?"

"Nah, just the usual drunk guys who won't take no for an answer." Hailey hugs herself, pressing her arms against her chest. "I always go when Dani does. Someone has to be sober enough to look out for her."

There's an awkward silence and then Hailey starts to say she'll go now, but I ask her, "Before you do... how do you know Sarah Buchanan?"

Hailey's eyes narrow. "Who?"

I show her the message I got and Hailey says, "Oh, that Sarah. We're not actually friends. I added her because we have to do a project for AI-Based Tech together. She's very quiet and shy and I asked to work with her because I felt bad that everyone else was pairing up and she didn't seem to know what to do." Hailey pushes a stray lock of hair behind her ear. "Funny you should mention her. I ran into her at the party last night."

"Really? It doesn't sound like she's the type."

"I didn't think so either. She seemed really uncomfortable, like her eyes were darting everywhere and she was sort of standing in a corner hugging herself and watching everyone. I guess she has awful social anxiety. She said she was pushing herself to do what normal people do and told me she didn't want to ruin my fun by making me hang with her." Hailey shook her head sadly. "Weird that she said this was an unverified rumor when I told her last night that we were trying to find out if anyone knew anything about Ellie disappearing. But she's so shy that I doubt she'd even question it if the Dean told her to pull your post so…"

My phone beeps. It's Alicia asking if I'm ready to go to breakfast, so I'd better hurry up and get myself that way. Hailey's words echo in my ears as I excuse myself to go take a shower and I can't help wondering why the Dean is so eager to keep Ellie's disappearance quiet.

five

"YOU NEED TO see it their way," Alicia says as we make our way toward the cafeteria across the street an hour later. The sun bounces off her jet-black hair, making it look like it's got purple streaks. "From their perspective, a phone call from a random kid isn't proof a crime's been committed, especially since you didn't bother to call the cops. Why didn't you, by the way?"

I stare down at my high-top sneakers. "It ain't been 24 hours yet." That's BS and I know it, but it's preferable to explaining why I don't trust cops, which would mean telling Alicia the whole story of what happened to me back home.

"Still," Alicia says. "It's up to them to find missing people. Not you."

"Not necessarily. I reckon if I'm going to be an investigative reporter I need to start looking into things on my own." I push my way past her to the cafeteria, where Ken's already sitting at a table by himself, hunched over his tablet while taking notes in a notebook.

"I didn't mean to hurt your feelings," Alicia says, following me to the table. "I'm just saying, maybe the Dean was trying to prevent a panic that also could have been prevented by you leaving this to the cops."

I glare at her, caught between pushing the point further and making myself look good to Ken. "You're probably right," I say, "but I don't think I can let this go, not when there's a chance that girl could still be alive. If the worst happens, I want to be able to look her little brother in the eye and tell him I did everything I could to bring her home, all right? Besides, nobody's safe if there's some predator on campus making students disappear." I throw myself in my seat. "So what do you say? You guys gonna help me find her?"

Ken says, "I said I would, didn't I? If you have a plan, tell us and we'll see what we can do."

Alicia hesitates, but then she says, "I'm in, I guess, but only to the extent of making sure you don't get yourself killed." She climbs into her seat. "What do we know about this girl?"

"Not much beyond her being a grad student that works in the neuroscience lab," I say, "but I'm about to change that cause soon as I get some food I'll check out her Instagram."

Alicia nods. "I guess I can talk to my peer mentor," she says. "Jessica works in the lab too—I know cause she's always trying to convince me to apply for a junior researcher position but I don't have time. Anyway, maybe she knows something we don't about Elllie."

"Good idea," I agree. "Mind if I come with you?"

"I guess not," Alicia says.

I hate leaving Ken out so as I get up I say, "You feel like looking at her socials for us?"

"Not really," Ken says, "but I'll do it if you really want." He brushes my fingertips with his, smiling that same soft smile as last night. My heart pounds and I hope it ain't written all over my face how much I wish he'd kiss me. "Tell you what," he says. "I'll be on standby for now, and when you find something substantial for me to do, I'll get it done for you, okay?"

My stomach sinks with disappointment and I ain't sure if it's about his offer or the fact that we aren't any closer to kissing than usual. "K," I mumble, adding that I'll be right back before following Alicia to the other end of the cafeteria, where Jessica is picking at an omelet with her fork. Even sitting down, I can tell she's taller than average, probably about the same size as Dani, who's always complaining about being a giant cause she's but an inch short of six feet. She's got the same jet black hair as Alicia, but wearing a half-ponytail in the middle of hair down past her shoulders instead of having her hair cut at an angle to frame her face. Her skin's a darker shade of tan than Alicia's and her brown eyes are bigger.

Alicia says something to her in Spanish, introducing us, I reckon. Jessica twists the sun charm on her necklace nervously as she answers. Then she turns toward me and says, "You are the one who made the post last night saying Ellie is missing?"

I raise my eyebrows. "You saw it before it was deleted?"

Jessica nods. "I didn't want to believe..." She lets her breath out slowly. "Last night Ellie was supposed to meet me at the library but she never showed. I should have known then something was wrong." She blinks back tears. "How did you know before me she was missing? I learned it only this morning when there was no answer at her apartment and a neighbor told me she didn't think Ellie had been home all night."

"That must have been rough." I glance at the empty seat next to her. "May I..."

Jessica shrugs. "I do not own the cafeteria tables. But do not think I forgot my question, either. How did you know?"

I let my breath out slowly. "Bobby called my show. He was beside himself with fear for his sister, but his Daddy cut him off."

"Oh no," Jessica says. She shakes her head sadly. "I am sure he had the belt taken to him for this." She lets her breath out slowly. "He should have called me, not you. I am the one who knows her."

"What's done is done." I deliberately keep my voice soft. "You mind if we ask you a few questions? Off the record, I promise."

Jessica's face trembles. "I have been through this with the police once already this morning. I called them after I learned Ellie has been missing all night."

"I'm sure that was hard," I say, "but the more we know, the more we can help. You and Ellie are close?"

"We are… friends," Jessica says, getting stuck on the last word.

"And they work in the research lab together," Alicia adds.

Jessica says something in Spanish and Alicia responds, frowning. I cross my arms, wishing I'd taken Spanish in high school so I'd have a chance at following their conversation.

"Want to fill me in?" I ask when there's a lull in the conversation.

"Sorry," Alicia says. "She said she was going to talk to Ellie about me joining the lab last night but she doesn't think it's a good fit for me anymore anyway."

"Dr. Armstrong hired a junior researcher already," Jessica says. "Alicia was not quick enough to get the opportunity. It is too bad because I think she would have been a stronger applicant than this Sarah, who is not pre-med."

My breath catches in my throat. Sarah? It's a common name, so it's likely a coincidence, but still, if it ain't, that girl is getting around. "Sarah Buchanan?" I ask.

Jessica shrugs. "Maybe? I forget her last name. Anyway, I will not waste your time with this lab talk that does not concern you." She sighs deeply. "If I knew the last time I saw Ellie might be the last, I would have done things differently."

"What do you mean?"

Jessica checks the time on her phone. "I have only a minute before I have to leave for the lab." She throws the phone down and stares into space, wasting precious seconds. "I last saw Ellie at 6 pm or so. She came to my apartment and I helped her get ready for a... a date." Another hesitation. Is that the way Jessica speaks, or is she hiding something?

I want to push her on that, but I don't know what to ask. "This date have a name?"

"Mark Anderson." Jessica's eyes narrow. She asks Alicia something in Spanish.

"Yes," Alicia says. "I know him." She turns toward me. "Mark's a TA in my neuroscience class. All the straight girls fight each other to get into his study session because they think he's cute."

Jessica's eyes widen—she'd best not have a problem with Alicia being gay.

I rush into the next question before she can make an uncalled-for comment. "So Ellie had a date last night?"

"Y-yes." Jessica puts her necklace charm under her blouse. "She never likes to take the time with her hair but she let me do it for her and she had soft curls like feathers falling down to her shoulders. And her dress. I have never seen her wear one that shows off what she has so perfectly." Jessica's voice is soft and her cheeks are going red. "Anyway, she went downtown and I went to the library. She promised me she would help me get my paper ready for publication when she was finished, but three hours later she didn't return and her phone went to voicemail. I should have known then that she was in trouble but I assumed there was a reason..." She twists her sun charm. "And now she is kidnapped or worse."

"We don't know that for sure," I say. "But if something did happen, you reckon this Mark —"

"If I thought this I would never have let Ellie go out with

him." Jessica shakes her head while I try to make sense of that. What does she mean, let her? What would she have done if Ellie defied her? She goes on, "I would hate to think I am this poor a judge of character, so no, Mark did not do anything to Ellie."

"What kind of mood was Ellie in?" I ask.

"Let's put it this way. I was lost in her smile."

"That's good, at least, I reckon." I cross my arms. "Where did they go?"

"The Burnt Olive," Jessica says. "I told her the Burger Bistro was better for a date, but she wanted to please Mark so they went there instead and then it seems she vanished into thin air." She blinks hard. "I really have to go to the lab now, so if you will excuse me."

"One more question," I say. "Is it possible Ellie had an ex-boyfriend before Mark who was jealous?"

Jessica's jaw tightens. "No, this is not possible. She did not have other men in her life." Her phone buzzes. "And now I must get to the lab. Ellie will be so upset if she falls too far behind on her research."

"What kind of research does she do?" I ask as Jessica stands.

Jessica shakes her head slightly, making her sequined earrings bounce. "This is confidential," she says, "but I will say it is brilliant enough to take the world by storm." Her voice shakes slightly, but she covers with a cough and she sounds normal again as she excuses herself before she walks off.

She's hiding something. I'm sure of it.

Dani and Hailey have joined us by the time we get back. I'm glad to see that Dani looks like she's in decent shape; she's got a large coffee and a plate of eggs in front of her that looks like enough to feed three people.

"Here," she says, pushing her plate over to me. "Peace offering cause I screwed up last night."

"I ain't mad," I say, "though I won't say no to getting bacon and eggs without having to go through the buffet." I sit down and shovel eggs into my mouth like there's no tomorrow.

"Cool it," Ken says. "I don't want to have to practice my Heimlich on you."

"Yeah," Dani adds. "If you worked up that much of an appetite talking to Alicia's friend, she must have said something good. Take a break and tell us."

I gulp my water. "She was... evasive." Alicia's eyes narrow and I say, "You thought so do, didn't you?"

"Not really," Alicia says. "I mean, yes, she was holding something back, but it's probably because she didn't know how you'd react if you knew she was into Ellie."

"She wouldn't if she saw this table," Ken says. "Besides me, not one of us is straight." He looks at me, then away, his skin turning an even deeper shade of brown. Is he attracted to me despite what he says or am I seeing what I want to see?

"She doesn't know that," Alicia says. "She didn't even know I'm a lesbian." She takes a sip of orange juice. "But she was upset when CJ asked her if Ellie had any ex-boyfriends that might have wanted to hurt her. I could tell."

"Same." I take another forkful of eggs. "Say, you don't think she was jealous enough to — "

"Of course not!" Alicia snaps. "What is wrong with you? Haven't we moved past thinking one woman having a crush on another is a crime yet?"

"Let's not make this into something it's not." Ken takes a sip of his coffee while I stare at Alicia's orange juice, trying not to let my aggravation get the better of me. "No one's saying Jessica being into Ellie means she's up to no good. But you have to admit CJ's got a point. Look, this woman helped someone she has feelings for get ready for a date with some guy an hour before she disappeared. You really gonna tell me it never crossed your mind that she could have been insanely jealous?"

Alicia's eyes narrow and her jaw tightens. "I'm getting a blueberry muffin," she says, pushing away from the table.

"Alicia...," I say, but she's already gone.

"Don't worry," Dani says. "You know how Alicia is. She'll cool down soon enough."

"Yeah," Hailey agrees, pushing her hair behind her ear. "How about you go over with us what Jessica told you? Maybe we can figure out how it all fits together."

"Okay." I let my breath out slowly. "We can add to the timeline Dani helped me sketch out last night." I open my digital notebook and go over Jessica's claims about helping Ellie get ready for her date before heading to the library.

Hailey types that into her phone and I say, "What's that you're doing?"

"You'll see," Hailey says. "Go on."

"Okay, right. So according to Jessica, she and Ellie were supposed to meet back up in the library at 9 but Ellie never showed."

"Which makes sense," Dani says, "cause we figured out yesterday Ellie disappeared sometime between 7:45 and 8:45."

"Jessica wait around in the library the whole time?" Ken asks.

"I can find out, maybe," Hailey says. She works in the AV room at the library, so I suppose she has ways of finding out who was in the building. "No promises, though. I don't have access to the database I need." She types something else into her phone. "In the meantime, here. I just set up a digital whiteboard for us. It has a timeline and a column for each suspect, see?" She shows us her phone; each column has an area for a name and photo, and underneath that, there's a place to fill in

Means, Motive, and Opportunity. "Clues go here," Hailey says, pointing to a blank area on the bottom. "Upload photos and we can drag them wherever we want, and there are lots of other cool features to play around with. But the important thing is, as soon as each of you accepts the invite, you can update it in real-time and it'll sync on all of our devices, so if someone finds something, just enter it and we all have access."

"Impressive," I say, taking out my phone and clicking on the link to accept the invite.

Dani grins. "Hailey's tech skills are her superpower."

Hailey's cheeks darken. "I do what I can."

Alicia comes back with a huge blueberry muffin and several little butters. "We ruled out Jessica yet?"

"Maybe," I say. "How about you —"

Ken puts his finger on his lips as he grabs his phone.

"What..." I begin.

Ken whispers, "Police coming this way and I don't want them getting ideas til we're sure." He pats my shoulder as I turn my head to see what he's talking about.

A tall, completely bald man heads toward our table. The man wears a police badge in a belt loop; otherwise, I'd have supposed he was a school administrator. He's wearing a light grey suit jacket and slacks the same color, a red tie, and a white dress shirt. The colors look especially good on him because of his skin tone, which is two shades darker than Ken's.

"Excuse me." The cop's deep voice echoes off the walls. "Which one of you's Cassandra Jennings?"

I stand slowly. "Call me CJ. Please," I say, trying to hide the tremble in my voice. I can't think of any reason he should, but I can't shake the feeling he's fixin' to take me to the precinct for questioning.

six

"CJ, THEN," THE cop says. "My name's Benjamin Cooper. I'm a detective with the Missing Persons/Homicide division of the Cedarwood PD."

My eggs go down the wrong hole and I have to cough them back up. "Homicide?"

Detective Cooper holds up his hand. "I didn't mean to scare you. I'm not here in connection with a death. In fact, I'm hoping to prevent one." He pulls out an empty chair and sits backward on it, facing me. "Campus Police called me after a student named Ellie Bishop was reported missing. But you knew Ellie was in trouble already, didn't you, CJ? That's why you posted that flyer last night."

Ken puts his hand on my shoulder. I shiver at his touch. Again.

"Don't say another word," he says. "Not til we get you a lawyer."

Cooper shows off a set of bright white teeth. "If you want to call an attorney, I'll wait. But here's the thing: Ellie's disappearance has all the signs of an abduction, and the longer it takes for us to find her, the more likely it is that whoever has her will kill her. So it might be better not to waste time waiting to make arrangements with an attorney right now, especially since you aren't in any trouble."

I rub the back of my neck, trying to get rid of the throbbing headache that's come on all of a sudden. I don't trust this cop any more than any other. Just because he hasn't arrested me yet doesn't mean he's not hoping it ends up that way. Still, time's been ticking away and he's right that Ellie doesn't have a second to spare.

"All right," I say. "I'll forget the lawyer for now, for Ellie's sake."

Cooper nods approvingly. "That's the right decision, CJ. How about you and I go over to that empty table in the corner so that we won't get distracted?" His voice goes up like he's asking a question, but its strong, firm tone tells me that No is not an option.

"Don't worry," Ken says as I stand. "We're not going anywhere til you get back." He locks eyes with Cooper, then looks away.

I sink into the empty seat across the room and clasp my hands in front of me so I don't fidget and get mistaken for someone with something to hide.

Cooper asks me if Bobby or Ellie are friends of mine and follows it up by asking why Bobby called my podcast when I'm a stranger to him. Then he asks me what I did after I got the call from Bobby.

I swallow hard, trying to get some saliva going, before I explain how I found out who had called me. "I felt like I hit the jackpot when I found out that Ken's sister knew Bobby," I say as I wrap up, "but Ken didn't think it was a good idea to involve her, not even as a messenger."

"Really." Cooper's tone is neutral, but I can feel the skepticism oozing out of the air around him. "That must have felt like an unnecessary roadblock."

What in the world is this? Is it me he's after or Ken?

I need that water more than ever, but I don't have it so I have to make do without it. "H-have you met Vicki yet? The girl's super smart but when it comes to people, it's another story."

Cooper's head bobs slightly. "I see. Well, let's keep the focus on finding Ellie. Have you done anything else to try to find out where she is?"

"Nothing that's worked." I explain about the missing persons' flyer that the page admin deleted and the conversation I had with Jessica.

"Jessica Gomez?" he asks.

"I reckon so. I only know her first name and that she works in the lab with Ellie."

Cooper nods. "That's the woman who reported her missing. I daresay you've got more out of her than we did."

My face goes hot. "Off the record, is Jessica a suspect?"

"I can't comment on an ongoing investigation. But at this stage, everyone who interacted with Ellie recently is fair game until they're ruled out, so you can imagine we will be verifying the information she gave you." Cooper takes a thin leather wallet out of his pocket and pulls a card out of it. "Now, I'm not naive enough to think that you're going to stop trying to find Ellie on your own just because I'm on the case too. But I can't do my job if I don't have access to all available facts. So if you find out anything that might be important or helpful, I expect you to call me immediately. Understood?"

"Yes, sir." My voice is flat.

"Excellent. I look forward to working together to bring Ellie home. By the way, do you think any of your friends might know more? Your boyfriend, for example? What's his name, Ken?"

I stare at Cooper, confused. "I don't see how. He doesn't know Ellie any more than I do."

"Right. Of course." Cooper's chair scratches loudly on the

floor as he pushes it out from the table. I have an impulse to stop him and tell him about that text I got last night, but my better angels stop me. There's no point, not when it came to nothing and he's got Ellie on his mind. So I keep it to myself while I watch him leave.

Ken's in trouble. I know it almost as surely as I know the cops are in the wrong forest, never mind barking up the wrong tree. Ken wouldn't. He couldn't.

If I had any doubt left about looking into Ellie's disappearance, it's evaporated now, cause it's clear the cops are gonna waste so much time looking at Ken that Ellie doesn't stand a chance of making it home alive.

My phone buzzes. It's a text from my advisor, Dr. Blanton, asking me how soon I can get to his office to meet with him and the Dean of Students.

What the hell?

seven

I TAKE THIRTY seconds to fill my friends in before I grab my bag and rush across campus. Dr. Blanton's office is one of a dozen in the journalism department; after I go through an automatic glass door and tell the receptionist who I'm here to see, I have to wait to be called back to his tiny cubicle.

Even though he seemed to be in a hurry for me to get here, he takes his time being ready to see me, which is just as well cause I need to catch my breath. I grab my phone and start scrolling Ellie's Instagram account while I'm waiting so that at least I'm not completely wasting my morning.

Stories only stay up for 24 hours, so anything Elle posted before yesterday morning's long gone, but she has a photo of her and Jessica in the lab yesterday afternoon with an arrow pointing to Jessica and the words BEST FRIENDS 4EVA! In the photo, Jessica's hand is on Ellie's shoulder as she looks at something on her computer. Jessica's smiling, but her eyes are narrow and she seems to be staring at nothing.

Alicia's right: Jessica's got feelings for Ellie. I ask myself again whether it's possible she did something stupid over them.

The Story changes to a photo of Ellie sitting in front of a

mirror, wearing a low-cut red dress. Jessica's behind her, her hands in Ellie's hair. It has the caption: NEW LIFE STARTS TONIGHT! in black letters on two white stripes that look like paint. So Jessica was telling the truth about helping Ellie get ready for her date. But what did Ellie mean by that caption?

The Story fades into a video of Ellie, sitting on a stone bench. There are flower beds behind her and cobblestone paths leading somewhere off-camera. Ellie's blouse got red and yellow petals painted onto a navy blue background. It's over-sized and makes her chest look flat; I wonder if she prefers baggy clothes for the same reason I do.

I dig in my pockets for my earbuds, but the receptionist tells me to go ahead to Dr. Blanton's office now. I check the timestamp before I put my phone away and get up. 18 hours ago, so I've got a few hours before Ellie's message disappears forever.

Dr. Blanton's office, if you can even call it that, is a small cubicle that has just enough room for his desk, a small book-shelf behind it, and two metal chairs facing it. That tiny space makes my stomach do flip-flops, and not in a good way, at the best of times, and it's worse today cause Dean Northrop is standing by his desk, crossing her arms. She's not a tall woman by any stretch of the imagination, though she towers over Dr. Blanton because he's sitting behind the desk. She's intimi-dating to me, with her perfectly combed layered hairstyle, pearl necklace and earrings to match, and dark blue dress and heels. She is wearing silver-rimmed glasses and a stern expres-sion on her face, which is more round than oval. Her skin is a pale peach color, while Dr. Blanton's is light brown.

Dr. Blanton introduces her to me as "Dean Northrop," not giving any first name to go with the last. "She's the Dean of Students and my immediate supervisor," he says, chuckling nervously.

"Dr. Blanton and I have been talking about last night's unfortunate events," Dean Northrop says. "He thinks that having a student cover the story of Ellie Bishop's disappearance would be a valuable learning experience, and he recommended you. I wanted to meet you to see if you are the right fit for this assignment." She gestures for me to take a seat. As I sink into mine, she says, "I'm trying to find the right words to explain to you the competing priorities you will have to balance. Our first priority, of course, is for this student to be found alive and returned safely to campus. However, it is vital you report on this issue in a way that does not reflect badly on the university. Students are scared, you see, and if a peer reporter gives them the impression that the school is generally unsafe, that will be extremely problematic. We also don't want any parents of prospective or current students getting the idea that their children could be hurt or killed and deciding they don't want them here. So you will have to balance the need to find the truth with the need to protect the university's reputation. Do you think you are up to that task?"

My throat feels so tight I can barely breathe. If I say what I really feel, I ain't getting this assignment, and that'll make it harder to find out what happened to Ellie. But I can't lie, either.

Dr. Blanton comes to my rescue, saying, "I explained to Dean Northrop that you would be working under my supervision and that I will be assisting you to navigate the political concerns."

"I appreciate that, sir," I say, my mouth so dry that my tongue practically sticks to the roof. "I reckon with your help I can get this done." I turn toward Dean Northrop. "I do have one question, ma'am. Why did you direct your assistant to remove my post with the missing persons' flyer?"

Dean Northrop pulls her blouse down even though it doesn't look out of place. "She was following protocol. In

these cases, we need to have police confirmation before dissem-
inating what could be a baseless rumor that gets people riled
up. But I'm glad you asked that question because this is the
sort of thing I'm talking about. Please do not post information
that has not been proven to be true. That only invites panic."

I want to call BS on her response, but again, I know better.
"I understand," I say quietly.

"Good," Dean Northrop says. "We will allow you to cover
this story on a trial basis. Please run any ideas for stories past
Dr. Blanton before you begin working on them." She holds
out her hand. "Congratulations on obtaining this position."

I shake hands with her cause I'm expected to. Hers are as
cold and clammy as I thought they'd be, and immediately
afterward her phone beeps and she says she has to run, something about getting her daughter that I don't follow cause I
ain't listening.

"What was all that BS?" I say quietly in case she's still
hanging around.

"That," Dr. Blanton says, "is your first lesson in how to
deal with powerful figures that might not want you to dig too
deeply. You handled it admirably." He smiles slightly. "So you
know, I'll give you free rein in who and what you want to
investigate related to Ellie's disappearance. But I will be
guiding you as to how to navigate the choppy waters you are
soon going to find yourself in."

I nod without understanding.

Dr. Blanton says, "I have sources in the police station who
may be of use to you. I could introduce you if you'd like."

My stomach does flip-flops for the second time in an hour.
"I... um, how do I know they're telling me the truth?"

Dr. Blanton crosses his arms. "I would not offer you a
source I did not absolutely trust."

"I meant no disrespect. It's just..." I hug myself. "I had a
negative experience with the police back home, and the detec-

tive in charge of this case wasn't much better so I find it hard to imagine sitting down with a cop for long enough to get anything useful."

"I understand. I have plenty of reasons to be wary of cops, too, as you might imagine. But as reporters, we have to push those feelings aside and talk to whatever sources are willing to speak with us. Otherwise, we could miss out on valuable information."

"Yes, sir." I swallow hard. "Let me see what I can find out on my own first, but then if I need to I'll talk to your source."

Dr. Blanton's smile fades. He's disappointed in me. Crap. "Of course," he says. "When you're ready, let me know." He dismisses me, adding, "This investigation could get dangerous for many reasons. Please don't try to do everything on your own."

I promise I won't and hightail it out of there.

I take the bus back after lunch so I can finish checking out Ellie's Instagram. I don't care what Dean Northrop says about protecting the university's reputation; I'm going to do whatever it takes to find out what happened to Ellie and bring her home.

Her video is still there. I hit Play, ignoring the feeling that Ellie's someone I want to get to know better. She's missing, possibly kidnapped—this is no time to start crushing on her.

"Hi guys!" Ellie says brightly, but I can tell her smile's plastered on when she wants to cry cause there's no light in her eyes. She plays with the charm on her necklace, drawing attention to it. It's a crescent moon and when she twists it between her fingers, I see writing on the back.

"I made a decision today and I wanted to tell you about it." Ellie looks away, then back at the camera. "I, um, I know you've heard the rumors about me. The only way out is to come clean. It's true. You'd be justified in thinking the only reason I'm team leader is... you know. It's not, but..." Ellie blinks hard. "Listen. I'm going to get out of this uncomfortable situation, okay? But don't any of you ever make the same mistake I made. If someone is pressuring you to do something that makes you feel gross, walk away. Believe me, it's not worth it. Nothing is."

I stare at the video, watching it over and over. What was Ellie involved in that had her so upset? Whatever it was, she was fixin' to call it quits, and that could have been a reason for someone to make her disappear.

I play the video again, a dark thought crossing my mind. The rumors had to do with how she got her job, so could she have slept with someone, a boss or something like that? My fingers fly furiously across the keyboard, trying to find out more about Dr. Armstrong since he runs the lab.

On the neuroscience lab website, Dr. Armstrong's got a bio full of accomplishments I barely understand and a nice headshot that's credited to someone named Chloe Lancaster. The photo displays a good-looking guy around my parents' age with curly brown hair that's streaked with gray and an easy smile. Could he have taken advantage of Ellie? Something about his photo feels off, but I don't know for sure why, and for all I know I could be mixing him up with the man who kidnapped me.

My phone rings while I'm arguing with myself about whether Armstrong's giving off predator vibes or not. I don't recognize the number, but I answer it anyway. There's all this noise, like a whole bunch of people talking all at once, and then the call drops.

My heart's pounding, but I tell myself to cut that out cause I don't have time to worry about some stupid prank call.

I switch back to IG and stab at the screen, well aware that

Ellie's sad video was likely her last message to the world before she disappeared.

The only photo Ellie posted that night is of her at the bar at the Burnt Olive. Her hair falls down in soft curls and she's got glittery silver eyeshadow on and lip gloss that's somewhere between pink and purple. She's wearing a different top than the one in the video; this one's the red dress she was wearing in her earlier photo. Up close it looks even more low-cut than in the other photo. She's got a silver chain around her neck that goes well with the deep red of her dress, but if she's wearing the same necklace as earlier, the charm ain't visible.

The caption reads:

Looks like I'm going on a date with myself. Tell me I'm worth it. #fallfromgrace #stoodup #waitingforever #BurntOlive

Wait, so Mark stood her up? Then what? There ain't any pictures of food or her eating, with or without a partner—did she leave after all?

I shake my head sadly, aware this was the last selfie she took before she disappeared and if I don't hurry up and find her, it might be the last one she ever uploads.

The Burnt Olive's the best place to start. A quick search leads me to the discovery that it's closed til suppertime tonight. I want Ken to go with me to talk to the staff and see what they know, but he's stuck watching Vicki til late.

Dani's my backup plan, but she doesn't answer her phone, so I have to wait to try to catch her at home.

She's halfway out the door when I get back and doesn't have time to talk. As she rushes past me, she calls, "I hope you don't mind that I let your visitor use your computer."

What visitor? I walk cautiously into the room.

A child is sitting at my desk, playing a pinball game on my

Mac. He's short and stocky, with hair the same color and texture as what I just saw on Ellie's video.

"CJ!" The boy runs to me, practically knocking me over in an attempt to hug me. "I tried to call you from the bus stop but I got scared and didn't say anything."

So that's what that dropped call was about. I let my breath out slowly, relieved it wasn't anything more nefarious. "Bobby, right?"

"Yes, ma'am," Bobby says, sounding more like a child from where I come from than one born and raised here. "Vicki said I could come talk to you about Ellie. Did you find out what happened to her yet?"

eight

I UNTANGLE MYSELF carefully from Bobby, not wanting him to feel rejected even though I'm not comfortable with some child I've never met before hugging me. Kneeling so that I can look him right in the eye, I say, "I wish I could say that. All I can do is promise not to give up til I find her."

"Do you think she's alive?" Bobby's voice shakes.

"I sure hope so." I put my hand on Bobby's shoulder. "We didn't get to finish our conversation when you called my show. Would it be all right if I ask you some questions about Ellie?"

Bobby nods. "I like talking about her. It makes me feel like she's still here."

"You're real close with her, huh?"

"Yeah." Bobby sighs. "She helps me feel safe when Daddy gets mad and she never ever treats me like I'm stupid or weird." He blinks several times in succession, reminding me of the way Vicki tugs at her hair when she gets upset.

"Sounds like a good big sister." I squeeze Bobby's shoulder. "What made you think she was in trouble when you called me?"

"Cause." Bobby looks at the ground. "She didn't call to say goodnight. She always calls at exactly 8:15. But that night, nothing, and she didn't pick up her phone when I called her instead." He hugs himself and rocks back and forth slightly. "Daddy was wrong! He said that I was worried for no reason and he punished me for calling you. And then today the police told me she's missing!" He leans his head on my chest.

I hand him a tissue. "Far as I'm concerned, you did the right thing, calling me and trying to get Ellie help. And now I'm trying to find out if there was anyone Ellie knew who might have wanted to hurt her. Did she ever tell you someone was bothering her?"

Bobby shakes his head. "She wouldn't talk to me about things like that. But sometimes when I'm visiting her I spy on her." He smirks slightly and his eyes sparkle.

I'm torn between telling him that ain't nice and letting it go so he'll trust me. "Did you ever hear anything that could give me a clue where she went?"

"One thing," Bobby says, "but she and Jessica made me promise not to tell."

Jessica again. I knew something wasn't right about that girl.

"This ain't the time to keep secrets," I tell Bobby. "Now that Ellie's missing, the more you can tell me about what's been happening in her life, the easier it'll be for me to track her down."

"Okay. But when you find her, you can't tell her I told."

"I won't." My heart pounds. Is Bobby going to tell me something that could break this wide open? "What is it you know that you ain't supposed to tell?"

Bobby wriggles. "Ellie has a boyfriend," he says, "and Jessica doesn't think he was a good one. I heard her telling Ellie, 'What that man is doing to you is not right.' Then I dropped my phone by accident and they heard me. Ellie was super mad. She pulled the door open hard and I thought she was going to slap me in my face."

"I sure hope she didn't do that."

"Uh uh. She never hits me no matter how mad she gets." Bobby swallows hard. "Anyway, she made me tell Jessica that I was eavesdropping and then Jessica told me not to tell anyone what I heard. I didn't want to because grown-ups aren't supposed to ask kids to keep secrets, but Ellie said this was different because I knew she and Jessica would never hurt me and that if Daddy found out he'd be super mad at her."

"What would your Daddy do if he got mad at her?" I don't want to ask the question, but the way Bobby's talking, I have to. There's a chance Ellie's father's the one who made her disappear, at least til Bobby tells me there ain't.

Bobby stares at his feet. "I dunno exactly. Maybe stop paying for her to go to school?"

I get the same feeling I did from Jessica earlier, like Bobby knows something he ain't telling, but he's no bigger than Vicki so I don't feel right pushing him. "Do you know who they were talking about?" I ask.

Bobby shakes his head. "I didn't even think Ellie liked boys. I thought..." He swallows hard. "Never mind. It isn't nice."

The way Jessica talked about Ellie pops into my head. Maybe it wasn't so unrequited after all. "Bobby," I say gently. "Is Ellie gay?"

Bobby stiffens. "Course not. Daddy calls Jessica bad names because she is, so Ellie can't be."

My heart pounds. The casual way Bobby mentions his dad's hatred of gay people makes me worry that poison's got in his head too, and that hits too close to home for me.

"Jessica's there a lot, huh?" I say, changing the subject. "Do you like her?"

"I guess." Bobby stuffs his hands in his pocket. "She and Ellie are always in private when she's there."

I want to ask more about Jessica, but I don't know what to

ask, so instead I say, "You visit Ellie a lot, right? Did you ever see anyone hanging around who felt wrong to you?"

"Nuh uh. Sometimes Ellie's friend Chloe comes over and she's kind of weird but she's nice, and anyway Ellie said there's no reason to be scared of her just cause she's different."

Chloe. I've seen that name recently. "How is she weird?"

"I can't explain it. She seems to like to be by herself even when we're all together, I guess." Bobby's phone beeps "Shit!" He throws his hands over his mouth, trying to push the word back in. "I'm sorry, I'm sorry. I didn't mean to say the S word. It just came out. I swear it did!"

"Doesn't bother me any. What's up?"

"I have to go, that's what! Daddy checks where my phone is at 3:15 to make sure I got home safely and if he finds out I'm on the other side of town I'll get in really big trouble!" Bobby grabs his bag from the floor next to my computer. "I gotta go."

"Can I walk you to the bus stop, at least?"

"I got here, I can get back." Bobby's halfway out the door before he adds, "Thanks for talking to me."

"You call me anytime, okay?" I tell him.

Bobby nods and runs out of the room. As the door slams shut behind him, I sink down on my bed and take out my digital notebook, trying to make sense of everything he just told me.

I spend the next hour going through my notes and trying to get my thoughts together. The only thing that's clear to me is that Bobby's scared to death of his daddy. If the man takes his belt to him when he gets out of line, he might have done more than that to Ellie if he found out about her doing something he didn't like.

I pace back and forth, not wanting to think a father could make his own daughter disappear. But Bobby's denial that

Ellie was gay and his belief she escaped the wrath his daddy reserved for Jessica won't leave me. And Jessica lied to me, too. She denied that Ellie had any boyfriends other than the one date with Mark, so what was it that Bobby overheard? And how did all that tie in with the video she made, which I have no doubt is connected to what happened to her somehow?

My phone rings, making me jump. It's Dani.

"Sorry I couldn't talk before," she says. "And sorry about last night. It was pretty shitty of me to get drunk when I was supposed to be searching for Ellie."

I bite my lip. I want to tell Dani I'm disappointed, but how can I be when I knew going in what she was like? "I wish you'd have kept your word, but too late now, I reckon."

" I'll make it up to you, I swear. No more parties, no more alcohol, just clearheaded, sober Dani being a good friend."

I believe her but I don't. Dani's got all the good intentions in the world, but when it comes to partying, she can't seem to help herself. I say, carefully, "Can't say I don't appreciate you wanting to. Listen, from Ellie's IG it looks like Mark stood her up last night, but I won't know for sure til I talk to the people who work at the Burnt Olive. Want to come out with me tonight?"

"To eat too? Cause if you want to take me to dinner, I never say no to good food and good company." Dani's tone is light and flirty, the way I so often wish Ken's would be.

"Tell you what," I say. "I'll pay for dinner if you'll be by my side when I talk to whoever I can about Ellie."

"Deal," Dani says. "On one condition."

"What's that?"

"Lose that baggy sweatshirt. I want you to wear something that shows off how good you look."

My stomach tightens. Dani wants me to show off my figure, and I just can't do that. My goddamn chest gets me read as female no matter how hard I try to show the world I ain't one.

Still, if I don't give in, I'll end up at the Burnt Olive by myself, and something tells me that nothing good can come of putting my nose in Ellie's disappearance without someone there to watch my back. "Okay, fine," I say, leaving out I'll be wearing a men's dress shirt and slacks.

I sure hope I ain't leading her on, but too late now. Dani's already told me to be ready by the time she gets out of class at 7, so I'm good and stuck. What have I got myself into?

nine

"WHY ARE YOU WEARING BOYS' clothes on a date?" Vicki asks, wandering into Ken's room while I'm looking through his closet for a shirt to borrow.

"It's not a date," I say quickly. Ont he off-chance Ken's more interested in me than I think, I don't want him to think I ain't available. "And I don't feel comfortable wearing girls' clothes."

"Why?"

"Vicki," Ken says. "Stop asking so many questions."

"It's all right." I stare at the line of dress shirts in Ken's closet, trying to get my words together. "You know how if your pigtails aren't exactly right, you feel out of sorts? That's how it is for me when I have to wear girls' clothes."

"Oh." Vicki hopes on one foot while tugging at her pigtail —did I overwhelm or confuse her? She says, "We had an assembly in school today that required me to miss math and history. Guess which one I was sad about."

Ken and I exchange glances. Ken says, "Not a good time, Vicki. Go set the table for dinner before Mom comes home and finds it undone."

"You gonna kiss CJ after I'm gone and see if you can get her date out of her head?"

Ken glares at Vicki. "I'm not playing around. Stop getting in my business and go set the table."

Vicki giggles to herself and runs off—is she mad or amused?

Ken checks to make sure she's not listening at the door before slamming it closed. "Sorry about her."

I shrug. "She's nothing but a child. She doesn't know any better."

"Don't let her fool you. Just cause she's autistic or whatever doesn't mean she doesn't know when she's up in someone's business that isn't hers." Ken rubs his hands together. "Not to be a hypocrite, but can I ask you something?"

We're standing close enough that if this was the movies, Ken would lean in to surprise me with a kiss that awakens all my pent-up feelings for him. I breathe in sharply as I nod.

"What's up with you and Dani? You're not... this isn't a first date, is it?"

I laugh. "Course not. The Burnt Olive's the last place anyone saw Ellie but Dani won't go with me to find out what anyone knows unless I have supper there with her."

"Dressed to the nines. She know you're not taking her out for anything but work?"

"She'd best." I twist my hands inside out and back again. "I'm not into her, Ken. Or most women. You know that, right?"

Ken looks me up and down. "You think I don't know what you are? I've known from the second I set eyes on you that you feel like a guy on the inside."

That's not exactly it either. Man fits better than woman but it still doesn't feel right. "Kind of, but... Look, I don't need any label, all right? I'm CJ, that's all."

"One of the things that makes you so cool. You're one-of-a-kind." Ken smiles widely and his eyes are sparkling.

I look away. I can't let myself think he means it the way I want him to. "So far I've got a couple ideas about what happened to Ellie." I tell Ken about my theory about Ellie's dad, and my other one about Ellie sleeping with Dr. Armstrong. "I don't know how I can find out about Bobby's dad just yet, but the lab's another story. I have some more questions for Jessica, and maybe we can get other people to talk to us too. Want to come with me tomorrow morning to see?"

"Long as it's after 11. I got class til then." Ken fist-bumps me. "Now let's get you ready. Move over and let me find you a shirt."

Dani looks me up and down when we meet outside the Burnt Olive, making me feel self-conscious about the stiff white dress shirt and grey slacks I'm wearing. "Wow. It wasn't exactly what I expected, but you clean up nice." Her eyes sparkle, but does she secretly disapprove?

I make a production out of rifling through my messenger bag for a flyer to show the manager. "Come on."

"K." Dani's got a cheery tone in her voice but there's a heaviness under it. "Hope they won't kick us out for asking questions. This place is nice."

I have to admit Dani's right. The Burnt Olive's fancy for a restaurant five blocks from campus. The railings going up to the entrance have an ornate design and lights wrapped around them. There's both a revolving door and a regular entrance. the second of which is attached to a wheelchair ramp.

The inside's even more elegant, with a bar behind the hostess station and a woman wearing a dress shirt and bow tie standing behind a platform. The waiters all wear the same uniform: a white dress shirt, black slacks, and black bow tie. I wouldn't mind working here.

"Can I help you ladies?" the hostess says.

I stare over her shoulder at the bar, trying to compare it to the one in Ellie's photo, so I won't go off on anyone. I'm wearing Ken's clothes and I've got my hair cut short as a boy's. How am I a woman?

"Before you seat us, would you mind bringing this to the manager?" I hand the hostess the flyer. "This girl vanished into thin air and we heard the last place anyone saw her was right here last night."

The hostess's eyes widen. "So it's true. I didn't know that girl's name, but I know her face very well. She came in every Tuesday at 6:30 on the dot."

So Jessica lied again, or at least, made it seem like Ellie going on her date here was something special. "She ever come here with a Mexican girl?" I ask. "Taller than me, wears a sun necklace?"

"A couple times. Now that girl... when she was with her, Ellie's face just lit up."

"And the other night? "

"You'd be down too if your date was so late it felt like he was standing you up after you'd gone to a ton of effort to look nice for him, wouldn't you?"

Dani and I exchange glances. She says, "So he bothered showing up eventually?"

"She had far more patience than I would have, I'll tell you that much. She must have sat at that bar by herself for half an hour, checking her phone constantly and looking more and more upset. If it was me, I'd have asked for a table for one and not let him join it, either."

"Wow," Dani says. "You're pretty pissed on her behalf."

"Like I said, she was in here a lot. Nice girl, big tipper, never had a bad word to say to anyone. Those are the kinds of girls the world walks all over, and it's not right, you know?"

I know it's a long shot, but I ask if there was anyone else at the bar who might have given Ellie a hard time.

"It was too busy to keep an eye on her all the time," the hostess says. "But no one treated her bad as far as I know, except the asshole who kept her waiting forever. When he came in he didn't apologize or anything, just came up to me and said he hoped we still had a table for them. I didn't want to seat him, but what could I do? I gave them menus and a table in the back and that was that." She crosses her arms. "You don't think that jackass did something to her, do you?"

"We hope not," Dani says, which saves me having to figure out how to answer.

The hostess takes out some menus. "Let me show you to a table before I get in trouble. But listen, if you give me a flyer I'll ask the manager about putting it in the window. Maybe someone saw something."

We thank the hostess and exchange the flyer for a menu. She seats us in the back of the restaurant, far away from everyone else.

"She reckons we're on a date too," I say, trying to keep my tone light.

"Would that be so bad?" Dani asks. "I mean, you are cute even though I don't get why you won't wear anything femi-nine." I look away, my cheeks reddening. Dani says, "Sorry for being too forward. I... like you."

I stare down at my menu, not wanting to hurt Dani's feel-ings but not knowing what to say. It's not that she ain't cute, but no matter how much I focus on the sparkle in her eye or how her hair's almost long enough to sit on, I can't make myself feel for her what I feel for Ken. "I'm flattered," I tell her. "But - "

Dani's jaw trembles. "But you don't feel the same."

"I don't want to hurt your feelings." My voice is soft. "Sometimes I think I like someone as a friend and then all of a sudden here comes wanting more, so it could happen, but right now, the feelings ain't there."

Dani stares down at the table. "At least you're honest. And I drink too much, so why would you want me that way anyway?" I can't see her eyes, but I know she's got that look in them you get when you want to cry but you can't.

I pat her hand. "Let's focus on Ellie, okay? The longer she's missing, the more likely she is to turn up dead."

"If she isn't already." Dani's voice is flat.

I swallow hard. It's been a day since Ellie disappeared, so the probability of finding her alive is slim to none at this point. But it happens sometimes, doesn't it?

"I refuse to believe she's dead unless there's a body," I say.

"I don't like thinking it either." Dani shudders. "A student at our school disappearing is scary enough."

I drop the menu, surprised. Dani doesn't seem like the type to be scared of anything. "If it helps any, I doubt it was random, given what she was dealing with. Hours after she said she wanted to get out of something uncomfortable, she vanished, so..."

Dani nods, but her eyes are wide and her lips pressed tightly together like she's trying not to say something. I put my hand over hers even though it's a bad idea given the circumstances, and promise her we'll get to the truth before Ellie's kidnapper can come after either of us, trying to sound more sure than I feel. It's been over a day and we're no closer than we were, other than being aware that Jessica's told a bunch of lies and Ellie's dad is a piece of work.

"I hate to say it, but it's looking more and more like Jessica's involved," I say. "Every conversation we have leads to a new lie she told, and some of them seem pointless. Why would she make it sound like the Burnt Olive was Mark's idea when Ellie always came here on Tuesdays?"

Dani shrugs. "How would that help her even if she did do something to Ellie? Mark looks worse, if you ask me. Where was he all that time?"

"You reckon he was setting things up to make Ellie disappear?"

"Maybe. Til we talk to him we won't know. Alicia has an in; see if she can get you an interview with him."

"I suppose she will if it takes the heat off Jessica. She doesn't want to hear anything about her being involved." I grab my phone. "I'll ask if she ever confirmed Jessica's alibi while I'm at it."

The waitress comes to take our drink orders while I'm texting and I can't help wondering what she knows, but she disappears again before I can ask her anything except to get me a ginger ale. Soon as she's gone, I tell Dani that Ken and I are going to go talk to Jessica again at the lab tomorrow. Dani offers to skip her class to come with us, but I manage to talk her down from that terrible idea.

Alicia texts back:

> I'll try but M doesn't lead my TA study session & I doubt he even knows who I am because there are SO many people in that class!

I can't help noticing she's skipped answering about Jessica. I'm about to text her again when she texts back:

> PS The librarians I spoke to said Jessica looked familiar but they couldn't remember if they'd seen her last night or a different night. But she's not lying. I'm sure of it.

I show the text to Dani. She agrees that we have to find out for sure what Jessica's story is before Alicia gets hurt.

After supper, Dani suggests we check out the area around the restaurant for clues. My stomach sinks; I should have thought of that. And worse yet, the outside of the restaurant makes it clear how impossible it's going to be to track Ellie's movements after she left. There's one tiny camera on a light pole outside the restaurant, but no matter which way she went, she'd have gone out of range almost immediately. There's a bus stop on the corner, so if she went that way she'd have blended in with the crowd—but did she?

"Now what?" I ask. "We don't even have a clue which way she went."

"Maybe, maybe not," Dani says. "If she comes here every week, she probably lives near here."

"Unless she jumps on the bus after."

"I don't think so." Dani's head is bent over her phone as she types something. "Remember, she had to be back by 8:15 to call her kid brother. So she probably stopped in here on her way home, took an hour or so to eat, and then headed off to..." She grins as she shows me the phone.

Google Maps is telling us that there are student apartments two blocks to the east.

"Let's take an after-dinner walk and see which one's hers," Dani says.

"K." I shove my hands in my pockets, more grateful than I want to admit for Dani's help. I'm the one who's supposed to be a reporter, but I'm better at interviews than at thinking things through. Maybe Dani's the one who ought to be working with Dr. Blanton, not me.

"She was probably in a rush," Dani says as we pass by several stores—a bakery, a boarded-up place that still has a

Chinese restaurant sign above it, and a bookstore. "Mark made her late and she needed to get home to call Bobby. So if she wasn't paying attention and someone followed her..."

I try to run, but he grabs me from behind, pressing his hand over my mouth and pinning my too-skinny arms against his chest...

"He had a car waiting," I say, my mouth so dry I can barely force the words out. "He forced —"

"Maybe," Dani says. "If it was even a he. You were suspicious of Jessica, remember?" She frowns. "You okay? You look like you're about to hurl."

"Y-yeah. It just hit me how much danger Ellie's in, that's all. I mean, we knew it from the minute we learned she disappeared but..." I shake my head slightly. "We're running out of time to find her and I don't know if we ever will."

"Of course we will," Dani pats my shoulder. "You're not doing this alone, you know. Ken and Alicia might be skeptical, but I'm all in and I'm pretty sure Hailey is too. And as soon as this light changes, we're going to find out where she lives and maybe that'll be a major breakthrough."

"I sure hope so." I make myself smile for Dani's sake, then force breath out of my mouth, trying to shake the lingering sense of dread that always comes with my memories of my abduction.

Halfway down the block, we find a student apartment that has Ellie's last name on the buzzer box. BISHOP, handwritten in black marker on buzzer #408. No one else has 408, so it's clear she lives alone—no point to mashing the button, then.

Another dead end. Damnit.

"What's this?" Dani bends down and picks up a small silver thing that's half hidden in the dirt by the corner of the building. It's a crescent moon charm. The circular clasp that attaches it to a chain is broken in half, and the side Dani's holding is engraved in Spanish:

Para Ellie. Eres mi media naranja.

ten

I STARE AT the charm in the palm of Dani's hand, trying to get my thoughts together. "You reckon Jessica gave her that?"

"Maybe. It's not like she's the only Spanish-speaking person in all of Cedarwood." Dani swallows hard. "Ellie must have fought someone off. I bet they pulled her necklace hard enough to break it." Even though Dani's voice holds steady, I know her well enough to know she's close to tears.

"Could be she let them break it so someone would find it and know she was taken against her will," I say as Dani takes a photo to upload to the digital whiteboard. My ears are buzzing and my stomach's doing flip-flops, but my voice goes flat as if I don't feel anything at all. "You got a plastic bag or something so we won't lose that?"

"A tissue?" Dani opens her pocketbook. "I hope whatever happened wasn't too brutal."

"Yeah." I hold my hand out as Dani wraps the charm in a tissue.

"What are you going to do with that?" she asks.

"Confront Jessica. She'd best sleep well tonight cause tomorrow she's going to be made to confess the truth about her and Ellie and everything else she's been trying to hide from us."

"N-not give it to the cops?"

I stiffen. "Doubt they'll do anything with it besides say we contaminated it. If we want them to find Ellie, we have to lead them to her." I put the charm carefully into a mini-pocket in my jeans and button the flap so it can't fall out before I squat down. "This is where you found it, right?"

Dani nods slightly. Her eyes are wide; it must be hitting her how much danger Ellie's in right now.

I check out the area. It's a big patch of dirt to the side of the entrance that I reckon's going to be grass once the seeds start growing. There are too many sets of footprints to keep track of; Ellie's are probably buried under everyone else who walked across the dirt instead of going up the stone path to the door like you're supposed to, and some of the footprints are smeared so there's no telling what's what.

My eye's drawn to a spot just under the wall. Four oblong marks, like fingers, attached to a square...

"That a handprint?" I ask Dani.

"There's a second one here," Dani says, pointing. She grabs her phone and takes photos to upload to the whiteboard. "And look," she says after, She kneels and grabs something out of the dirt with two fingers. "Hair."

My eyes follow the thin, dark strand to the wall behind it. It's brick and empty except for some windows going up four stories, but it's all scuffed up from about halfway down to the bottom.

I stand up slowly and point to the wall. "Get that too." I turn my back, trying to think. In my mind's eye, someone grabs Ellie from behind, pressing a gloved hand over her mouth, dragging her away to a waiting car...

No. That was me way back when. Ellie obviously fought

back cause otherwise her necklace charm wouldn't have fallen to the ground.

I hug myself, trying to make sense of it all. "She was attacked right here, that's for sure," I say flatly.

Dani puts her hand on my shoulder, making me flinch. "Sure looks that way. Here, move over so I can get the photos." I slide over, hoping I ain't ruining any of the evidence by the way I'm moving. Dani takes more photos and says, "I hope Hailey can enhance these after we upload them cause there's not enough light." She gestures toward the windows. "Ugh, what an ugly view."

"Yeah." I tilt my head up at the windows, wondering if anyone happened to see Ellie getting attacked. If they did, they should have done something to help, but I reckon they might have been too scared to get involved.

"You know anyone who could tell us if someone called 911?" Dani asks.

I shrug. "Dr. Blanton might. But I doubt anyone did cause the cops didn't know anything about Ellie disappearing til Jessica called them this morning." My neck hurts from staring up at the windows. I rub it as I add, "But maybe someone saw something out one of these windows even if they didn't call for help."

Dani glances at her phone. "If the manager'll let us knock on doors tomorrow that'll help. In the meantime, maybe you can ask people for tips on your podcast page and then share it on your personal profile and I'll share it on mine. If someone's seen something, we'll find out. Come on."

I walk slowly away, my head held high, but I'm fighting the urge to run. If the fight was as bad as I think it was, Ellie could be seriously hurt. For all I know, it's too late already.

I can't shake the dread rising from my stomach as Dani and I board a bus back home.

. . .

The next morning, I tell Ken about the charm as we're walking across campus to the science building. "I didn't tell Alicia," I say, "cause she's so defensive of Jessica."

Ken shrugs. "Maybe she's right. Just cause Jessica gave Ellie this—if she did—doesn't mean she ripped it off her neck." He bites his lip. "How do we know whatever happened wasn't a robbery gone bad?"

Doubt fills my body. Ken's right; it could be someone random. But still. The video message. The hostess' claim that Ellie seemed depressed. All the lies Jessica told us. Everything adds up to foul play, and not by a random stranger who just wanted her necklace. "I hope not," I say weakly. "If she got kidnapped or worse cause someone wanted a cheap piece of jewelry, that'd be more than I could bear."

Ken puts his hand on my shoulder. "It's senseless no matter what the reason. Is it any better if Jessica did something to her cause she was jealous than if some dude wanted her necklace?"

"I guess not. But mugging doesn't feel right." I bite my lip, wondering again if I'm suited to investigate this or if I'd be better off farming it out to someone else and just writing the final report up for Dr. Blanton to give to the Dean.

"Ken! CJ! Wait up!" It's Alicia's voice. I ain't really in the mood when she's so pro-Jessica, but I'm not going to snub her either, so I stop and wait. She runs all the way across the quad to get to us, and by the time she gets there she needs her inhaler to help her catch her breath.

"You'll be okay once that takes hold, right?" I say after she puts it away.

Alicia nods. "This is nothing, trust me." She breathes in sharply, making fear shoot through me.

"Where's the fire, anyway?" Ken says.

"Dr. Armstrong made an announcement this morning about Ellie being missing that was super weird. I taped it along with the rest of his lecture. Here." Alicia's still breathing too hard for my liking as she pulls up the recording on her phone.

Dr. Armstrong's voice is soft. "As you know, I hate to pre-empt any part of my lecture. However, the administration has given me the sad news that Ellie Bishop, the lead researcher in my neuroscience laboratory, has gone missing. Ellie is a phenomenal researcher. She is working on some innovative projects that will greatly impact the field of neuroscience, especially as it relates to the effects of violence on the brain. If she is not found and returned safely so that she can resume her work, the loss to the scientific community will be unspeakable. Therefore, if anyone knows anything, I urge you to speak with Campus Safety or the local police."

"That's what he has to say?" I cross my arms. "Would he care if she wasn't his top researcher?"

"That was my thought exactly," Alicia says. "She WORKS for him. Where the hell is his empathy?"

"Maybe he just didn't know what to say," Ken suggests. "Just cause he's focusing on her research doesn't mean he doesn't care about her."

"Uncomfortable situation. The rumors about how she got her job are true. Remember?" Alicia's voice is hard. "He was doing something to her. He had to be."

"Seems like," I agree, "but only way to know for sure is to talk to him."

"Mind if I come with?" Alicia asks. "I want to ask Jessica what she thinks."

My stomach sinks. How are we going to confront Jessica with Alicia there? "Sure thing," I say, feeling like I can't turn her down without a lot of explanations I don't want to give. "You should know something too. Dani and I found this last night and we think it was a gift from Jessica." I take the charm out of my pocket and show it to her.

Alicia reads the inscription. "That's so beautiful. I hope

someone tells me someday I'm their *media naranja* too." She bites her lip. "It literally means half orange, which is a poetic way of saying soulmate, don't you think?"

"You reckon it was from Jessica?" I ask, wishing Alicia would stay focused on what's important.

"Probably. The edges match that sun necklace she always wears." Alicia shakes her head. "Poor Jessica. If Ellie was her secret girlfriend, losing her this way has to be a punch to her gut."

I'm quiet for a second. "We have to ask her why she left out that she was involved with Ellie last time we talked to her. You know that, right?"

Alicia crosses her arms. "It's obvious why. Not everyone can be out and obviously Ellie and Jessica weren't."

"Maybe," I say. "It's still a lie she told us on top of a few others and we need the truth."

Alicia's eyes flash. "I'm glad I'm coming with. This has to be handled with sensitivity, not by accusing Jessica of doing things she'd never do." She pushes past me before I can say a thing to her, leaving me no choice but to follow her as fast as my legs can take me.

eleven

THE RECEPTIONIST DOESN'T WANT to let us into the lab or even call Jessica down to talk to us. She says the cops have already taken up a lot of the researchers' time with their official investigation and she doesn't see the value in disturbing them again for a bunch of student reporters. "Besides, a lot of the information in the lab is confidential, so we can't let people who aren't vetted properly inside."

"What's the vetting — " I begin, but Alicia interrupts to say she's Jessica's mentee and sure Jessica wants to talk to her.

"I'm not sure if she's here," the receptionist says. She makes a call, then tells us, "Sarah'll come out to meet you. She's the most junior member of the lab, but she knows what she can and can't say."

Sarah. The same one who killed my post about Ellie the other night.

The lab door creaks open. Sarah is a tall girl, dark-haired like Ellie but with longer hair that is piled into a bun on the top of her head. Her cheeks are too pink for her pale white skin and I'm surprised she wears that type of blush because the rest of her makeup is dark: black eyeliner and mascara and purple lip gloss.

"I'm the youngest, so they sent me out to take care of you," she says, flashing a self-deprecating smile. "Come, I'll talk to you in the conference room."

I exchange glances with Ken. Alicia is texting someone, probably Jessica, and I'm sure she's still seething. I keep my thoughts to myself as Sarah taps her student ID against the security door and holds it open, gesturing for us to follow her.

"So terrible about Ellie." Sarah fidgets with her hands. Her fingers are long and she wears a silver ring with small diamonds in it on her middle finger. "Awful." She stops fidgeting and pushes her hair behind her ear instead.

"So then you know my post about her being missing ain't BS, then?" This wasn't the way I'd planned to go; it just slips out, and worse, my voice rises of its own accord too.

Sarah reddens. "I-I told you, that was the Dean's decision. I didn't agree but I don't get paid to fight with her so..." She laughs nervously. "Anyway, what do you guys want to know?"

"Anything you can tell us about Ellie and her life," I say. "We're grasping at straws here."

"Right." Sarah pushes her hair behind her ear. "I don't know her very well. I mean, I've heard rumors."

"What kind of rumors?"

"Nothing important. Besides, you shouldn't speak ill of the... missing, right?" Sarah's eyes dart all over the place.

"It's all right," Ken says. "Whatever you say's just between us. The way we see it, if you heard rumors, so did other people, and someone might have got upset enough to hurt Ellie so..."

Sarah goes pale. "Okay, okay. But it stays between us. I don't want Jessica to complain to Dr. Armstrong that I was telling lies to ruin Ellie's reputation." Sarah rolls her eyes while Ken and I exchange glances; I reckon he's wondering what that's about as much as I am. "Um, people say that Ellie slept with Dr. Armstrong and that's why he made her the lead researcher."

My stomach sinks. "Who told you that?"

Sarah shrugs. "It's one of those things that everyone in the lab knows. Like an open secret." She holds up her hands. "I didn't say I believed it, just that everyone laughed at me for not knowing it already."

"Does Dr. Armstrong know what people say about him?" Ken asks.

Sarah shrugs. "If he does, he won't care. He's one of those rare people who actually doesn't give a shit what others think." She laughs nervously. "People will probably say the same thing about him and me soon cause last night, we were in his office til late and then we left together."

It ain't lost on me that Sarah just gave me an alibi for when Ellie vanished. "You reckon he'd make time to see us soon so we can hear his take on what might have happened to Ellie?"

Sarah pushes her hair behind her ear. "Oh. That's not up to me," she says, grabbing her phone. " I'll Airdrop you his assistant's details. Her name's Chloe and she does his calendar."

"Let me ask you this," I say as she does it. "There anyone in the lab who might be jealous enough to hurt Ellie?"

Sarah's eyes dart back and forth. "I hope no one would be that petty. I mean, yeah, Ellie's published more than everyone and she's twice as gorgeous as me and Jessica put together, but we're all here to advance our education, right? Getting jealous is so middle school."

I'm dying to ask her why she's so nervous but I'm afraid she'll clam up if I do. Instead, I ask, "We heard that Ellie went on a date with Mark right before she disappeared. You think there's any chance he — "

A shadow falls over us. "Jessica," Sarah says quietly. "You're back."

"I am," Jessica says, coming into the room. "Do you have news about Ellie?" she asks. Her face trembles. "She's not... they did not find a body, did they?"

"No, ma'am," I say. "But we did find this, last night." I show her the charm.

Jessica's eyes widen. "So I was not the only one who kept mine." She bites her lip.

Alicia says something to her in Spanish and Jessica answers in kind, then says in English, "Okay. I am aware you have questions about this and maybe about why I didn't tell you I was close enough to Ellie to give her such a thing. If you will come to the garden behind the building with me, I will explain everything."

twelve

I RECOGNIZE THE garden behind the neuroscience building as soon as we follow Jessica through the gates. There are stone benches scattered here and there, and one of them is in front of a flower bed.

This is where Ellie filmed her last Story.

Jessica throws herself onto a bench."The garden is Ellie's favorite place. I keep coming here ever since I learned she was missing, as if I think it can give me answers."

"I reckon I can understand that." I sit down next to her even though I ain't been given permission. "So you and Ellie…"

"We are friends." Jessica's voice is flat. She plays with her sun charm, twisting it back and forth, before she adds, "But for a while we were more and I had hoped maybe…" She swallows hard.

Alicia says something softly in Spanish. Jessica shakes her head and says, "I had to keep it secret because Ellie cannot come out to the world. It is not safe because of her father."

"Jessica?" I say gently, knowing I can't push too hard even though I still have my doubts about her. "Is it possible that if he found out he'd do something to her?"

Jessica stiffens. "It is not her we need to fear for. It's Bobby. He is still a child and stuck at home with this man who does not deserve him."

"Bobby let slip he thought Ellie was gay," I tell her, "but he said the next second he had to be wrong because his daddy wouldn't allow it."

"This is correct." Jessica bites her lip. "Ellie would not let me visit her at her father's home anymore because after I left the first time, the father said he needed to give Bobby a spanking to get the gayness out of him." Jessica blinks back tears. "This is why it ended, because I could not stand pretending we were nothing to each other when we were everything."

"Yet you still protected her secret."

"Of course I did." Jessica stares at her feet. "I told you, we had Bobby to consider." She's silent for a long minute. "Ellie is bisexual, so it is not a total lie for her to be with a man, but her heart never stopped beating for me."

I exchange glances with Ken. I've got no doubt Jessica's sincere, but I still can't shake the feeling that she might have been jealous enough to hurt Ellie after her date with Mark. Still, accusing her directly won't do us a lick of good, so I say, carefully, "It must have hurt so much to see her go on a date with Mark then."

Jessica's face trembles. "Of course it did. But if you are asking did I make her disappear because I couldn't have her, the answer is no. I am an adult. I would not lash out violently because I cannot have the girl of my heart." She blinks hard. "If I wanted to hurt anyone it would be Ellie's father. He makes both his children miserable and he killed our relationship."

Alicia asks something in Spanish and Jessica responds. Alicia says, "She says the only reason she doesn't believe he did it is that he always comes home at 6:30 to keep an eye on Bobby.”

“He takes a train from the city,” Jessica adds, “the same one every time.”

I add that to the digital whiteboard. “Why didn’t you tell us all this in the first place?”

“I told you,” Alicia says, her voice hard, “she didn’t trust strangers, even if I told her you were okay.”

I glare at her. “Let her speak for herself.”

Alicia scowls, but Jessica says, “You are both correct. I was the one who lied by omission so I need to be the one to answer for it. I didn’t want to invade Ellie’s privacy, even now when she is missing. It was not only for Bobby. It was for her.” Jessica blinks hard. “I told one more lie. The proposal I was planning to discuss with her the evening she vanished had nothing to do with the research lab. I had asked her earlier if she would let me give her another chance and she said we would talk about it after her date with Mark.”

Ouch. Double gut punch. And this woman expects me to believe she wasn’t involved? “Why was she so hell-bent on going out with Mark?”

Jessica swallows hard. “She had her reasons.”

I glance at Ken, silently willing him to take over. He knows how to push in ways I don’t. He must have read my mind cause he says, “Being cagey’s not gonna help us trust you now. What reasons?”

Jessica shakes her head slightly. “I know you cannot understand this, but I need to protect her privacy even now.”

I cross my arms. “Does this have anything to do with the video she made?”

“You saw it before it disappeared.” Jessica’s voice is flat. “I should not be surprised. So did over 10,000 other people, most of them after she went missing. Before, few people cared.”

"Maybe they didn't know who she was until she made the news with her vanishing act," Ken says.

"But you do care," I add, "so how about you tell us what that was all about?"

Jessica's eyes dart up to the right; maybe she's trying to come up with a suitable lie. She says, slowly, "There is an ugly rumor that started even before she was appointed to the lead researcher position. She is always a magnet for jealousy in the lab because she knows not only how to research but how to get it published and she is so driven to succeed she has outperformed men who are in their fifth year when this is only her second."

"Any of these men threaten her?" Ken asks.

Jessica shrugs. "If they did, she didn't tell me. They used the rumor to discredit her instead, saying her success can be attributed to her offering sex with powerful men in exchange for what she wants."

Alicia scowls, disgusted, but I say to Jessica gently, "As ugly as that is, Ellie said it was true."

"I am aware." Jessica's voice is flat.

"So then she and Dr. Armstrong..."

"Ellie gained every accolade by her own hard work! She does not need to sleep her way to the top." Jessica is fidgeting with her necklace charm, twisting it quickly between her fingers; I reckon she believes the rumor no matter how much she's protesting.

"I'm sure," I say. "But Sarah also told me that everyone knows that the two of them are sleeping together. You have any idea where she got that from?"

Jessica's jaw tightens. "Sarah is too quick to believe what she hears," she says, "especially if it makes Ellie look bad."

"So they don't like each other, then?"

Jessica hesitates. "Ellie does not dislike anyone," she says, "but Sarah has had to work hard to prove herself. Dr.

Armstrong knew I was recruiting qualified undergraduates to assist us in the lab but he cut me out of the process to put Sarah in that position, and Ellie did not like having her authority as lead researcher undermined too." Jessica sighs deeply. "I should return to the lab," she says, "but first, can I have Ellie's charm? It is all I have of her right now and I need something to hold onto or I will not make it through the day."

I ain't about to give it to her, not when it's evidence and she hasn't really proven that she's innocent. "In a minute," I say. "First tell me this. Bobby said he overheard you telling Ellie that some man wasn't doing right by her. Was that Mark or someone else?"

Jessica freezes. Her eyes dart up to the right again before she says, "It is Ellie's story to tell, no one else's, and I am sure she does not want any more gossip repeated about her than already exists."

There seems to be no point in pushing her; I should just give her the charm even though I still don't completely trust her. "All right, fine. One more thing and then you can have this. The librarians said they couldn't remember if you were in the library or not the night Ellie disappeared. You have another way of proving it?"

Jessica's eyes narrow. "After all this, you still think there's any possibility I hurt Ellie?"

"Of course not," Alicia says. "We just know how the cops are, so..."

Jessica stabs at something on her phone. "Here," she says, shoving her phone at me. "I hope my library login history will settle this so I don't have to hear any more hurtful accusations."

I see a screenshot that says *Library Record*, but the phone blinks and then cuts off.

"I can't see anything," I tell her, handing her the phone.

Jessica tries to turn it back on, but it won't. "Damn it. The battery chose the wrong moment to drain completely."

Of course it did. I bite my lip, not seeing any good coming out of saying so.

"Tell you what," Alicia says. "I'll stick around while you charge it and then you can text it to me and that'll be that."

Jessica nods. "I cannot let you in the lab for confidentiality reasons but we can wait together in the conference room for the phone to be ready." She holds out her hand as she turns toward me. "I know you have no reason to trust me, but I am asking you to please give me Ellie's charm anyway. I am doing her work on top of my own in the hope that it somehow brings her back alive, and it would be a lot easier to do if I had a piece of her by my side."

I still don't like the idea, yet it feels cruel to deny Jessica something that gives her so much comfort. "Here," I say. "Please don't forget to give Alicia your login history. The sooner we clear you, the sooner we can find out what really happened to Ellie."

Jessica has tears in her eyes as her head bobs slightly. "I wish my word was good enough, but I understand you do not know me."

"I believe you," Alicia says, and adds something in Spanish as they walk off together.

I ain't sure what to make out of that. It seems ridiculous to worry that Alicia could be going off with a kidnapper, but at the same time, Jessica still ain't being 100% truthful with us.

"Let's go," Ken whispers. "We'll get to the bottom of this together, okay?"

I follow him out of the garden, wishing so badly that he had his arm around me that it hurts.

thirteen

KEN TAKES ME to the student union to grab a drink and debrief. The last thing I need is coffee when I'm so wound up that I can barely sit still, so he gets me a chai tea instead and remembers that when I ask for it I mean iced, not the hot stuff that's the default up here. My heart does flip-flops as he walks across the room to the coffee stand. I doubt any other man would be half as considerate.

Even though usually I hate being babied, him taking care of me makes me wish desperately for something I can't have. I grab my phone and text Hailey to ask her to look into Jessica's library login if she can. I doubt Jessica'll remember to get us a screenshot, and Alicia's too caught up in believing in her innocence to ask for it. Besides, screenshots can be doctored, so I'd rather someone I trust checks out the original.

When Ken comes back, he hands me my tea and says, "Drink first, then we'll talk."

The thought flashes through my mind that he's treating me the way he does Vicki when she's upset. I gulp my tea, trying to push down my irritation. Ken's jaw tightens, but he ignores it.

"Now," he says, "how serious are you about Jessica being behind this thing?"

"I don't know," I admit. "She seems genuinely heartbroken over Ellie's disappearance, but I ain't the best judge of when I'm having the wool pulled over my eyes." If I was, I'd never have been catfished by a pedophile. It's been half a decade and I'm an adult now, but that still doesn't mean I trust myself not to get fooled twice. "Anyway," I say, letting my breath out slowly, "if Hailey gets her hands on Jessica's login record and it turns out she was telling the truth about being in the library when Ellie disappeared, that's that."

Ken nods. "Long as you don't get stuck on her when there's other people who are just as suspicious. My money's on Ellie's dad. If he'd beat a kid Vicki's age to punish him for his sister being attracted to women, who the hell knows what he'd do if he found out Ellie slept with Jessica."

"Or with Armstrong. He's the type who would blame her even though Armstrong's the one with all the power." I shudder.

"You got a good point. Though we have to find out for sure if he —"

"Why would Ellie lie about that?" My voice rises of its own accord. "Being seen as a victim ain't fun, especially when half the people you know are more interested in blaming you for it than holding the man responsible who shattered your world."

Ken holds his hands up. "I'm not saying she's lying, Ceej. But doesn't what we've learned about verifying sources come into play when all you have is a video stating something ambiguous?"

"It ain't ambiguous, but whatever. I don't want to fight." I chew on my straw, breathing hard. I thought Ken was different, that maybe I could trust him with what happened to me, but now I ain't so sure.

"Me either." Ken stirs his coffee with his straw. "You know what we need? To move around some." I roll my eyes but he ignores that. "I'm serious! Whatever happened to Ellie's pretty heavy, and we're both all wound up. Getting some fresh air while we run around'll help."

I shrug. "Seems like a waste of time to me, but if you want…"

"It's not. You'll see." Ken unzips his backpack. "Besides, bet you can't resist throwing this around." He takes out a piece of wood shaped almost like the top of a circle. It's dark brown with the tips painted red.

"What in the world is that?" I ask.

"What, doesn't everyone carry a boomerang around with them?" Ken smirks. "Vicki gave it to me last Christmas. She was real proud of making it in her woodworking class and she dragged me out in the snow to show me that it always comes back when you throw it, long as you use your right hand."

"I'm sure she knew the laws of physics behind it, too," I say, my lips stretching into a small smile. "You actually like it or are you carrying it around so you won't hurt her feelings?"

"Both," Ken says. "I didn't have any reason to play with it til now, but I think it's just the thing to get your mind off Ellie for a little bit."

I push my tea away, my smile fading. "I don't want a distraction. I want to solve this."

"I know." Ken spins the boomerang on the table as if it's one of those fidget spinners Vicki sometimes plays with. "But sometimes when you stop pushing so hard for answers, they pop into your head. Give your brain space to figure stuff out, all right? Besides, we haven't had any time to make each other laugh since this Ellie thing began."

My cheeks grow hot. "I feel so bad having a good time with you when someone could be torturing Ellie right now."

I shiver involuntarily as Ken puts my hand between his.

"Us being miserable too won't bring her back faster. Now are you gonna race me to the park or what?"

My phone rings. It's a text from Alicia, with a copy of Jessica's login history. I stare at the screenshot without bothering to read the message. It shows Jessica's name and email address and then it lists the last five logins.

The top one has last Tuesday's date on it and says she logged in at 6:45 PM and didn't log out til 9:30 PM.

I stare at it awhile, my heart pounding. "Jessica's clear," I say. "Or she will be soon as Hailey verifies this." I forward the screenshot to Hailey before showing it to Ken.

"That's good news, right?" Ken says. "One less person we have to worry about, especially with Alicia being buddy-buddy with her."

I nod, but I can't figure out what I'm feeling. Part of me's glad my instincts were right, but I'm also still skeptical even though it would be a ridiculous amount of effort to go to for Jessica to forge her login history when all she had to do was not show it to us in the first place. "It is, but it isn't," I say slowly, "cause if it ain't her, we're no closer to finding Ellie than we were before."

"We'll get there." Ken stands. "Let go of what we can't control, that's what I say. And you owe me a race, so let's get moving."

"But —"

Ken starts running, calling over his shoulder, "You really gonna let me win just like that?"

I don't feel like it, but sitting here sulking ain't gonna do anything for me, so I squash my cup and throw it in the trash before running after him.

The park's three blocks south of campus, but we don't stop running except to wait on the light on University Drive, which turns red when it sees us coming and refuses to change back for a good five minutes. Ken jogs in place to keep the momentum going, so I do too. I ain't about to give him a head start. When the light finally goes green again I dart across the street before he has a chance to react and down toward the park, not stopping til I'm past the open metal gates and the brown signs warning everyone that the park closes at dusk.

"First one to the field wins!" Ken calls, but I barely hear him. My foot hits the field at the same time as his does, and not a moment too soon cause my ankles are screaming for oxygen and my heart's pounding. The field is a mix of grass and dirt halfway across the park; you can see Ellie's building from here. There are bushes on one side of the grass, separating it from a nearby pond.

Ken says he was there a half second before I was and I say I was first. He holds up his hands and says he'll give it to me if I let him throw the boomerang first.

"Fine with me." I laugh nervously. "I hope this thing doesn't sink down to the bottom of the pond when I throw it."

"Nah. I told you, it's supposed to always come back." Ken hands me a bottle of water out of his backpack. "Here. Let's rehydrate first."

We sit cross-legged on the grass, drinking water and catching our breaths. Ken says, "I didn't know I got a girl who was so competitive."

"I'm not exactly a girl, but thanks." I take a sip of water.

Ken's cheeks get darker. "Sorry," he says, looking away. "I forgot. What do you want me to call you?"

I shrug. "Friend, I guess, cause that's what we are."

Ken's shoulders slump as he looks me up and down. "Yeah," he says. "I guess so." He pats my hand. "Just out of curiosity, if you had a boyfriend, what would you be to them?"

"Asking for a friend?" I ask lightly. My ears are buzzing from all the exercise I just did and I'm feeling light enough inside I can almost believe he wants me that way.

Ken stares at the grass we're sitting on. "Yeah. For a friend."

I shrug, my stomach sinking. "Partner, I suppose," I say. "But I'd have to find a man who ain't worried what it makes them to be dating me, so it probably ain't gonna happen any time soon, if ever."

Ken looks away from me as he crushes his empty water bottle. "Right. I was just talking hypothetically." He tosses the bottle toward a nearby trash can. It looks like it's gonna bounce off the rim, but it goes in. "Let's play." He stands. "Unless you're still too scared of it going into the pond to try it out."

"Me? Nah." I make myself smile even though my good mood's melting away like the last of the snow when the sun comes out. "Let's give it a try."

Ken takes the boomerang out and tosses it in my direction. Before I can catch it, it turns in the air and heads back toward him.

"Whoa, this really does work how she said." I run after the boomerang. "I hope Alicia hasn't forgotten to see if she can get Mark to talk to us. We need his side."

"Now you're talking. But don't go in with guns blazing. That'll just scare him off." Ken stares at the boomerang in my hands. "You gonna toss that back or what?"

"Sorry." I try to throw the boomerang, but it doesn't do that fancy spin back, instead nosediving into the bushes. As I run to get it, a horrible smell hits my nose, so pungent I have to pinch my nostrils close while I push through the branches, or try to. They're sagging and won't move, like something's holding them down.

When I shove against the bushes, I see it.

The body.

The hair's all tangled up in the branches and the legs are hanging down, barely touching the ground. There's a bruise on the right knee, or at least it looks like it—it's hard to tell from what little I can see—and more on what's left of her neck. The face is swollen and the skin is discolored and barely recognizable as human, and her eyes are completely red. The awful smell is so strong now I expect I'll be sick any second, and there are flies and other bugs crawling all over.

It doesn't look like the photos and video at all, but I know without a doubt what I'm looking at.

It's Ellie, and she's dead.

fourteen

KEN'S CALLING ME, asking if I found the boomerang. It sounds like he's very far away even though I know he's only on the other side of the grass.

Where in tarnation is that stupid toy?

There. Stuck in a branch in front of Ellie.

I gently pick it up, half tempted to ask Ellie if she hid it so I'd find what's left of her. I turn and push my way through the bushes as fast as humanly possible, trying to get out of there before I lose what's left of my mind.

"There you are," Ken says. The light goes out of his face all at once. "What's wrong?"

"I found... I found..." I make myself breathe hard through my nose, trying to force out the words that won't come naturally. "It's Ellie. She's in the bushes." My voice shakes. "She's dead."

Ken squeezes his eyes shut as he crosses himself. "You're sure it's her?"

I nod. "Someone threw her out like yesterday's trash. Could be she wanted me to find her so I could put her to rest. We have to lay her flat and put a blanket over her or something."

"No!" Ken's voice is louder than I ever knew he was capable of. I flinch as he puts his arms around me, hugging me tight. "We can't mess with the body, not til the cops check it out. There could be evidence they need to put away whatever bastard did this to her. You gotta leave it alone, okay?"

I stiffen. "I won't touch her. Just let me go. Please let me go."

Ken releases me. "Show me, okay? I need to know what to tell 911." We get as far as the bushes when he wrinkles his nose at the smell. "I can see her from here," he says. "No need to get any closer. Come on."

We get out of the bushes and Ken calls 911. I sit cross-legged on the grass, staring into space while he describes what's left of Ellie, my eyes burning but no tears coming out. I sure hope the cops take it more seriously than the ones back home did after I escaped my kidnapper. Will they look into what really happened, or will they assume Ken and I killed her and drag us off in cuffs just so they can call it a day?

After he hangs up, Ken puts his arm around me as he tells me the cops are on their way. "How you doing?" he asks softly.

I shrug. "Been better." I pull out handfuls of grass and toss them over my shoulder. "Y-you don't reckon they'll blame us, do you?"

"Better not. But how about I call my mom and see if we need to get a lawyer down here?"

I don't want Ken to bother his mom over this, but I can't find the words to say so. I lean on his chest and let him hold me while he makes the call. His heart beats in my ear and I don't ever want to pull away from him again.

I need to say a prayer for Ellie since that's all I can do for her now, but instead I keep thinking about what happened to me back home and how my kidnapper might have taken my life from me when he'd gotten everything else he wanted if I hadn't managed to escape his vehicle in time. I don't even know where the strength came from to fight my way out with my hands bound behind my back. All I know is that something snapped in me then and my body moved by itself as if it had decided on its own that it wasn't letting him take a single thing more from me than he already had.

And now I feel more helpless than I did then. Ellie's dead, and I have no idea who killed her or how to prove it.

A sob escapes from my throat despite my best efforts.

Ken strokes my hair. "It'll be all over soon. Listen to my mom, okay?"

I pull tufts of grass out of the ground, trying to calm myself, while Ken puts the phone on speaker and moves slightly so he can keep holding me against his chest while I talk to his mom.

"CJ?" Mrs. Hansen's voice is firm. "You there, baby?"

"Yes, ma'am." I try to keep my voice as steady as hers so I don't embarrass myself.

I do my best to pay attention as she instructs me to answer the cops' questions but explains I need to tell them I'm represented by counsel if they try pinning Ellie's death on me. My mind's still stuck on how much it sucks that I didn't get to Ellie before she died and I have to keep pulling it back to what Mrs. Hansen is saying so I don't waste her time when she's trying to help me. By the end, I ain't sure if she's really hired a lawyer for me or if I'm just supposed to say she did if the cops treat me like a criminal. I hope I won't have to find out, but I wouldn't put it past them to find a reason to arrest me.

After we hang up, Ken holds me tighter while I pull up more grass and try not to cry. I want to kiss him so badly it hurts, but I know better than to allow myself to go there.

The cops' flashing lights give me a headache as they approach. I make myself sit up properly anyway.

As I rub the back of my neck, the police detective I spoke to before comes up to me. He's got another detective with him, a woman with short, jet-black hair and bronze skin. She's shorter than him, but not by much, and her arm muscles bulge as she puts one hand on the butt of her gun like she's expecting to have to pull it out.

"CJ, right?" the male detective says. "I'm Detective Cooper, in case you've forgotten, and this is my partner, Detective Estrada. Come talk to me while we're waiting for the forensics team. I want to hear all about how you stumbled across this body."

Ken asks to sit with me, but Cooper says he can cover more ground if Estrada questions him at the same time.

I follow Cooper to a picnic table far enough away to be private but close enough to where Ken's sitting with the other detective that I can see them out of the corner of my eye.

"I'd say it was nice to see you again, but I know these are not the most pleasant of circumstances," Detective Cooper says. "Your boyfriend told the 911 dispatcher that you were the one who found the body?"

I nod, not bothering to correct him about who Ken is to me, and explain how I came to be in the bushes. Cooper asks for details that I don't have the answer to, like how long I was there and if I noticed anything else strange. All I can tell him is that Ellie's hair was caught on a branch and that her smell made me sick.

"I'm sorry that happened," Cooper says when he's finally done making me relive this.

"Not as sorry as I am," I sniff. "I wish I'd found her alive. Even if she was all messed up from being kidnapped, she'd still have a chance to move forward with her life." A sob escapes. Cooper waits for me to compose myself; he's silent so long I feel a need to say something more. "Was she dead the whole time I've been searching for her?"

"We'll let the forensics team determine that." Cooper

glances down at his legal pad, then back up at me. "I have to ask, did you touch or move her?"

I shake my head. "I wanted to lay her to rest but Ken stopped me so it wouldn't mess up the crime scene before you could look at it."

"Ken seems to know a lot about the proper procedure for dealing with dead bodies," Cooper comments.

I don't see what this has to do with the price of beans. "His mom works for a big criminal law firm in the city."

"I see. Well, I'm glad he didn't let you interfere with the body. Now, how familiar are you with this park? Have you been here often?"

I shake my head. "All I knew about it before today was that Campus Police said it's dangerous here after dark."

Cooper raises his eyebrows. "I see. So you wouldn't know what type of traffic this area gets or how likely it is that someone might dump a body here."

"You saying she was killed elsewhere and they threw her away after they were done with her?"

Cooper hesitates. "How about I stick to asking questions and you stick to answering them?"

As far as I'm concerned, that's confirmation. "T-throwing her away like that's even worse than taking her life. Who would do that?"

"I agree." Cooper's voice is soft, though it ain't lost on me that he sidestepped the second half of my comment. "One more thing, CJ. I know you were trying to find Ellie alive. Have you come across any information that might be helpful in finding out what happened to her?"

I rub the back of my neck. I'm sure he's already looked at Ellie's socials, but I tell him about the video anyway, then think hard about that moon charm. He ain't gonna like that I kept it from him, but does it matter? Ellie's dead and noth-ing'll change that.

"There's something else," I say, my mouth dry. Cooper silently pushes a bottle of water across the picnic table to me. I sip it, more to buy myself time than anything, then explain, haltingly, how Dani and I found the moon charm and how I used it to get Jessica to talk.

Cooper frowns. "Are you telling me you think Jessica killed Ellie?"

"I did," I say slowly, "but she has an alibi. Look." I show him the screenshot.

"I'm going to Airdrop that to myself, okay?" Cooper says. As he does, he adds, "We'll look into whether this document is real. But first I need you to tell me why you were suspicious of Jessica in the first place."

I bite my lip, thinking. Now that I'm 99% sure Jessica's innocent, I don't want to get her in trouble she doesn't deserve. But holding things back'll only blow up in my face. "She told me some lies," I say, "but she explained them. She and Ellie used to be more than friends, but Ellie ain't out so she did what it took to protect her privacy. But for a while there I reckoned that she was jealous because Ellie went on a date with a man, and since he was the last to see her alive it seemed to add up."

Cooper frowns. "Wait. Ellie was into women but she dated a man?" He holds up his hand as I start to explain. "Never mind. That doesn't matter unless it was a motive for someone to kill her. What's this man's name?"

I give it to him.

"Okay. Now, where is the charm you found now?"

I stare down at the table. "Jessica has it."

Cooper breathes in sharply. "That complicates things. Why did you not turn this item over to my team right away?"

"C-cause it was contaminated anyway from us touching it so we reckoned we might as well use it to get Jessica to tell us the truth."

"Bull." Cooper raises his voice slightly, making me flinch. More quietly, he says, "Jessica's obvious lies made you suspicious of her. Please have enough respect for me not to do the same thing to me. You did not hold onto this evidence because you thought it was contaminated. You did it because you wanted to use it in your own investigation, didn't you?"

"Y-yes sir," I say, staring at the table. The wood is splintered in spots, making it not the safest place for people to sit and eat. "Am I in trouble?"

"No. I do not believe that you deliberately obstructed justice and we'd only tip off the killer that they left evidence behind if I were to make a big deal out of this. But if it happens again, I will not be so forgiving. This evidence could have helped us bring Ellie's killer to justice and now we might not be able to use it. Investigating on your own is one thing, but the last thing I need is you making it harder for me to do my job. Do I make myself clear?"

"Yes, sir. I apologize."

Cooper nods, but I'm sure my apology isn't cutting it. "I need to speak to your friend directly about that charm. Please give me her contact information."

I hope Dani won't be too upset, but I have no choice but to cooperate.

"She might not like me talking out of turn," I say after I do, "but something happened and I reckon it's related." I tell Cooper how Dani offered to look for Ellie at the party and show him the text I got threatening her.

Cooper frowns as he forwards it to himself. "If your friend was drinking at that party, I hope you will advise her not to do that again for a while. Until we have the person who killed Ellie in custody, we can't assume the killer won't strike again, and a young woman whose judgment is compromised is an easy target, especially if someone already has it in their head to threaten her to intimidate you."

I bow my head. "Yes, sir. She's aware."

"Good. Is there anything else you haven't told me that might be relevant?"

I shake my head. I should tell him about the handprints, but I'm too exhausted to speak.

Cooper pats my shoulder as he stands. "There are no words for how sorry I am that you had to make this gruesome discovery. Take it easy, all right? And know that my team is gathering clues and we aren't giving up on Ellie any more than you are." He gets up and walks away before I can answer.

His partner is still talking to Ken, so there's nothing to do but sit and wait. I stare into space, half-watching as a bunch of cops stretch yellow police tape around the bushes where Ellie's still lying. It's just like on TV, so much so it's tempting to pretend none of it's real.

Except it is, and I can't get the image of Ellie's body in those bushes out of my mind. What was left of her had been too disgusting to look at for long, so I don't know what her face looked like—was fear written all over it? I'd wager she thought of Bobby and worried about how he was going to get on without her, especially since now he was stuck with his daddy. Tears spring to my eyes and I can't help thinking how badly I failed him.

The cops finish mounting their yellow tape and move into the bushes to look at Ellie. I want to know what they're finding, yet the thought of them poking and prodding at her remains is so disturbing I can't bear it and turn my head toward Ken's table to distract myself.

Ken's hands are clasped in front of him. He's looking the cop in the eye as he answers a question, but his shoulders are the tiniest bit slumped and I can see his muscles bulging through his shirt sleeves.

Is that detective accusing him of something?

I ain't sure God'll listen, but I say a prayer anyway,

promising Him that if Ken's allowed to come back to me I'll tell him how I feel about him. I reckon it worked, cause the next second, the detective walks away and Ken heads toward my table.

I don't get the chance to keep up my end, though, cause as soon as Ken sits down, a cop kicks us out of the area. Pushing through all the reporters who have somehow found out already about me finding Ellie's body is exhausting and I can barely speak when Ken asks me if I'm okay.

"I can't shake the memory of her lying there like that," I say, my voice shaking. "She was so full of life on that video and now…"

Ken squeezes my shoulder. "Let me take you home. The sooner we get out of here, the better."

I don't want to, but when I get into his car, my whole body feels heavy and I can barely keep my eyes open, so I have to let him take me to the dorm and tuck me into bed like I'm still younger than Vicki.

I don't remember dreaming when I wake up again, but I must have cause I've got this feeling that I need to go check on Bobby. I hurry to wash my face and get changed so I can bike down to the Bishop house; I have the address from when I looked up who called me the night Ellie disappeared.

Their house looks nicer from the outside than I expected. It's bigger than Ken's and it has a freshly cut lawn and a flower garden in front, as well as a path and steps made of stone that lead up to a porch with a bench swing, where Bobby is sitting and hugging himself.

Bobby's eyes widen when he sees me and he puts on an obviously-forced smile. "CJ! You came!"

"I reckon you heard about Ellie." I sit down next to him. "There's no words for how sorry I am. I'll swear on anything you want I tried my hardest to find her alive."

"I know." Bobby crawls into my lap before I know what

he's about to do and clings to me, leaning his head against my chest. "I don't understand why someone would do this to her."

"I don't either," I tell him, "but I'm fixin' to find out. Whoever it was will pay for taking her from you and that's a promise." I put my hand on his shoulder, not daring to do more than that even though he clearly wants to be held. "Your daddy know you're out here?"

"Yeah." Bobby's voice goes flat. "I think it's cause he's sad. When I asked him if he had to go back to work today, his shoulders started shaking and he yelled at me to go outside and leave him alone."

"Everyone handles things in their own way, I reckon." I squeeze Bobby's shoulder. "I know the last thing you want right now's to answer more questions, but I have to know, did your daddy get home the same time as always the night Ellie disappeared?"

Bobby swallows hard. "Course he did. What kind of question is that?"

The front door creaks open before I can answer and a voice I only I only half-recognize says, "Bobby, who are -"

I look up as Bobby's daddy comes all the way out of the house. Mr. Bishop is taller and thinner than I imagined. He's lost most of his hair but I can see Ellie in him, especially round the eyes.

"Who the hell are you and why are you touching my son?" he says.

I get my hands off Bobby, putting them up as if his daddy has a shotgun. He doesn't, but the way he's talking is like the way a protective father with one would. "I don't mean any disrespect, sir. I'm CJ Jennings, the reporter Bobby spoke to on the air the night Ellie disappeared."

"Yeah, right." Mr. Bishop looks me up and down. "I know

what your kind does. My son isn't gay and he never will be. Get away from him."

"No, Daddy!" Bobby said. "CJ is my friend! She's helping us find out who hurt Ellie so that we can make them pay."

"Bobby," Mr. Bishop says, his voice as quiet and threatening as the man who abducted me, "shut up and get in the house."

Bobby shrinks back but stares at his father. His daddy takes a step toward him and he runs into the house as fast as his little legs can carry him. He turns his head over his shoulder before he disappears and I feel as if his eyes are screaming at me to help him. Then the screen door clangs closed and he's gone.

"I apologize for disturbing you, Mr. Bishop," I say, hoping that leaning into being as respectful as I've been taught to be to my elders will help dissipate Mr. Bishop's anger before he hurts Bobby. "I wanted Bobby to know that I'd done everything in my power to find your daughter alive and that I'm not going to rest now until I find out who killed her and bring them to justice."

Mr. Bishop's face softens, then hardens again. "You'd better not broadcast any lies about Ellie or you'll be hearing from my lawyer. And stay away from my son. I will not let someone like you take advantage of him."

Someone like you. He thinks I'm no better than the man who abducted me cause I dress like a man when he can tell I was born with a female body. Disgust rises in my throat and I have to breathe deeply to stop myself from puking.

"Yes, sir, I understand." I stand. "I truly am sorry for your loss. Tell me one thing. Do you know if Ellie was having any problems with this man she went on a date with right before she disappeared?"

Mr. Bishop's eyes narrow. "More lies. Ellie didn't date cause she knew if she lit the money I was spending on her education on fire, there'd be serious consequences. You tell that perverted girlfriend of hers that she'll pay for what she did to my little girl." He punches his open palm with his fist. "Now stop with the insinuations and get the hell out of here."

I keep my voice as calm as I can. "Yes, sir. But I am trying to get your daughter justice so if you think of anything that can help, here's my card." I give it to him, then turn and walk away, aware that he's going to throw it away as soon as my back's turned.

fifteen

I FINALLY GET a chance to look through the tips people have sent me while I'm on the bus back to campus. There are a ton of responses on my post, but half of them are people with no profile photo and names like Nunya Nunyabiz trying to start crap, saying I must hate myself for being such a shitty reporter that I need to ask the Internet to do my job for me or that I should wake them up when I report on something actually worth caring about. Some of them joke around about being responsible for her disappearance, too, saying, things like, "Oh yeah, it was me 😂😂😂😂"

It disgusts me how easy it is for people to not only dismiss Ellie's death as no big deal but make fun of me for wanting to get justice for her. When I posted this last night, I thought she was still alive and so did the people saying this shit, but still. How can they be so cruel?

My eyes hurt and I want to lean back and close them, but I don't let myself. Ellie needs me to keep fighting for her, and the key to her murder might be hidden among all these laugh reacts and people who think it's hilarious to say they did it.

I have a ton of DMs both on my podcast account and my

personal profile, but I don't have the energy to look at them and I'm relieved when Dani texts:

> Hailey & I both have news. Meet @ Alicia's.
> PS Are you okay??

My head's pounding, but I tell Dani I'm fine before texting Ken about the meeting. His parents ain't home yet, so he's stuck there with Vicki, but he says he can get away with video chat as long as we don't mind if he gets interrupted.

Everyone but Ken's there by the time I get to Alicia's, making her front room feel tiny. She's lucky enough to live by herself in a suite-style dorm that's more like an apartment, except she's got a shared bathroom with her next-door neighbor.

"We ordered pizza," Dani says. "I made Alicia get half black olive for you."

I pat her hand and make myself smile, grateful for her attempt to make things normal, while Hailey sets up a video link on her tablet and texts the logon info to Ken so he can join us.

"You sure everything's okay?" Alicia asks while we're waiting. "I can't imagine how you felt when you found her."

"Be glad you weren't there." I swallow hard. "I wish I could forget it, but it's burned into my brain, and so's my conversation with the cops." I sigh deeply. "Seemed like they were harder on Ken than me."

"They were," Ken says. I flinch; I hadn't realized he'd made it on. "Nothing I can't handle, though. I figured the tall Black guy who called the body in would be on the top of their list." His eyes narrow, but he makes himself smile. "Anyway, sorry I'm late. Vicki had all this drama cause she can't find this diver toy she's gonna use in her bath later. You'd think she's the one who had someone die the way she went on about it."

"I reckon that's how it is for her," I say. "When I was a child, losing a favorite toy was like losing my best friend."

There's a knock on the door. Alicia opens it and Jessica's standing there, holding a bottle of sparkling cider. Her ponytail is too loose, as if she didn't make much of an effort, and there are tears drying on her temples. She smiles slightly and holds up a bottle of sparkling cider. "I b-bring this to toast to Ellie's memory."

Alicia holds her arms out, but Jessica says, "It is not right. You are my mentee."

"I don't care," Alicia says. "We're friends, and I know Ellie meant a lot to you."

Jessica lets Alicia hug her. While she does, Hailey says, "We know you didn't kill Ellie. I authenticated your screenshot."

Jessica nods. "I appreciate this." She puts the bottle of cider carefully down on a table before sinking down into a spare beanbag chair and turning toward meh. "I am sorry you had to find her, but at least we know now." She blinks back tears.

I reach for her hand to pat it. She hesitates, then grabs mine and squeezes it, then lets me go.

Hailey says, "There's something else, too. I enhanced the photos you guys sent me last night." She opens her phone. "Not to be insensitive or anything but did Ellie look like she'd been dragged through the mud?"

"She was barefooted," I say, "but I can't recall if her feet were muddy. Why?"

"Because," Hailey says, "I think we have proof positive she was killed at the apartment, not the park." She opens the photo and presses some buttons to project it on the tablet screen. All I see is a bunch of smeared footprints that tell us nothing, but she says, "That's exactly it. It's like someone was dragging their feet."

"Or they were dragged," Dani says.

"I agree with this hypothesis." Jessica points. "There are footprints on either side."

I glance at it. It's hard to tell which footprints are relevant cause there are about a hundred of them smushed together.

"That could be nothing," I say. "There's too many."

"Yes, but if we presume someone dragged her away, then their footprints are mixed into these." Jessica turns toward Hailey. "Is there a way you can use your photo tools to isolate the footprints we need to see?"

"I wish I could," Hailey says, "but I don't have access to that kind of tech."

Jessica's face falls. Her disappointment makes my eyes burn, but I don't let myself cry.

"Let's just update the whiteboard," I say, "if you haven't already, Hailey." I swallow hard. "I don't like recalling how Ellie looked but I'll add it."

No one answers. The air feels heavy as I open the whiteboard app.

After a few minutes, Dani says, "Um, maybe it'll cheer us all up if I play this tip I got in my DMs today?" She lets her breath out slowly and says, "You should have it too, CJ, I think this person sent it to both of us."

"This person doesn't have a name?" I ask.

"It was on Social Strands. Their profile name is April Dixon, but they have a drawing for a profile photo instead of a real picture, and they're not in the student group. Anyway, here." Dani opens the DM and shows us all the tipster's profile photo. It's one of those cartoon avatars that AI makes from real photos. The drawing is of a girl with brown hair that hangs down and is tucked behind one ear. Her face is oval and her skin is peach. I can't tell from the drawing exactly who she is, but I swear I've seen her someplace before.

Jessica's eyes widen as Dani shows her the profile.

"You know who that is a picture of?" I ask. "She seems familiar to me but I can't place her."

Jessica nods. "It looks just like Dr. Armstrong's assistant, Chloe. But I don't know why she would use a profile with a fake name." She sighs. "I hope she has not fallen apart since Ellie's death. Ellie was a close friend to her."

"Friend or..." I begin.

Jessica swallows hard. "It would be worse for Chloe if it were more, though I think she is straight. Anyway, was the tip worthwhile?"

"You tell me what you think," Dani says, and hits Play.

A female voice whispers, "I saw a silver car double-parked in front of the Burnt Olive and messing up all the traffic. A woman with long, dark hair got in the car and started it just before Ellie left the restaurant, and then she drove in the same direction like she was following her to her apartment. I think she might have been the killer, do you?" I listen closely, wondering why this girl's whispering and trying to guess who she is. The voice isn't familiar. It sounds like it could be any girl on campus, but something feels off about it that I can't quite put my finger on.

Alicia frowns. She turns and says something to Jessica in Spanish, talking so quickly that even if I knew more than a few words, I wouldn't be able to follow her. Jessica answers, speaking their native language just as rapidly.

"Not to be rude," Ken says, "but is there something you guys want to share with the rest of us?"

"Sorry," Alicia says. "I just got really upset." She crosses her arms. "Whoever sent that tip has to be lying. Jessica has a silver car and long dark hair. If we hadn't been able to prove her alibi, we might be fighting right now about whether she killed Ellie."

I raise my eyebrows. "You reckon someone's framing her?"

Jessica nods. "Not just anyone," she says. "Chloe, who I

thought loved Ellie. And who also has a silver car so since I am proven innocent it would be easy to think she is confessing while pretending not to." She swallows hard. "The evidence suggests she is trying to make you think I killed Ellie, so the most logical conclusion is that she did so herself, but that does not match who I thought she was at all." Her face trembles.

Alicia puts her hand on Jessica's shoulder.

Hailey says, "Let's not jump to conclusions. Forward me that voice clip, Dani, and a link to the profile. I want to analyze them to see if I can find out whose phone sent it and whether it's a human voice or AI-generated. Certain abnormalities in the pitch variation make me suspect the latter, but I won't know until I run some tests."

Jessica smiles slightly despite the tears in her eyes. "This reminds me how Ellie would never accept the first conclusion anyone came to. She had a rule in the lab that when drawing conclusions you had to list at least three different possibilities and your analysis of which ones were possible and what was most probable. She would be honored if we used her method to find out who killed her."

Alicia says, "And on that note, how about we take a break to toast to Ellie? The pizza should be here any minute, too."

"Good idea," Jessica says. She opens the cider and pours it into red plastic cups for all of us, then picks hers up and says, "To Ellie's spirit and to our newfound friendship. It comforts me to think her last act was to bring us all together to get justice for the theft of her life." Her voice shakes slightly and she takes a deep breath and forces it out.

"We will," I tell her as Alicia's phone buzzes. Alicia asks Jessica to come with her to get the pizzas from downstairs and Jessica gets up slowly to follow her.

"How soon before you know something about that tip?" I ask Hailey while Jessica and Alicia are out of the room.

"The AV room is closed now," Hailey says, "but I can run

some tests tomorrow after my 9 AM class. So probably midday?" She opens the small section of her backpack and fishes for something inside. "Before I forget, this is for you guys." She takes out a plastic bag that has several tiny clip-on mics. "These are Bluetooth," she explains. "If you connect them to your phone, you can record without anyone knowing. We have them all semester; I signed them out at the end of my shift today."

I thank her as I put mine carefully in my pocket. Dani says, "So... whether or not that tip was AI, how do we find out whether any of it's true?"

"I can help with that," Ken says. "I don't know what color it was, but there was definitely a double-parked car by the Burnt Olive that evening. I know cause I got stuck in traffic down there."

I frown. "When you were on the way to the studio to get me?"

"No, earlier." Ken sighs. "I had to run an errand for my mom and it took way longer than I expected cause of that stupid double-parked car. It took up the whole lane so everything slowed to a crawl while everyone tried to get around it."

"Vicki must have loved that," I say.

Ken swallows hard. "That's why I was so pissed about it. Vicki, um... she wasn't with me. I left her home by herself cause it wasn't supposed to take more than ten minutes tops and she was in a mood about having to go out when it wasn't part of her usual routine." His cheeks darken. "I should have dragged her along anyway. I was irresponsible, leaving her without supervision for nearly an hour. And worse... it was right around the time Ellie was killed so now there's no one to back me up about where I was."

My throat tightens. "That what the cops were pressing you about?"

Ken nods. "Don't worry. My mom's lined up a lawyer in

case they decide not to drop it. She's mad as hell that I left Vicki alone, but she said being stupid's not against the law and she won't let me go to jail for it."

"Who is going to jail now?" Jessica says, coming back in with Alicia. "Black olives was the right choice, by the way. It happens that was also Ellie's favorite."

"I'm glad," I say. "And nobody. Ken was just telling us that he was stuck in traffic near the Burnt Olive the night Ellie disappeared because of a double-parked car."

Jessica's eyes widen. "So the tip had truth inside it."

I nod. "Do you reckon there's any chance Chloe really did double-park there?"

"That is one of our three explanations," Jessica says, "but it is a highly unlikely one. She is too afraid of the police to risk implicating herself even if there is an innocent explanation for her presence at the Burnt Olive that night."

"If she's that scared, she's not thinking clearly," Ken says. "Maybe she's trying to stop the cops from catching her by telling on herself in the hopes we'll assume she would never do any such thing."

"That's too convoluted," Alicia says.

"Either way," I say, "we need to talk to Chloe and find out what she knows about this April Dixon account." I bite into a piece of pizza. It might as well be cardboard cause I'm not paying any attention to how it tastes. "Sarah gave me her contact info so that I can try to arrange an interview with Dr. Armstrong about Ellie. Maybe I can get her to arrange one for herself while we're at it."

"I will introduce you tomorrow," Jessica says. "On Fridays she works for Dr. Armstrong in the afternoon because she has a class at 10 AM. I will have coffee with her before her class and convince her to meet with you."

"And in the meantime," Alicia says, "in the interest of not

getting stuck on one suspect, how about CJ and I have a chat with Mark? He was the last to see Ellie alive, so..."

Jessica's eyes are wet with tears. "These are good plans," she says, "but now I want to try to salvage my dinner, so let's have no more of this." She grabs a piece of pizza and bites into it, blinking hard.

I sure hope we can get answers tomorrow, cause Jessica can't go on like this.

"So what do you reckon?" I ask Dani as we walk home from Alicia's. "Is that tip for real?"

Dani shrugs. "Either way, it doesn't make any sense. If it's real, Chloe's telling on herself in an effort to frame Jessica."

"And if it's fake, someone wants us to think Chloe's doing that. So I suppose maybe someone's framing her, not Jessica."

"I guess." She sighs. "It would help if we knew anything about Chloe other than what Jessica told us."

I take out my phone and Google Dr. Armstrong, recalling he had a photo credited to Chloe. Her last name's Lancaster, which is enough to go on. When I look her up, I find her listing on the lab website and learn she's a nontraditional student, which means she's doing her undergrad degree late, who works for Armstrong part-time while studying psychology. She has a photo next to her bio; I saw it before, but this time it makes me freeze up and stare at it cause now that I know what Dean Northrop looks like, I see a younger version of her in Chloe.

"Interesting," Dani says, "but not incriminating. Anything else?"

I hit the Back button and scroll down. Pay dirt -- there's a news article in the Cedarwood Courier with the headline:

Dean Speaks Out on Daughter's Arrest: 'She's an Addict, Not a Criminal.'

I click on it. The article is very short and has a photo of Dean Northrop at a podium next to one of Chloe being escorted up the courthouse steps in handcuffs. It says simply that Dean Northrop responded to the arrest of her daughter, who was alleged to be responsible for a string of burglaries on campus, and that the Dean made a statement via Chloe's lawyer to the effect that they believe Chloe's crimes were the result of a drug problem and will be asking the judge to sentence her to rehab.

"And she's still the Dean?" Dani says. "Wouldn't something like this end her career?"

"It ain't like she's the one who broke into people's houses. She can't help what her daughter does." I stop dead in my tracks as something hits me. "Wait... what if the situation Ellie was in wasn't what we think? Jessica said Chloe was Ellie's friend. What if Ellie knew Chloe was back on drugs and decided she was sick of covering it up?"

"That's a motive for murder, that's what. But we don't have any proof."

"Not yet, but maybe after we meet her tomorrow we'll get some."

"I hope so." Dani's phone rings. She goes pale as she checks the display. ""C-Cedarwood Police?"

"I had to tell them about the charm," I tell her. "I'm sorry I didn't give you a heads-up."

Dani swallows hard as she answers. "Hello? Y-yes, this is her. Um... is tomorrow okay? It's kind of late. I can do that. I have class at 11, so as long as I'm on a bus back by 10:30. Yes, that works. Thanks."

She hangs up the phone. "The cops want to see me," she

says flatly. "I managed to get them to wait til tomorrow, but they have some questions about that charm we found. I hope I didn't make myself into a suspect by not insisting we give it to them right away."

sixteen

WHEN WE GET HOME, Dani drinks an entire bottle of water in two gulps and I know she wishes it was something stronger.

"How about I ask Ken's mom to get you a lawyer?" I ask. My phone buzzes just then. Speak of the Devil—it's him.

I answer. "Hey, I was just —"

"It's Vicki," Vicki whispers, her voice so low I can barely hear her.

"Vicki," I say quietly. "What are you doing up this time of night?"

"The cops were just here, that's what!" Vicki sniffs.

Fear shoots through me. "It'll be all right," I say, keeping my voice even for Vicki's sake. "What did they want?"

"I don't know. I heard them say they wanted to confirm the timeline or something like that, and Mama said that Ken was represented by counsel and then they left. Are they going to arrest Ken? He didn't do anything wrong."

"Try to relax. The police have to ask a lot of people questions when something bad happens like what happened to Bobby's sister. It doesn't mean they think Ken hurt her." I feel horrible about pretending everything's fine when I'm just as freaked out as Vicki is, but it won't do for her to panic.

"I hope Mama chased them away for good," Vicki says. "I was just reading this book about falsely convicted prisoners throughout history and —" There's footsteps in the background. Vicki whispers, "Uh oh."

Mrs. Hansen says, "Out of bed when you're supposed to be asleep, and taking Ken's phone without permission. Give it here." She gets on the line and says, "Who is this?"

"It's CJ," I say. "Vicki called me because she was worried about the police visit."

Mrs. Hansen is quiet for a while before she says, "I'm sorry she bothered you. Everything's fine."

I swallow hard. "I was worried about Ken earlier. They questioned us separately when we found the body and he said they were looking at him because of their biases."

"It wasn't anything we didn't expect after what happened," Mrs. Hansen says, "but that doesn't mean we're letting it go any further. I know Ken's rights and I made sure he knows them too, and he's got the sharpest lawyer in the five boroughs. So no one's going to railroad him, and that's a promise."

Vicki asks in the background, "What does that mean, 'railroad someone?'"

Mrs. Hansen sighs. "I'd better hang up since a certain little pitcher is using those big ears of hers in ways she knows she's not supposed to. You just relax as best as you can, baby. You had a hard day, but God's got brighter ones ahead. You'll see." She hangs up before I can reply.

"What was that?" Dani puts her water bottle down.

"I ain't sure. Ken's mom's not talking and Vicki only overheard bits and pieces. But best as I can tell, the cops wanted to question Ken again and his mom wouldn't let them."

"Fuck." Dani sits down next to me. "I wish they'd stop

grasping at straws and look at someone who actually has a chance in hell of being involved."

I search the mess on my desk for my earbuds so I can listen to rain sounds and try to calm myself. "I'm coming with you to the police station tomorrow if that's all right. I want to know what they think they got on Ken so we can get to work disproving it."

Dani nods. "I could use the moral support anyway. In the meantime, what about that double-parked car? You think it was actually Chloe's?"

"Dunno." I give up on the earbuds. My time's better spent trying to clear Ken's name anyway. Instead, I use the voice-activated search on my phone to get news articles about the traffic jam, in the hopes someone published a picture of the car. If they did, maybe we can ask Jessica if it matches Chloe's.

"Or find out where she lives so we can check it out ourselves." Dani yawns. Her eyes blink closed, then open. "Fuck. I'm falling asleep. You gonna be okay if I turn in?"

I promise her I will and get to checking out search results. The only article I find is on the online version of the *Cedar-wood Courier*. I click on it and the article starts to load, complete with a picture of the traffic around the Burnt Olive that night, but then the screen changes and it informs me I have to subscribe for access.

I glare at my phone, but then I get an idea and do an image search instead. If I can find the photo associated with the arti-cle, that's good enough for now.

Pay dirt. There's a black-and-white photo of the traffic jam, probably taken from a local traffic camera. It's hard to see the double-parked car cause all the cars trying to get around it are blocking my view, but the roof is visible and comes out gray in the photo.

I download the photo and use an AI app to colorize it. I can't be sure the colors are right, but I reckon they are cause I recognize Ken's car in the back of the line of traffic, and it's dark blue like it's supposed to be.

The roof of the mystery car that caused all the trouble is silver, just like the tipster said.

I flip back and forth between the color photo and the original, not sure what to do next. On my third go-round, I notice something in the corner and enlarge the photo with my fingers.

It's a timestamp from the traffic cam. 7:58 pm.

I almost jump out of bed with excitement. That means we have proof that Ken was stuck in traffic around the time Ellie was killed. There's no way he could have gotten down three blocks before 8:15 when she missed her call with Bobby, not with that mess on the road.

I save the photo to my phone. Now all I have to do is convince Cooper tomorrow and he'll have to leave Ken alone.

The chairs in the precinct lobby the next morning are made of the same cheap plastic as the ones in the precinct back home that messed my mom's back all up the time she had to come down cause of what happened to me. Fortunately, we don't have to sit on them too long; Cooper comes out a minute or so after we check in with the desk sergeant.

"Daniela, I presume?" he says to Dani.

"I prefer Dani," Dani says, "But whatever you want to call me is fine." She rubs her temples as she gets up.

Cooper nods at me as I start to follow them. "I'm sorry, CJ, but witness interviews are private."

"So she's a witness and not a suspect?" I ask.

Cooper's eyes narrow. "Nice try, but you know I can't comment on that. Now, if you'll excuse us—"

"How about you give me a comment about something else, then?" I have no business being so disrespectful to someone in a position of authority but I don't see any other way to get the answers I need. "What's up with questioning Ken? You saw how he was when we found the body. You have to know he ain't got anything to do with this."

Cooper sighs, then gestures with his head for us to both follow him down the hall.

His office, if you can even call it that, is even more cramped than the little cubicle Dr. Blanton's got. He's got files and papers everywhere, all on top of each other, and behind him there's a big whiteboard like you see on the TV with Ellie's name and picture on the top and suspects' names written in black marker underneath. I want to check it for Ken's name, but Cooper's shoulders block that area of the board altogether when he sits down at his desk.

"Here," he says, taking a card out and pushing it across the desk. "This is the contact info for Roberta Martin, our press information officer. All official inquiries go through her."

"Yes, sir. Thank you." I pocket the card. "Unofficially, have you checked the traffic cam footage around the Burnt Olive yet? Cause if you that'll prove Ken didn't do it."

Cooper raises his eyebrows. "I never said that your boyfriend was a suspect. But let's not waste time playing games. Show me whatever it is you came here to show me so I can get back to doing my job."

I show him the photo and point out the timestamp. "The way I see it, Ken couldn't have gotten three blocks down to kill Ellie any too quick, and she was gone within the next fifteen minutes."

"Believe it or not, I've seen this same footage." Cooper crosses his arms. "But here's the thing. If Ken was on my suspect list, I couldn't cross him off based on this. It's possible the traffic cleared soon after this still image was taken, which would have allowed him to get to the scene of Ellie's apartment in time to attack her."

I stare at him. Why is he so determined to get Ken for this? "And you think it was him and not whoever drove that car? We heard it went the same direction she did too."

"I didn't say whether the car did or didn't move. This is all hypothetical." Cooper leans back in his seat. "Look, CJ, I can't confirm or deny that your boyfriend is a person of interest in this case. But what I can tell you is that anyone I question in connection with this murder will get a fair shake from me. I will not make an arrest until I have a solid case against an individual, and I will not allow anyone's biases to determine the direction of our investigation."

Dani interjects, "Do you know who the driver of the double-parked car is?"

Cooper smiles slightly. "I thought I was the one asking questions here. In fact, I'd like to get back to that." He nods at me. "Please wait for Dani in the lobby. I will return her to you as soon as possible."

So that's that, then. I hope Dani can turn the tables on him and get the info we need, but I don't ask. Instead. I pat her shoulder and reassure her I ain't going far before returning to the lobby, where I throw myself on one of those stupid plastic chairs and shove my earbuds in to listen to the voice note again and again, trying to figure out for myself whether it's AI-generated and getting nowhere.

When Dani finally comes out, I can't tell if the tears in her eyes are from exhaustion or cause something happened.

"How'd it go?" I ask, pushing away how bad I feel that I gave her name to Cooper in the first place.

Dani shakes her head. "I'll tell you when we're far enough away from here for me to feel normal again." She pushes past me before I can answer, leaving me to wonder what went wrong and how bad it was.

seventeen

DANI DOESN'T SAY a word on the bus home. It's too early for Hailey to have anything. I start to text her anyway, then erase it, not wanting to make her sorry she got involved in this by bothering her too much.

Jessica texts:

> Chloe canceled our coffee date. She is not feeling well and is resting so she can possibly get to work in the afternoon.

Great. Either this illness is a hangover from doing speed or Chloe's avoiding Jessica so that she won't find out the truth. I start to show Dani, but she has her earbuds in and her eyes closed, so I leave her alone.

When we get back to our room, she throws herself on my bed and stares into space. I sit down next to her and say, gently, "Feel like talking?"

Dani shrugs. "I did it to myself," she says flatly. "It wasn't just the charm. I shouldn't have listened to you about not turning it in but..." She swallows hard. "I rubbed my temples one too many times and he assumed I was hungover when actually, my head hurts cause I was so freaked out I barely slept. And that opened the door to a lot of bullshit about how maybe I got drunk enough to hurt her when we both know I was sober til I went to that party. But hey, I'm a party girl, right? Dani the Drunk, can't help myself when the alcohol's freely flowing. Good thing I was on the phone with my mom when Ellie died, though if they call her before I get a chance to give her a heads up she'll be so upset that I'll probably wish I was in jail."

I put my arm around Dani, but she pulls away. "Don't waste time feeling sorry for me. Get ready to question Mark cause if he did it, maybe no one you care about'll end up in jail."

My heart pounds. "There's no chance you're going to jail," I say carefully, "cause your mom'll back up your alibi no matter how mad she is that she's put in this position."

"It's not just that. It's..." Dani swallows hard. "My dad left when I was four cause he decided he'd rather keep drinking than keep being my dad. So how do you think my mom'll feel when she finds out half the reason I'm a suspect is I drank too much that night?"

My phone beeps and I know without looking at it's Alicia. "I have to go," I say, "but I don't like leaving you alone when you're like this."

"Don't worry." Dani makes herself smile. "I'm not stupid enough to try to buy a six-pack when I know the stores around here are cracking down on that shit. I'll call my mom while you're gone and assuming she doesn't jump through the phone to drag me back to Connecticut, afterward I'll see what else I can find about Chloe before we meet downtown."

"If you're sure," I say. "We could use your analytical skills when we meet Mark."

Dani shakes her head. "One student who's not in his class is okay, but two might feel like a shakedown. Let's not scare him away." As I turn, she says, "Ceej?"

I turn back around. "Yeah?"

Dani swallows hard. "I'll be cleared soon, but you should know that they're still seriously considering Ken. That detective tried to see what he could get out of me about him too."

My heart pounds so hard I can barely breathe and my ears start buzzing, but I nod and say, "Guess it's a good thing I'm interviewing Mark, then. Like you said, the sooner we prove someone else did it, the less likely it is someone I love ends up in jail."

Dani's eyes widen, but I turn tail and hurry away before she can ask me if I mean 'love' the way it sounds when it comes to Ken.

The elevator up to the fourth floor of the science building takes forever to come, and it doesn't help that Alicia won't stop talking about the cops questioning Dani. "She doesn't have any more motive than Ken does," she says while I mash the call button over and over, "but she's right that she did it to herself with her drinking. She's not quite as bad as my brother, but still."

This is the first I'm hearing of Alicia's brother, and I don't want to know any more. The elevator finally comes; as I push my way into it, I say, "You reckon Mark'll give us anything useful?"

"I hope so. I barely know him." Alicia lowers her voice. "Maybe after we're done, we should stop by Dr. Armstrong's office and find out if Chloe's really sick or what."

"She ain't supposed to be in til afternoon anyway." I run my fingers along the paneled walls as we walk down the hall toward the TA office. "You ever met her?"

Alicia shakes her head.. "She brings him his briefcase and his laptop at the beginning of class and comes back to help him pack up at the end, so I've seen her on the stage in the front of the auditorium, but I've never spoken to her." Her eyes widen. "He has office hours on Mondays and Thursdays so I could use that as an excuse to meet both of them next week, I guess."

"Could be," I say, "but if they see through you…"

Alicia swallows hard. "I'll be careful," she says. "I want to ask him if there's another spot open in the lab anyway." She puts her hand on the doorknob to the TA office. "Anyway, here we are."

The TA office is one big room with a bunch of long tables in it like we used to have in high school chemistry class. The room is light and airy, but also busy; various TAs are sitting with students, going over class material with them, and the room buzzes with a thousand conversations as we push our way toward the back to talk to Mark.

Mark's at the furthest table, and someone's sitting across from him, blocking my view. The man's about as tall as Ken, maybe taller, and he sits up straighter than anyone I've ever seen. His head is full of auburn curls but there are gray streaks near the nape of his neck, so it must be a dye job.

The man's saying something to Mark about lesson plans for next week.

So this is the infamous Dr. Armstrong. Just knowing I'm in the same room with him makes my stomach feel so tight with anxiety I might throw up.

eighteen

DR. ARMSTRONG LOOKS up. "You have students," he says, "though I daresay this isn't about the joy inherent in understanding the neurological basis of perception." He nods at me. "You're the young woman who discovered Ellie's fate, are you not?"

Not a woman, thanks. But I ain't about to get into that with him. "Yes, sir. Alicia is in your introductory class and she reckoned she'd be able to get me an audience with your TA here."

"What a delightful way you have of speaking. You aren't from here, are you?"

"No, sir, but with all due respect, I didn't come here to discuss that. We need to talk to Mark. From what we understand, he was the last person to see Ellie alive."

I'm hoping for some sort of reaction, but Armstrong's face might as well be made of stone. He loses his half-smile, but by the time he says, "Of course," it's back. "Please don't take too long. Mark needs to understand his role perfectly in our upcoming lessons." He turns and gives Mark a cold stare before moving aside, plopping himself down at the table in front of ours and busying himself with something on his phone. I can't help noticing that he's holding the phone at arm's length in order to read whatever's on his screen.

"Don't worry, Dr. Armstrong," Mark says as we sit down. He's a short guy whose full beard makes him look even tinier than he is. He clasps his hands in front of him. "This will be a short interview, ladies. Like I told the police, I don't really know much. Besides, Ellie was a private person who I doubt would want her business spread all over campus via a podcast. You aren't going to do that, are you?"

"Course not." I cross my arms as I sit down. "I heard you kept her waiting half an hour that night."

Mark shrugs. "Why does it matter? Obviously, she was still alive when I got there." He tilts his head forward, and I can't help thinking he's checking Dr. Armstrong's body language for signs of approval.

"If it doesn't matter, you won't mind telling us where you were," Alicia says.

Mark scowls. "My life, my business. Ellie wasn't killed while I was unaccounted for." His voice is even, but I pick up on his defensiveness anyway.

"Be nice, Mark," Dr. Armstrong says. "Humor the young ladies." He doesn't look up from his phone as he adds, "Mark is embarrassed that his professional life cut into his ability to socialize. He and I were going over some things for the next day's classes."

I have my doubts on that score. "If there's security footage or something that can corroborate that, we won't have to waste any more time."

Mark scowls. "Dr. Armstrong told you where I was. He never lies." He leans forward. "Look, it wasn't my tardiness that killed her, so you can drop this. Now, Ellie was also very much alive when I left the Burnt Olive, even if she was a little drunk. And that's all I know. So if you'll excuse me—"

"Not yet." I cross my arms. "You left before she did?"

Mark's eyes dart to Dr. Armstrong, then away. "I had to. Like I said, she was drunk. And she was acting like we were on a date when we weren't. She was wearing this low-cut red dress and she was all over me."

Alicia raises her eyebrows. "And you weren't into her?"

Mark blushes. "I-I would be but... look, I'm not the kind of guy who takes advantage, okay? And anyway, it was a set-up."

"A set-up?" I ask. "How do you mean?"

"Isn't it obvious?"Mark clasps his hands in front of him and looks me dead in the eye. "Ellie wasn't as good at playing straight as she thought. Everyone knew it, even if they didn't say so, and they also knew she and Jessica had broken up and that it was ugly. So it was obvious she wanted to use me to get back at Jessica, and I don't like being used. You understand that, girls, don't you?"

It's the third time I've been misgendered in as many minutes. I breathe in sharply, refusing to let it get to me. "How do you know how things were between Ellie and Jessica?"

"Cause," Mark says. "I was the guy Ellie always turned to when things were shit. But I guess she did it one too many times cause... well, you know what happened to her."

Alicia crosses her arms. "Jessica told me that you spread rumors about how Ellie got her job. Did you?"

Mark's jaw tightens. "Of course not."

I twist my head over my shoulder to look Armstrong in the eye. "You might want to do something about whoever did. Some people are saying Ellie got her job by jumping in bed with you."

Alicia elbows me and shakes her head slightly. I reckon she's right that I've gone too far, but too late now. I refuse to turn away as Dr. Armstrong slowly looks up from his phone to stare at me.

"I pay no attention to gossip and innuendo, and perhaps it would be best if you don't either," Armstrong says. A shiver goes down my spine as he stands. "I think you ladies have taken up enough of my TA's time. You will have to excuse us now." The way he looks at me makes me wonder if he knows exactly what he's doing when he misgenders me.

"We will," I say firmly, "soon as Mark tells us where he went after he left the Burnt Olive."

"You mean did I lie in wait in the parking lot for her?" Mark laughs. "Of course not. After I turned down Ellie and her pathetic offer of revenge sex, I went to see a girl who actually wanted me."

"This girl have a name?"

"Yeah, but I'm not telling you." Mark crosses his arms. "Unlike Ellie, I keep my private business to myself."

"I'd think you'd want to be able to back up your alibi," I say.

Mark laughs again. "You're not the cops. I have nothing to prove to you." He nods at Dr. Armstrong. "I'm done with these two playing detective. If they won't leave, call Campus Police."

"I'm quite certain that won't be necessary." Armstrong gestures toward the door. "Come, ladies, I'll walk you out."

I shove my hands into my pockets and shuffle my feet as I follow him to the elevator.

Armstrong says, "I assume you are eventually going to put bits and pieces of these interviews into a podcast about Ellie's life and death."

"I reckon so." I haven't actually thought about what I'd do beyond finding the truth, but Armstrong doesn't need to know that.

"This is a wonderful project," Armstrong says, "and one I'd very much like to be a part of." He takes a card out of his wallet and hands it to me. "I could provide quite a lot of insight into the neurology behind this seemingly senseless act of violence as well as give your listeners a sense of what Ellie was like as a researcher. Oh, she was so delightful to work with. Such a quick mind housed in the most beautiful of bodies."

I bite my lip so my disgust won't show on my face as Armstrong hands me a card. "Chloe is on top of all her communications on my behalf and will undoubtedly respond within an hour of your email," he says. "I will make sure of it."

"I heard she's out sick," I say carefully.

"Yes, that's right. But my point still stands. Email her as soon as you can so that we can get this interview started." He bows slightly. "Pleasure to meet you ladies. I am sure I will be seeing you again soon, both of you."

He walks off and I let my breath out slowly, feeling like I can finally take air into my lungs.

nineteen

THIS TIME ALICIA'S the one to mash the elevator button over and over.

"Can't get away fast enough, huh?" I say.

"Nope. Stupid slow elevator." Alicia lets her breath out slowly. "It wasn't just me, right? He was controlling every word Mark said, and thanks to that asshole, Mark tried to frame Jessica."

"I read it the same." I cross my arms. "If that voice was AI-generated, you reckon he's behind it?"

"I don't know. Maybe." Alicia mashes the button again. "Come on already!"

"Hey. Maybe it's a good thing the elevator's slow." I lower my voice. "Armstrong's with Mark, so might be a good time to duck down to his office and see what we can find out."

Alicia frowns. "Chloe's not due in for another hour, if she comes at all."

"Right," I say, "so maybe no one's there and we can take a peek at what certain people might be hiding."

Alicia swallows hard. "Bad idea. A, the office'll be locked, and B, if for some reason it's not we'd be doing something illegal."

I cross my arms. She's right, but doing things by the book ain't helped anything. "Not like we're gonna go into any locked areas."

Alicia shrugs. "He probably has someone else working for him when she's not there, but maybe they can tell us a little about him. I'd do that much. But no crossing lines, and if no one's there, we leave."

I reckon that's fair, though I can't promise I'll stick to it if an opportunity arises to find out something we ain't supposed to know. I double-check check my mic is connected before I follow her down the hall.

Armstrong has a real office, not like Dr. Blanton and his cubicle in the back of the journalism faculty room. It's behind a door that has his name on it.

I try the door; it ain't locked. I open it a crack and then freeze.

There's a girl sitting at a desk next to an inner door that I guess is his real office, doing something on a computer.

It ain't Chloe, but it ain't a stranger either.

It's Sarah.

twenty

SARAH GESTURES FOR us to come in. "So we meet again," she says. "What's up?"

Alicia and I exchange glances. I say, "Dr. Armstrong told us that his assistant could help us get him on my show to talk about Ellie. But I thought you work for the Dean."

Has Sarah gone pale? She straightens a pile of papers on her desk as she says, "I do, but Dr. Armstrong asked me for a favor this morning so I skipped my class to help him out."

Alicia and I exchange glances. "You sure that's a good idea?" I ask. "Most of my classes, I'd be lost if I skipped."

Sarah shrugs. "It's just one day. Anyway, that's not why you're here, is it?" She double-clicks with the mouse. "Have you cleared this with Dean Northrop? After all, it's school equipment you're using so she has final say."

My throat tightens with anger. First deleting my post about Ellie, now this. "She ain't ever had to approve my podcasts before."

"You never reported on things that could make the school look bad before," Sarah says. "Besides, she didn't meet with you about covering Ellie's death so you could keep her out of the loop."

I cross my arms and glare at her. Alicia comes to the rescue, saying, "Do you really think she'd have a problem with Dr. Armstrong sharing his expertise as a neuroscientist? That's what he wants to do, talk about the neurobiology behind violent crime. Unless... is there something you know about Dr. Armstrong that CJ better stay away from?"

Sarah's eyes narrow. "Of course not. Why would there be? He's so kind and generous, and he has this way of making you feel special." Her voice is soft and her cheeks are slightly pink.

"I sure hope you don't have a crush on him," I say carefully. "You know that can't go anywhere."

Sarah's blush gets deeper. "You never know. There has to be a reason he asked me to do this for him, right?" She lets her breath out slowly. "Anyway, I booked an appointment with him for your studio on Monday afternoon. If Dean Northrop doesn't like it, make sure to let Chloe know to cancel it."

That soon? My heart pounds as I thank Sarah. "Speaking of Chloe, how well do you know her?"

Sarah's eyes dart to her screen, then away. "Um, I don't really. I mean, I've seen her around. Sometimes she comes to Dean Northrop's office when I'm working, especially lately. They started carpooling after Ellie died." She plays with the scroll wheel on her mouse, flicking it for no apparent reason. "I guess Chloe's scared she's next cause she's not driving herself to work anymore."

Or she doesn't want to be in the car she used to dump Ellie's body after she killed her. "Is that the only way she's been different since the murder?"

"I guess. Like I said, I don't really know her. Though I'll tell you something if you promise not to tell Dean Northrop. She's super protective of Chloe and I don't want to lose my job."

Alicia and I exchange glances, agreeing silently to go for it. "Go ahead," I tell Sarah. "Your secret's safe with us."

"Thanks." Sarah bites her lip. "Um, Chloe has mental health issues. I know cause I have access to Dean Northrop's calender, and once a week she leaves early to take Chloe to a psychiatrist in the city."

"That doesn't necessarily mean anything," Alicia says. "Lots of people do therapy."

"Yeah, but it's a psychiatrist, not a psychologist, so that means she's on meds. Plus, maybe I'm wrong, but I feel like Dean Northrop's trying to keep it secret by taking her all the way into Manhattan instead of using someone local, know what I mean?"

"Or maybe it's cause she doesn't want her to be judged," Alicia says. "I'm on antidepressants; that doesn't make me unstable."

"I-I didn't mean..." Sarah sighs. "Never mind. It's just, if you ever meet Chloe, you'll know right away something's off about her."

Alicia's jaw tightens. I take over, asking, "You reckon it's possible Chloe killed Ellie?"

"It's possible. After all, she lives in Ellie's building and I heard that's where it went down." Sarah's phone dings. She glances at it, smiling slightly. "Dr. Armstrong's on his way back. I'll tell him about the appointment as soon as he gets here, I promise. But I'm sure he won't want to walk in on me gossiping about Chloe so..."

"Right. Of course." I gesture with my head for Alicia to follow me.

Sarah calls, "Oh, CJ? Before you go, can I ask you something? Who's that girl with the super long hair you hang out with?"

I freeze. Why is she asking about Dani? "My roommate," I say carefully. "Why?"

"Cause she's cute," Sarah says, "so I was hoping you'd know if she was single."

Oh. That's all she wants. "Ain't for me to say," I tell her, "but I'll pass on the compliment."

Sarah blushes the same way she did when she was talking about Armstrong, making it obvious Dani ain't the only one she's got a crush on. I whisper as much to Alicia in the hall after we leave.

She shrugs. "Hopefully it's one-sided, not like what Ellie said happened."

"Thing is, she's the one who deleted my post about Ellie and now she's saying Dean Northrop could cancel Armstrong's appearance on my show."

Alicia frowns as she mashes the elevator button. "So what?"

"So, maybe she's doing it to protect him. I-if Ellie was fixin' to expose him, he has as much motive as we thought Chloe did before, and he's creepy on top of it."

My phone beeps before Alicia can answer, but from her narrow-eyed look I can tell she disagrees. I glance at it and see that Hailey's texted:

> ANALYSIS DONE. Meet me and Dani @ the bakery next to the Burnt Olive & I'll go over it.

"Coming?" I ask, showing Alicia the text.

"Um." Alicia pushes her hair behind her ear. "I think while you're doing that I'll get with Jessica and find out what she knows about Sarah."

I'd rather not have to fill Alicia in later, but her plan makes sense so I fist bump with her before heading downtown, eager to find out what Hailey's learned.

twenty-one

DANI AND HAILEY look so right together through the bakery window that I hate to have to disturb them. Their foreheads are nearly touching and even though they ain't holding hands, they should be.

They sit up straighter as I come in. "First things first," Dani says. "After the morning we both had, we deserve sugar." She pushes a chocolate cupcake with blue frosting and sprinkles toward me. "For you."

"Thanks." I climb into the seat they've saved for me. "I hope you don't mind I invited Ken too. He'll be here in a minute."

"Course," Hailey says. "But I have to bounce soon, so I'm going to go ahead and share what I have to share and then you can tell him after."

That's two people I'm obligated to repeat this to now. Better than nothing, I reckon, but I'm annoyed anyway.

Hailey pushes her hair behind her ear. "It was just as I suspected. There's no way that voice clip was human." She opens her phone and shows me a screenshot. It's one of those sound graphs that looks like a heart monitor reading, only the highs and lows are in green on a black background, and I can't make heads and tails out of it.

Hailey taps the graph. "You see how this is almost a flat line here? That's because there's not a lot of variety in the pitch. There's some, but not as much as there would be if a human was speaking."

I nod even though I don't really understand. "So someone had a computer record that tip?"

"Pretty much. There are AI voice generators now that sound close enough to human that they can fool people if they aren't paying close attention." Hailey takes a sip of her coffee. "The big question is, why?"

"Someone didn't want us to know who they are," I say. "Seems like they wanted us to think they're Chloe."

"Or Chloe did it herself," Dani says, "and wants us to think someone's framing her."

"Right." I turn back to Hailey. "We have any clue yet who this person is?"

"That'll be harder. The voice clip was sent via mobile, and cell phone IPs are harder to trace. I won't bore you with the details, but basically, the IP address moves around based on where the phone was at the time so it's more or less guesswork to figure out whose phone it is and where it was. Luckily, there's an app for that like everything else, but it's not necessarily accurate and in this case, either it's not, or someone was smart enough to use a fake name that they knew would taunt us."

"What was it?" I ask, wishing Hailey would hurry up and get to the point.

"Sorry." Hailey's cheeks darken with embarrassment. "I was trying to be dramatic." She takes another sip of coffee. "According to my app, this voice clip was sent from a phone registered to an Ellie Armstrong."

My eyes widen. I've heard that name before, but I can't

recall where. I think for a minute, then check something. "I thought so," I say. "The next caller after Bobby used the same phone, or at least, it was registered to the same name."

"Interesting." Hailey puts her hand to her chin. "What did they say?"

"The usual nonsense about someone's having fun with a man that ain't theirs to do it with. I only half paid attention, but I think they tried to make it sound like Ellie was a cheater. The voice sounded weird, like it was a prank call, and when I saw that name, as far as I was concerned it proved it."

Hailey nods. "So minutes after Bobby calls to say Ellie's missing, someone uses AI generation to complain that Ellie was sleeping with someone she shouldn't be."

"Which we know is true now cause she was sleeping with Armstrong." I cross my arms. "You reckon Sarah did it? She's got a big ol' crush on Armstrong so if she saw Ellie's video could be she got jealous."

"Stupid thing to be jealous of," Dani says. "Wasn't she listening to what Ellie actually said? Sleeping with him made her feel gross." She pushes her hair behind her ear. "Anyway, that call seems irrelevant, like someone was trying to throw us off."

"Or a prank like CJ said," Hailey says, "but I can't see why."

"I reckon that if it was Sarah, she knew the thing with him and Ellie would come out and she was trying to make us think bad of Ellie before it did."

"Maybe," Dani says. "But that doesn't matter. The tip is more important. And it's not totally fake, cause whoever it was knew there was a car double parked at the Burnt Olive that night. So it has to be someone who was there around the time Ellie left. But the question is, are they trying to frame someone or are they confessing without confessing?" She rubs her temples. "Trying to figure this out is making my head hurt."

"Figure what out?" Ken asks, sliding in next to me.

We give Ken the short version. He frowns and says, "If they're gonna frame someone, why not frame me? The cops are already stuck on me so..."

I pat his hand. "If we can ever crack what this is all about, they'll have to get unstuck."

Ken shrugs. "Lemme have a bite of that cupcake. It looks too good to leave alone."

I'm aware he's changing the subject, but since we've hit a dead end on the mystery caller, I don't mind. I hand him what's left of my cupcake as Dani's phone beeps to tell us the Burnt Olive's about to open.

There's already a crowd of students hanging around outside, waiting, which means it's gonna be hard to get the hostess' attention, and Ken's worried we won't have time to eat before he has to get Vicki from school. I brush his finger-tips with mine to keep him calm and fill everyone in about what happened at the science building this morning.

"She thought I was cute?" Dani says, surprised. She grins. "That gives us an in! All I have to do is get her to meet me and flirt with her til she opens up about whatever she knows about Ellie's death."

"I don't know," Hailey says. "That's messing with some-one's feelings. Not cool."

Dani pouts. "It's not like I'm going to make her think I'm madly in love with her. I flirt with everyone anyway."

A restaurant employee unlocks the door, cutting off the conversation. It's just as well cause Hailey's jaw is set and her eyes are narrow like she and Dani are headed for a fight if we don't change the subject.

The hostess recognizes us the second we walk up. "I guess you found your missing girl, huh?" She sighs deeply. "Such a shame. She was a sweet girl, from what I could tell. Just so you know, we did put your flyer in the window but I guess it was too late."

"Reckon so. You suppose the manager would let us take a look at the security footage from that camera outside so we can at least see which way she went?"

"Not her call to make. That's a city camera, hun."

"What about the cameras in here?" Ken asks.

The hostess bites her lip. "I'll ask, but no promises. We've been overrun with reporters since they found out Ellie was dead. How they all know she ate her last meal here I don't know, but it's not what we want to be known for and the manager doesn't want us talking to the press, period." She picks up a bunch of menus. "Four of you today?"

"Three, actually," Hailey says. "I got so caught up in this I almost forgot about my multimedia class." She hugs Dani and says quietly, "Think about what I said, okay?"

Dani's eyes are narrow but she nods slightly.

As Hailey leaves, I say to the hostess, "One more question. Did you happen to notice a car double-parked in front the last time Ellie was here?"

The hostess counts the menus in her hand before she answers, giving us the make and model under her breath. "We made an announcement it was about to get towed and the next thing I knew it was gone, so I figured some asshole decided to block the road instead of parking in the lot." Aloud, she says, "This way."

As we follow her, I ask, "So you didn't happen to see the driver?"

"No, ma'am," the hostess says. I scrunch my hands into my pockets, wishing I knew how she'd react if I told her I ain't a ma'am. "Just saw the car out the window and heard it start up soon after I made the announcement, that's all." She leads us to a table.

As we sit down, Dani shudders. "I have a feeling this is the same table Ellie ate her last meal at," she whispers. She stirs her water with her straw while I pat her hand. "So... is Silver Car Lady the killer or what?"

"Dunno. For all we know it ain't even a lady."

A waitress comes over just then to take our orders. I ain't really hungry after that cupcake, but I let her talk me and Ken into ordering a lamb gyro plate to share, and Dani gets a vegetarian one.

Before the waitress can go, I say, "We're looking into Ellie Bishop's death. Were you here the night she came in last?" I show her a photo of Ellie in case she doesn't know her by name.

"I wish I had been. I heard about her death, poor girl." The waitress crosses herself before she goes to put our orders in.

A couple minutes later, another waitress comes over from the table across from us that she's been bussing. "Is this yours?" she asks, holding out a paper.

I glance at it as I take it from her. It reads:

I'm the one who waited on that girl the night she died. I want to talk, but I can't here. Call me at this number. 516-555-4312. - Lisa

twenty-two

I **WANT** TO text Lisa back right away, but I know that could get her caught, so I make myself wait til we're done and halfway down the block.

After that, we discuss our next move. Ken's got to head back so he'll be in time to meet Vicki's school bus, but Dani's free, so she and I decide to talk to all the store owners between here and Ellie's apartment before we try to catch the manager like we originally planned.

The bakery closes at 7, so that's a dead end, and the Chinese takeout place next to it has a FOR RENT sign and a sheet of graffiti-covered metal covering the display window. Next door to that's an all-night convenience store.

"Perfect!" Dani says. "Someone must have seen something."

The store has big signs at the registers saying that they won't sell alcohol to anyone without checking ID and that they'll call the cops if you give them a fake one. Dani says, "If she was as drunk as Mark claimed, someone here probably noticed since they're so hardcore about this shit."

I don't think that follows logically, but it's worth a shot

anyway so I show the clerk behind the counter a photo of Ellie and explain what we're after.

The clerk says, "She passed by about 10 minutes to 8. She was crying pretty hard and walking fast."

"Did she seem drunk?" Dani asks.

He shrugs. "Maybe. I dunno. She didn't come in here to start shit so I didn't care."

"Right," I say. "Any chance you noticed someone following her, maybe in a silver car?"

The clerk shakes his head. "I was too busy to pay that much attention to some girl on the street."

The bookstore manager next door confirms Ellie came in regularly, but he wasn't on duty the night she disappeared, so he doesn't know anything, and the coffee shop manager says he was closing up for the night and not paying attention to who was walking by.

Across the street, there's a laundromat that's open all night, but the manager says he doesn't want any trouble and won't talk to us no matter what we say. The laundromat takes up most of the block, but there's a small thrift shop on the corner next to it.

A clerk at the thrift shop says, "We close at 7:30, so I was in the back taking care of counting down all the registers and putting the money in the safe til about 8. I wouldn't have seen anything, but I did hear loud footsteps and someone sobbing as they passed. And another thing, too. We got a donation in the drop box overnight, a really big one that had a lot of women's clothes. Some kid's clothes mixed in too but still... I read the girl was found naked, so you think maybe the killer dumped her clothes in the drop box?"

"Could be," I say. "You still have the clothes?"

"They've probably been sold already. It was a few days ago and they were nice. Flowery shirts and stuff like that."

"Was there a red dress?" Dani asks. "Show him the photo, Ceej."

I show the clerk the selfie Ellie put on IG. He frowns and says, "Might have been. I don't remember offhand. There were a lot of women's dresses in that batch."

We thank him for his time and move on.

Ellie's name has already been taken out of the list of apartments on the buzzer box when we get down the block to her building. It makes sense, I suppose. Her apartment's empty now, and it ain't like anyone was going to turn it into a museum. Still, it hurts to see that space where her name belongs. It's just another way the world's acknowledging that she's gone.

Dani takes a photo of the buzzer box so that we can start looking into who Ellie's neighbors were. There's no Dixon, which doesn't surprise either of us, but there is a Lancaster listed in Apartment 419, down the hall from Ellie.

"So Sarah was telling the truth about Chloe living in Ellie's building," I say.

"And she should be home if she's sick." Dani reaches over and presses the buzzer. There's no answer, not even after she presses and holds it for a full 30 seconds.

"Maybe she went to work after all," I say.

"Or she's not answering her door cause she knows people are looking for her," Dani says. "But whatever. Let's try the manager."

When I press the manager's buzzer, his intercom crackles to life right away. "Yeah?"

"We're friends of Ellie Bishop's," Dani says before I can answer. "Can we come in to talk to the residents about what they might have seen?"

"You cops?"

"No," Dani says. "Far from it."

"Then no." The manager hangs up.

I press the buzzer again, annoyed. The manager gets on and says, "If that's you again, nosey friends of Ellie Bishop, go away or I'll call the cops. My tenants don't need random people knocking on their doors and bothering them."

"Yes, sir," I say, "but how about you give us a few minutes of your time? Surely you knew Ellie well, right? We just want to know what happened to her."

"I don't know nothing."

Why is he so defensive? I have to think fast and can't worry about it, but it's strange. "Look, we ain't accusing you of anything, all right? But you know best what kind of tenant she was and who might have had a problem with her, so you can help us bring her family peace. Can you do that for them? Please?"

The manager hesitates for a second longer, then says, "Fine. Come into Apartment 100. But nowhere else." He hits the buzzer.

Dani sets up her mic while we go in.

In the lobby, the elevator has a big sign that says it's out of order and there's paint peeling on some of the walls. The railing feels loose as we tackle the stairs to get to the first floor, too; we lean our right hands against the wall instead to balance ourselves.

"Now we know what he was hiding," Dani whispers. "This is how the university maintains its off-campus apartments?"

"I reckon so," I whisper back. "I'd wager anything Ellie's dad didn't know. You think he'd put up with her living in this crappy a place?"

The manager's door creaks open and he beckons us into an office that looks like a converted apartment, with a kitchen behind him and an alcove to the right where his bedroom probably is. He's a short guy, wearing a suit too hot for the weather, and he introduces himself as Jon Gordon. When I sit down across from his desk, the strong scent of recently-smoked tobacco hits my nose even though it's against state law to smoke indoors.

"Railing's loose on the stairs," I tell him.

"Hopefully the elevator'll be fixed tomorrow and then people won't be using the stairs," Mr. Gordon says. "But I know you didn't come here to discuss that."

"No, sir. Like we said, we wanted to talk about Ellie Bishop."

"Right." The manager leans back in his chair. "If you'd told me someone was gonna kill her, I'd have thought you were clowning me. Sweet girl. Smart girl. Paid her rent on time, didn't have loud parties or nothing. If I'd known someone was bothering her, she wouldn't be the one six feet under, I can promise you that."

I stare at his crossed arms. He's got some muscles on him, but I can't see any reason he'd have used them to hurt Ellie if she was a model tenant. "You wouldn't happen to know if she had any problems with anyone here, would you?"

"If she did, it was news to me. She kept to herself except sometimes she'd have this Mexican gal over. I could tell that the only thing they were studying was each other's anatomy but they didn't cause problems, so what do I care?"

"So she got along with everyone?" Dani asks. "Even people who did make noise and have parties?"

"She wasn't the type to get in anyone's face. She was too quiet, if you ask me. Thought the best of everyone and there's people in the world that'll hurt you without a second thought. Guess she learned that the hard way."

"Guess so," I agree. My heart pounds and I don't know if I should push this, but I ask, "What about Chloe Lancaster?"

"What about her?" Mr. Gordon's eyes narrow and he scratches behind his ear.

"She ever have any problems with Ellie?"

Mr. Gordon crosses his arms. His chair squeaks as he shifts his weight. "I'm tryin' to find a nice way to put this," he says. "Not that I care that much about it, but she is the Dean's daughter so I gotta be careful, know what I mean?"

Dani and I exchange glances. "We ain't gonna tell anyone," I promise. "We just want to know if she could have hurt Ellie."

Mr. Gordon hesitates. "Doubt it," he says at last. "She ain't the type. Too skinny, for one thing. I doubt she has the strength to kill a bug, never mind a person. She's quiet, too, and her mom pays the rent for her, so there's no problem there."

"But you don't like her?"

Mr. Gordon shakes his head slightly. "She's not the kind of tenant I'd rent to if it wasn't for her family connection. You didn't hear this from me, but she's fresh out of rehab for hard shit. I'm all for people gettin' second chances, but that's not the vibe I want around here."

Why don't you fix the place up then? But there ain't a point to saying that, so I leave it alone. "Back to Ellie. Was she out of sorts the last few times you saw her?"

"I only ever really saw her first of the month. She liked to deliver her rent in person instead of using the app. She did mention she was going to be moving out come summer. Nothing personal, but she was planning on taking her kid brother full-time and kids ain't allowed to live here." Mr. Gordon leans back in his chair. "Listen, I got stuff to do so I can't take any more time with this."

"One more thing and then we'll be out of your hair," I say. "You have a tenant named April Dixon?"

"Never heard of her." Mr. Gordon stands. "Door's that way. And remember: leave my tenants alone."

Dani and I go. If things were different, we'd sneak up to try to talk to Chloe, but we don't need to get on Gordon's bad side. Instead, we go around the back of the apartment to check out the parking lot and see if Chloe's car is here.

The spaces are clearly marked by apartment number. We walk slowly around, looking for numbers painted on the floor or signs above the spots, something to tell us which one's Chloe's.

A chill passes through me as I pass by 408, which was Ellie's. It's empty—I wonder who took her car after she died, if she even had one. I force myself forward.

"Holy shit," Dani whispers as we get close. She gestures toward the car in Chloe's spot.

It's only got two doors and no power locks, but it's silver just like Jessica said it was, and it's the exact make and model the hostess gave us.

twenty-three

DANI CUPS HER hands around her eyes and presses her nose against the back window of the car. "It's too dark to tell for sure," she says, "but tell me if you see what I see."

I've got no idea what I'm looking for, but I press my nose against the glass. There's something sticking out from under a blanket on the back seat. It looks like it could be a necklace chain, but I can't really tell.

"That's what I thought too," Dani whispers. "If it is, it could go with that charm we found."

"Could be she put Ellie's body in her back seat and drove to the park to dump it." I swallow hard, trying to get rid of a bitter taste in the back of my throat. How could Chloe, or anyone, be so callous? "We ain't gonna get anything else out of this car right now, so let's go."

"And do what?" Dani asks, pulling on the driver's side door handle.

I hold my breath, not letting it out til enough time's passed I'm sure she hasn't set off an alarm. "Don't. I ain't in the mood for explaining to that manager why we're breaking into cars in his lot."

"You're right, I guess." Dani stops trying to break into the car and gets her phone instead. "Photos'll come out super dark, but maybe Hailey can enhance them." She turns her flash off so she can get a decent one through the back window before taking a bunch of the outside of the car, including the license plate and the registration sticker stuck to the windshield.

The door leading to the lot from the apartment creaks open as she's finishing up and footsteps come toward us.

Dani throws her arm around me and puts her mouth so close fear shoots through me that she's fixin' to kiss my ear. "Act natural," she whispers. It sends a shiver through me, and not the good kind. It's another echo of my abduction, of being bear-hugged so I can't fight and warned in a whisper to stay quiet.

I take as much air in through my nose as I can and let it out slowly as Dani says, "That vacant apartment is perfect for us, don't you think, babe?" My mouth's too dry to form words, but it doesn't matter cause she doesn't wait for an answer before she goes on, "Come on, let's celebrate."

She grabs my hand and we hightail it out of there. Dani's out of breath by the time we get across the street to the thrift shop and I have to stop and wait for her when I want to keep going til I get my bike. "It's fine," she says. "We're fine. No one's chasing us." She giggles. "Close one, huh?"

"Too close," I say. "Come on, let's make it home in one piece so we can figure out our next move."

Dani's face falls, but she says nothing, which is just as well cause I don't know how to begin to explain to her why I'm upset.

We get the bus home even though I have my bike, partially cause Dani doesn't have one so it would be impolite to take mine but mostly cause I want to send some emails to get my mind off the past.

First I text Alicia all our updates. Then I get Chloe's email off her card and take my time composing a message. I tell her that since Dr. Armstrong wants to be on the show, I'll need to do some background research, starting with finding a time to meet with her before Monday to get her perspective on him. After that, I text Dr. Blanton to ask him what I need to do to prepare for a guest on the show and explain the situation.

"You have a minute to tell me what I did wrong?" Dani asks as I send the final text.

"Huh? You didn't, what are you talking about?"

"I can tell you're mad at me." Dani crosses her arms. "Ever since we left the parking lot you haven't said a word other than to say it was too close for comfort. Did you think I was coming onto you? Because I wasn't, I swear. I just needed to get us out of there."

"It wasn't that." I bite my lip. "It's something I don't want to explain on a bus where anyone can overhear, but it doesn't have to do with anything you did. I promise."

Dani nods slightly, so I suppose she's satisfied with that, but when we get back to the room and I sign onto the digital whiteboard to update it, she says, "So... what set you off if it isn't me?"

I put my phone down carefully on the bed. "It's a long story. But something horrible happened to me when I was younger and once in a while something reminds me of it, especially since we took up this investigation."

Dani pours me a Coke from a bottle in the fridge and hands it to me. "It's not booze, but it'll do. Drink it and spill."

I shake my head slightly. "The details ain't important. All you have to know is I was... when I was fourteen a predator got his hands on me for a few minutes, but I escaped and am no worse for wear." My eyes burn but I blink back the tears I ain't got time for now.

"Holy shit," Dani says. She gulps her Coke. "My life hasn't

been a bed of roses either. But nothing that horrible ever happened to me." She puts her hand on my shoulder. "If you want to talk…"

"Not now. We got a dead girl in need of justice, she comes first." I pick up the phone again. "And a bunch of clues that don't seem to fit no matter which way I turn them. Chloe especially. It ain't like it's a secret she has a silver car, and she just might have used it to dump Ellie's body after she killed her. Why would she tell on herself with that tip?"

Dani shrugs. "We don't know for sure that that was Ellie's necklace in her back seat, or any necklace at all."

"I suppose. Still, she and everyone else involved with Ellie feel like a knot I can't untie to see who did what. And last time the clues lined up perfectly, I was all wrong. That's why I want to go over everything again and see what we missed." I open the whiteboard. "I reckon we should start with finding Ellie dead in the park. We know she wasn't killed there so —"

There's a knock on the door. It's Ken, holding Vicki tightly by the hand.

Shit. I totally lost track of time. Ken has to take Vicki with us to our expository writing class cause it starts an hour after she gets out of school, and I ain't anywhere near ready.

I hurry to get my stuff together, throwing papers off my desk and shoving them in my bag. I'm setting a terrible example for Vicki, but what choice do I have?

My phone buzzes, but I can't check it til I'm out in the hall, not when I'm already making Ken wait.

It's an email back from Chloe, so I guess she wasn't sick after all.

I stab at the screen to see what she wants. First thing that comes up is Dr. Armstrong's headshot; he's had her send it along to promote his appearance.

I skim the email, ignoring Vicki craning her neck to look

over my shoulder. I need to know if Chloe's willing to meet with me outside of Armstrong's presence.

But before I can get there, Vicki says, "That's the man I saw in the parking lot. Why do you have his picture on your phone?"

twenty-four

I STARE AT VICKI. If she's right, then could be Armstrong wanted to do to her that night what that pervert did to me. But it still doesn't add up, cause what on Earth would that have to do with what happened to Ellie?

"You sure?" I say weakly.

Vicki nods. "I didn't get a good look but I didn't have to. I always knew I'd recognize him if I saw him again."

Ken clears his throat. "Whether you're right or wrong, you're not supposed to be looking at other people's phones."

Vicki gets her angry smile on but says nothing. She silently tugs at her pigtail the whole way down to the lobby and grabs my hand instead of Ken's for the walk across campus. I try to talk to her but she won't speak, and Ken tells me under his breath to leave her alone til she gets out of her funk. When we get to the classroom, Ken reminds her to sit quietly and not disrupt the class. Vicki shrugs and stares at her notebook on the desk.

Her quiet anger hangs in the air, making it nearly impossible to concentrate, but this ain't the kind of class you can zone out in so I have to force my mind onto what I'm supposed to be doing.

Expository writing is all journal prompts followed by group discussions. Behind me, Vicki's pencil's scratching on her pad. It's a good sign that she's getting out of her bad mood, but it means later she'll bug me and Ken to read her attempt at the assignments and give each one a grade. Normally I don't mind, but today I want to talk to Ken about everything Dani and I found out, so I wish she wasn't here and then feel bad about it.

When class finally ends, I cut my phone on and find that Lisa's finally texted me back:

> Sorry for late response. Just got off shift. Can u come downtown to Royalty Coffee @ 12 pm tomorrow? (No need to answer unless you can't, just come.)

Vicki's on her toes, getting ready to look over my shoulder. I close the text and hug the phone to myself. All I need is her loudly asking questions about a source who's scared of getting caught.

"Vicki," I say quietly, not wanting to make her shut down all over again but needing to say something. "It's real important you respect my privacy. Sometimes I get messages from people who don't want anyone else to know who they are."

Ken says, "Weren't you told this an hour ago? Guess you need to spend some time in your room thinking about—" His phone rings, making an irritating chirping sound that has Vicki scurrying to put her hands over her ears. "Shit," he says under his breath. "It's my lawyer."

Vicki's eyes widen as Ken walks off to talk to his attorney. She tugs on my sleeve. "Are the police going to make Ken turn himself in?" she whispers.

"I'm sure that ain't it," I tell her, doing my best to keep my voice calm and even for her sake.

"I hope not." Vicki blinks back tears. "Who's going to

watch me after school and help me with my homework and tell me when I forget a rule if Ken goes to jail?"

I know she doesn't mean it as selfish as it's coming off. I kneel down so we're at eye level. "If the worst happens, I'll help out as much as I can and I bet we can get Dani and Alicia to pitch in too." Vicki nods, her face trembling. I ask her if it's okay if I give her a hug and she throws herself at me so hard I almost fall over as Ken approaches us.

"What's up?" I ask while I rub Vicki's back.

Ken swallows hard. "Cops have more questions for me. My lawyer says it's just routine still, but I got a bad feeling." He sighs deeply. "He thinks coming down tonight's best so we can show them I've got nothing to hide, but what the hell am I supposed to do with Vicki?"

I suggest I stay with her, and at first Ken ain't sure, but he doesn't have much of a choice so he agrees and texts his dad to let him know and ask him if I can take Vicki out to dinner to get her mind off things.

"Ice Cream Kitchen?" Vicki sniffs.

"Not happening," Ken says, coming back. "Dad says he doesn't want her routine disrupted," he tells me, "but we can get her something from the Burger King stand so you don't have to worry about her dinner."

Vicki's face falls, but she doesn't argue. She just holds out her arms and asks me to carry her as if she's a baby.

I pick her up, knowing she needs the comfort. She ain't heavy but she ain't light either, so I hope she'll be willing to walk at least part of the way to Ken's car. She throws her arms around my neck, clinging to me, and I don't blame her. Part of me worries I'm too late just like I was with Ellie and that Ken's about to be locked up for something he didn't do.

twenty-five

VICKI THROWS HER backpack on the floor when we get in the house and throws herself on the floor next to it, lying on her stomach and trying to make herself as flat as possible.

"Uh uh," Ken says. "If you're gonna sulk, do it in your room, and take that bag with you." Vicki seems like she's fixin' to ignore him, lying still like she didn't hear, but then she jumps up and grabs her bag, running away as fast as can be without saying a word.

"Oh boy." Ken sinks into the couch. "This is gonna be a rough night, Ceej. I'm sorry."

"I don't mind. I'd rather she be here with someone she knows cares."

"Yeah." Ken's voice is flat.

I pat his shoulder. "You'll be all right."

"Hope so. You'd think they'd move on from me already, but apparently my lack of an alibi's a sticking point."

"You never did tell me why you left her by herself. I know it wasn't cause you were off to kill Ellie, but I need to know what did happen so I can help get your name out of the cops' minds."

"If you weren't a reporter you'd make a great cop, you

know that?" Ken's tone is light and he's smiling, but I can tell he's close to tears. I take his hand without thinking and he lets me.

"Hey. It's me, CJ. You can tell me anything, okay? What happened that night?"

"Right." Ken squeezes my hand. "It's like this. Mom left me a bag of clothes she needed brought to the thrift shop. I was supposed to take them before Vicki got home but I forgot and, well, when I told her we had to go out after dinner she got all thrown off, I guess. She sat there picking at her dinner, not talking and not eating, either, and I didn't have time to wait for her to chill out cause I had to get this done before it was time to get you. So I figured, the thrift shop's ten minutes there and back and when she's in this mood she'll just stay in her room anyway. So I put her in there with her books and told her I'd be back soon and took off."

"The thrift shop across the street from Ellie's apartment?" I ask.

Ken nods. "That's another point against me. Even if they believe me, it's too close."

"Was it all Vicki's clothes or were some of your mom's dresses mixed in there?" I ask.

"I don't know why that matters, but it was all our old clothes mixed together."

Damn. So that lead we got from the thrift shop about someone dropping off a big batch of clothes was nothing. "K," I say. "And not judging you at all, but why'd it have to be done that night?"

"You're gonna think this is dumb."

"Never." I squeeze Ken's shoulder, resisting the temptation to pull him into a kiss when this is the complete wrong time to try anything like that.

"I didn't want to hear it from Mom. If she came home and found that bag still here, she'd go on for half an hour about how she depends on me to be reliable and how disappointed she was. Should have put up with it, huh? Then I wouldn't be in this mess."

"It's not like you knew someone was going to be killed. You did the best you could."

"Yeah, but I should have thought I might hit traffic. I was going downtown at rush hour." Ken shakes his head. "Sure wish I'd known to look out for Ellie long as I was stuck. I keep thinking I could have saved her."

"You couldn't, not any more than I could have." I put my hand over his. "Stop beating yourself up, all right?" Ken nods and I say, "How long were you stuck in traffic?"

"Long enough. I don't know exactly, but last time they said it was 37 minutes altogether so I guess that's what it is."

"The traffic didn't clear up while you were passing the Burnt Olive, did it?"

"It cleared up at some point. It was stuck, stuck, stuck and then it finally got unstuck. Why?"

"Cause there's traffic cam footage," I explain, "and I tried to show the cops you were stuck in traffic during the murder but that stupid detective said maybe it cleared up in time."

Ken's eyes narrowed. "I can't remember where I was when it cleared up or how much longer it took. My mind was on getting back before Vicki got herself into some kind of trouble. Once it moved, I went to the thrift shop lot, but the place was closed so I dropped off the clothes in the box and high-tailed it out of there. That's another problem. No receipt cause it was after hours."

I squeeze his shoulder. "You sure they're calling you as a suspect and not a witness? Maybe they just want to know if you saw that silver car."

"That wouldn't be worth all this hullabaloo. They're gonna try to get me to say I made the whole thing up about delivering clothes for Mom and that I was headed down there to mess with Ellie."

"With no motive? How dumb are they?"

Ken shrugs. "For all I know, I got the short straw and drew a couple racist cops, and if I did, it won't matter if it makes sense or not. And yeah, that's possible even though one of the detectives is Black too and the other's Latina."

I don't understand but I don't want to argue. Ken's the one who knows what it's like for him. "At least after this is over, we'll know exactly what they have on you besides this stupid alibi thing so we can get to work disproving it."

"Yeah, I guess." Ken puts his hands over mine. "Thanks for helping out with Vicki in a pinch."

Vicki comes back, so I guess she's over her silent fit. "Ooh, you're holding hands!" she says.

Ken drops my hand. I smile, trying to hide my disappointment, and say to Vicki, "You feeling better?"

"Now that I know you're in love, I am," Vicki turns toward Ken. "Are you gonna kiss her too before you go?"

Ken's eyes narrow. "That would be inappropriate. You don't go around kissing people who don't want to be kissed."

"Who says I don't want to be kissed?" The words fly out of my mouth before I realize what I'm fixin' to say. I put my hands to my lips, trying to push them back in, as Ken's eyes widen and he raises his eyebrows. "Sorry. Last thing you need right now is..."

"Don't be. I'm not gonna kiss you, not til we talk and make sure we're really on the same page, but you just gave me hope that the way I feel about you's not one-sided, and I need that right now." Ken brushes my fingertips. "We'll talk later, okay?"

"I'll hold you to it," I whisper, barely able to believe this is happening. "You know if we're together, it ain't exactly a straight relationship, right?"

Ken smiles. "You think I care what label people want to put on us? I want it to be you and me, not you and me and the rest of the world." His shoulders slump. "Hopefully I won't be too long." He tells Vicki sternly to be good and gives her a hug before he goes.

Vicki throws herself on the couch as the door slams closed behind Ken. I suggest we have our supper and Vicki hunches over and shuffles her feet to the kitchen table like she's 90 years old. At first, she picks at the bread instead of eating her burger but when I don't make her stop she gives it up and opens the burger and eats it with a knife and fork while looking at me every two seconds to see if I'm about to say something. After we're done she does the same sigh and shuffle to the trash before throwing herself back on the same spot on the couch.

I sit down next to her. "Feel like talking?"

Vicki shakes her head but says nothing, just picks at her bracelet.

I put my hand on her wrist. "You're fixin' to break that, and then you'll be upset."

"I'm already upset." Vicki's so quiet I can barely hear her, even if I strain. She stares at nothing for a while.

"How about a game of Rack-O?" I suggest. "You don't have to talk if you don't feel like it, except for saying Rack-O if you win."

Vicki silently slides off the couch and disappears down the hall, returning in a second with the Rack-O box. We set it up on the table and play half a round before all of a sudden she says, "CJ? If Ken gave the cops DNA, would that prove he didn't touch Ellie?"

I stare at the 15 card I just drew, half trying to decide where to put it and half mulling over Vicki's words. Finally I say, "I don't know, sweetheart. I reckon if his lawyer thinks it's a good idea, he'll bring it up."

Vicki nods. She watches as I put my card toward the front and throw out a 49.

"Hello, Mr. 49," she says to the card. "Let's give you a good home." She puts it in the back and throws out a 3. "Mama said Ken's fingers match bruises on Ellie's neck even though he didn't do it."

I'm sure Mrs. Hansen wasn't talking to Vicki when she said that, but I don't push it. My mind is racing, trying to figure out what that means and whether I should try to get more out of Vicki when I know her family wants her to break her eavesdropping habit.

I take the 3 and throw out a 38 that was in the front spot. "I reckon that means someone squeezed Ellie's neck, then."

Vicki shrugs as she reaches for a card, then tosses it on the discard pile. "Whoever really hurt Ellie must have been out of control," she says. "She had bruises on the back of her head and on her back and legs like they threw her down hard when they had their hands on her neck. Why did they do that? Wasn't it enough they made her not breathe?"

"I think you'd best stop listening at doors," I tell her, wishing I could get to my phone to add this to the digital whiteboard without her seeing. "You're hearing things that are too scary for you." I toss a card out.

Vicki gets her angry smile on as she draws a card and discards it. "That was not the card I needed to win."

"Happens sometimes." I pick up the card and put it in the back, throwing out a 12. "Rack-O."

Vicki glares at me and I'm sure we're in for another silent fit, but she says, "You had my card, so I win too." She picks it up and puts it in her rack and I let her. "Rack-o!" she says, and giggles, the first time she's shown any sign of happiness all evening. It only lasts til I tell her to help me put the cards up now that we're done and then the angry smile is back, but I'll take it.

After the game's put up, Vicki asks, "When's Ken gonna be back?" and I know she means she's worried he ain't coming home. I reassure her that it's probably soon and she asks to watch TV. Ken hadn't said Vicki was allowed and I suspect she ain't, but I reckon on a night like this it's okay to bend the rules.

Vicki turns on a kid's show I never heard of. Apparently, it's got a girl and her brother using magic to go back in time and solve ancient Egyptian mysteries. I can't make heads or tails out of it and only pretend to follow it while part of my brain tries to work out what this new clue about the bruises on Ellie's neck means and if it rules anyone out.

After the episode ends, Vicki begs me for another, swearing she'll turn off the TV as soon as her daddy comes home even if it's in the middle of the story. I doubt that and tell her to go get a book instead. I guess the TV did her some good cause she doesn't have a fit, silent or otherwise, though she leaves it for me to turn off while she runs to get something off her bookshelf.

At 8:30 on the dot, the front door creaks open and Mr. Hansen comes home.

Vicki jumps up off the couch and runs to greet him. "Daddy! Ken's at the police."

"I'm aware, Saturn. He just texted me that he's on his way back." Mr. Hansen looks over the top of Vicki's shoulder as he hugs her. "She didn't give you any trouble, did she?"

"No, sir. She didn't want to eat at first but once we got that burger in her, she was just fine."

Mr. Hansen nods. "Go get your bath ready," he tells Vicki. He kneels so he's at eye level with her and makes her tell him everything she's fixin' to bring into the bathroom and then adds, "Say goodnight to CJ first because now that I'm home, she needs to get going."

My stomach sinks, and not just cause I'm sick of being

misgendered. I was hoping to see Ken when he got back and make sure he was all in one piece.

Vicki gets her angry smile on. "CJ isn't staying to help me in the bath?"

"A big girl like you?" Mr. Hansen says. "I don't think so."

Vicki tries again, begging her daddy to let me meet her favorite bath toy, which she's christened Leonardo for some reason, and insisting she needs my help combing out her hair after, but after a while she runs out of ideas and has to go take her bath.

As soon as she's gone, Mr. Hansen thanks me for watching her and asks how much he owes me. I tell him he doesn't need to pay me, but he says he can't expect someone who ain't family to give their night up for free and presses three crisp $20 bills into my hand. I put them up right away so I won't be tempted to give them back.

As I do, he says, "I hope you're not offended that I would prefer you to leave now. I appreciate everything you've done for Vicki tonight and that you mean a lot to my son, but his legal situation is something his mother and I would rather deal with privately."

It stings a little that he doesn't consider me close enough to let me stay, but I need to respect Mr. Hansen's wishes, so I tell him I understand and pull the door open.

Ken's on the other side. "Leaving already?" he says.

"Your dad asked me to let you have some privacy with him," I say, "and I didn't want to be disrespectful." I brush his fingertips. "You okay?"

Ken nods. "I'm not out of the woods yet, but we're getting there." He comes all the way in. "They're gonna check the security footage at the thrift shop to see if I was there when I said I was. Cooper had this doubtful tone in his voice but the facts are what they are, so maybe he'll see it my way once he's got video evidence."

I try not to let it show on my face as I hug him cause it sounds like he's one step away from being in the clear. Ken hugs me back and whispers in my ear, "I'd kiss you but my dad..."

I nod in understanding and kiss his cheek even though I want so much more.

Ken's dad lets Ken walk me to the bus stop on the corner but tells him not to stay out long, so we can't really talk, though I do tell him what Vicki told me about the case.

He says, "We're never gonna cure her of listening to things that aren't her business and then spreading it around, huh? At least she got the details right this time. Cops say Ellie was strangled with someone's bare hands and mine happen to match the marks on her neck. They think I threw her so hard she hit the wall while I was choking her, so I guess that's what someone else did." He crosses his arms. "Way I see it, whoever killed Ellie has to be around my height cause otherwise, the bruises wouldn't line up right." He leans forward, looking for the bus. "Lawyer told me something else too. The forensics report says she didn't have sex that night, so she wasn't... you know, he didn't force himself on her too."

I nod, taking that in and trying to push away the memory of the man who kidnapped me pulling down my jeans in the back seat while my wrists were bound tight behind me. "S-so if not... where are Ellie's clothes?"

"That's the million-dollar question." Ken sighs. "I sure hope that security tape shows that the clothes I dropped in the box weren't hers or it won't prove shit about my innocence." The bus's headlights pierce the darkness as the bus comes slowly down the block. "That's you," Ken says. "Text me when you get in so I don't worry." He hugs me and says,

"We'll talk about everything once things settle down. I promise."

I keep to myself that I hope I can pull off finding the killer or things ain't ever gonna settle down in the way we hope.

The bus is only half-full. I grab a window seat and stare out at my reflection, trying to make sense of everything I've learned about Ellie's death, but coming up empty. I check my phone, finally able to read Chloe's email. She says she doesn't think it's a good idea for us to talk about Dr. Armstrong and sends me some links to his published research and a copy of his press kit, which has a page with his bio and a few press releases about the research he's done.

None of that's worth anything to me. It's all PR bullshit.

How am I going to get her to tell me something authentic?

I click onto my next email. It's from Dr. Blanton; he's attached a template for a contract I can give Dr. Armstrong so that he can't turn around and sue me for the fallout of what he says on the air and a link to Docusign so I can set it up to get electronic signatures.

More to get my mind off things than anything else, I do a preliminary Google search on Dr. Armstrong, typing in, "Neuroscientist Joshua Armstrong work history."

My eyes widen as a snippet comes up on the top of the page:

*Although he is a world-renowned **neuroscientist, Joshua Armstrong** has long been a controversial figure in academic circles. His **work history** includes numerous reports of inappropriate sexual behavior toward female students. Most notably, in 1999 he resigned from Los Angeles University following an accusation that he had impregnated a student. However.... [see more]*

I stab the link for the rest of the information but it gives me a 404 Page Not Found Error.

Damn it!

But still, it's obvious Armstrong's got a history, and it ain't the kind he'd want to get out. Nor is it the kind of thing that he'd stop doing just cause he was caught once.

But if Ellie went public with what he'd done to her, maybe his luck would have run out. And that's a strong motive to kill her if you ask me.

I need to find out more about the kind of shit he does cause if he killed once to keep Ellie quiet, he'll do it again, and I know at least one woman he could easily trick into sleeping with him.

You didn't die in vain, I tell Ellie silently. *I'll finish what you started, and that's a promise.*

twenty-six

I PLUG THE article website into the Wayback Machine, but it doesn't help. It tells me it's been changed several times but when I click on the original date, it only gives me a photo of Armstrong and the title of the article. I can't tell if it's my phone not loading or if that's all there is, but it'll have to wait til I get on a computer.

Dani's out when I get back, which gives me the space to myself to figure things out. I'm bone tired, but I make myself try the Wayback Machine again on my computer. No dice—it does the same thing and when I try to look at the next iteration I get the 404 notice. So that's that; the whole thing never uploaded to the archive and if I want to know what it says, I'll have to try another way.

I peel my clothes off and change into pajamas, wondering what in the world happened to Ellie's and why someone took them. Did the killer want to make us think something happened to her that was even worse than what did? The only other thing I can think of is that there was blood or something on her dress that would prove who did it, but it ain't like she was shot or stabbed; from what Ken and Vicki said, the killer strangled her with their bare hands. So what evidence could possibly have been left behind?

I lie in bed, willing sleep to come but getting nowhere. It seems like every clue that comes in makes things make less sense instead of more, like I'm turning a telescope lens the wrong way so everything gets blurrier instead of coming into focus.

I'm tossing and turning when Dani comes in and get up to talk to her, which doesn't help at all cause she tells me she and Hailey were working on sharpening the photos she took and that there's definitely a silver necklace chain in Chloe's backseat. "It's looking more and more like Chloe killed Ellie," she says. "All over her stupid drug problem. God, what a fucking waste."

"Maybe." I cross my arms. "But right now it seems more likely Dr. Armstrong's framing her. Could be he planted the necklace and made that fake account to make us think she sent that tip."

Dani frowns. "The phone was registered to Ellie Armstrong. But I doubt he'd be that obvious. Or that he'd kill his top student. That doesn't make sense."

"It does if you put what she said with what he did to someone else." I show Dani the snippet I found. "I can't get the whole article just yet. We're going to have to go to the public library for that, I reckon. But he's got a pattern of preying on students, and he's got away with it for 25 years, so if Ellie had incontrovertible proof and he knew his goose was cooked..."

"I guess." Dani swallows hard. "Everything you've told me makes me think he's cringe as fuck, but murder? That's a whole other level, especially since it seems like Ellie had just decided to go public." She crosses her arms. "You'd think instead of putting cryptic videos up, she'd file a complaint with the Dean."

"Could be she did." I lean forward, thinking. "We'll find out tomorrow."

"When you talk to the waitress, you mean?"

"That, and it's high time I gave Dean Northrop a progress report. I reckon I'll drop in on her before I go to talk to Lisa, and while I'm at it see what she knows about Ellie's problems with Armstrong."

Dani doesn't think I'll get too far on a Saturday, but the Dean's in half a day and I time it just right, getting to the Office of Student Affairs an hour before I have to leave to meet Lisa. It's a big office with several workers behind a counter, separated by cubicle wall dividers, each with the name of the department they work for. The Dean of Students, Dean of Admissions, Housing Director, and other administrators are all here.

My stomach sinks when I find Sarah working behind the counter for the Dean of Students. I'd hoped she wasn't on duty so I could get a read on Dr. Armstrong from someone else.

I give her my best smile anyway and tell her what I want. While we're waiting for Dean Northrop to be ready to see me, I lean forward and ask Sarah, "Say, do you know if Ellie filed a complaint against Dr. Armstrong before she died?"

Sarah's eyes widen. "I hope you're not going to accuse him of anything on the air. He didn't kill Ellie. He would never..."

"I didn't say he did. Though if she did file a complaint, it does give him a motive. So... did she?"

"What, and ruin her image as his star student?" There's a bitter note in Sarah's voice. "No, she wouldn't risk that. Probably the only reason she made that stupid video is that she thought people would stop talking about her using him to get a job if she came out and admitted to it. Not that it went viral til after she died, anyway."

I raise my eyebrows. "So then you don't reckon she had grounds for a complaint?"

"Of course not." Sarah's eyes are narrow and her forehead's shiny with sweat. "It's not like she didn't want it, and if she turned around and tried to say he forced her, she'd lose that job she wanted so bad. She wouldn't throw it away after everything she'd done to get it." She lets her breath out slowly. "Jessica's another story. That bitch was still in love with Ellie, I guess. She filed a bogus complaint against Dr. Armstrong, but thankfully, Dean Northrop saw through it and closed it almost the same day."

I raise my eyebrows, praying my thoughts ain't written all over my face. If Sarah's right about this, the Dean buried a complaint she ought to be taking seriously. And if Ellie took more drastic action to expose Armstrong, he wasn't the only one with a motive for murder.

I say, carefully, "Is Ellie the only one who filed a complaint against Armstrong the whole time you've worked here?"

"Jessica. Not Ellie. I told you that." Sarah flicks the scroll wheel on her mouse. "I've never seen any others," she says. "I'm sure there have been vindictive bitches before who got mad when he didn't give them good grades and made up stories about him."

"Right," I say. "So how does it work? Do you get the complaint first and pass it on to her?"

"You have someone to file one against?" Sarah's staring at the computer screen, not me, and her voice is flat. "I don't want to be rude, but I have work to do." Her phone rings before I can protest and it's Dean Northrop telling her to send me back.

I give her another big smile. "Saved by the bell, huh?"

Sarah doesn't smile back. "Her office is the first door on the right. You can't miss it."

The Dean is sitting behind her desk, her hands clasped in front of her like she's about to give a speech, when I come in. Her office is smaller than I expected the Dean of Students' to be; it's not cramped like Dr. Blanton's, but there's not a lot of open space either. She has the same two chairs in front of her desk for visitors that he has in his little cubicle, and the wall behind her is partially taken up by a bookshelf and partially by her diplomas. She got her Bachelors of Science in Biology from Los Angeles University and her Masters in Educational Administration here at CU, so I reckon she was promoted from within the university itself.

"I understand you've made some progress on our story," Dean Northrop says, her tone as crisp and businesslike as always.

"Yes, ma'am. I've spoken to several witnesses, and I have an appointment to talk to someone who worked at the restaurant where Ellie was last seen alive." I sigh deeply. "It does seem her killer might have been associated with this school."

"I see." Dean Northrop sips her coffee. "If that turns out to be the case, I suppose I will have to speak to the admissions department about improving our vetting process so that potentially violent students do not gain access to this campus."

"Could be, ma'am." I hesitate, not sure how much to tell her. I don't want to throw Mark under the bus when I ain't sure he had anything to do with this, but maybe she knows something I don't, and I need to gain her trust if I'm ever going to get anything out of her about her daughter or about that complaint that Jessica supposedly filed. "Have you ever had problems with a student named Mark Anderson? He TAs for Dr. Armstrong and he was at dinner with Ellie right before she disappeared."

Dean Northrop's jaw tightens, but she says, "I can't say I know that name offhand, so I'll have to say no."

I nod slightly, realizing that I need to take the plunge if I ever want to get anywhere. "I need to bring up a couple of sensitive subjects," I say.

"Please do. But first, I need to bring up one." Dean Northrop leans forward. "I understand that Dr. Armstrong plans to appear on your podcast."

My heart pounds in my ears. "He asked me if he could sit down for an interview on Monday," I say, careful to keep my voice calm and even. "I haven't decided yet how much of what he says will go into a broadcast about Ellie once this is all over."

"I see." Dean Northrop crosses her arms. "I know you probably are used to having free rein when it comes to producing your podcasts, and that is something I generally encourage. However, in this case, I must make an exception. Because we are dealing with a sensitive topic that could impact Ellie's family as well as the reputation of the school, I need to be able to vet all broadcasted items. Before you sit down with Dr. Armstrong, I need you to send me a proposal outlining the purpose of this interview and what you will be asking him. It cannot go forward without my approval."

My throat tightens with anger. "Even if I don't end up using what he says on the air?"

Dean Northrop takes her glasses off and rubs her temples. "I suppose if you keep it just between the two of you, it isn't any different than interviewing any other witness. However, I cannot allow you to use school equipment to record and possibly broadcast any part of what he says without permission."

I still don't like it, but antagonizing her won't do, so I say, quietly, "Yes, ma'am." I look away, trying to decide whether to bring up the complaint Ellie filed or the evidence against Chloe first. Finally, I say, "Sarah told me that someone filed a bogus complaint against him right before Ellie died. Is that true?"

Dean Northrop sits up even straighter. "I can't discuss that with you, unfortunately. Complaints against teachers are confidential. But I can tell you that if a student did file a complaint against him or any teacher at this university, I would have investigated it thoroughly, and I certainly would not allow my daughter to work closely with him if I did not think he was trustworthy."

Are her hands shaking slightly as she picks up her coffee mug or am I imagining that?

"Of course not, ma'am."

Dean Northrop nods. "Was that the sensitive topic you wanted to bring up?"

"One of them." I breathe in sharply, trying to stop the buzzing in my ears while I wonder if this even a good idea. "A witness told us that Chloe's car was double parked outside the restaurant where Ellie was eating that night and that she left at the same time as Ellie did."

"Chloe, as in my daughter." Dean Northrop's voice is flat. "They're mistaken, of course. Chloe has a car, but she rarely drives. Most of the time we carpool to campus in the morning and back in the evening, and anyplace else she would go is in walking distance of her apartment, including the restaurants downtown."

That begs the question of why Chloe even has a car, but I don't bother asking that. "Of course, ma'am. I was wondering if there was anything you know about her and Ellie's relationship that could help us clear up these rumors."

Dean Northrop pales slightly. "I knew they lived in the same building, but I didn't think they were familiar with one another beyond passing in the hallway on occasion. So there would be no motive and little opportunity for my daughter to harm Ellie." Her jaw is set and her lips are thin. She knows something she doesn't want me to know. I'm sure of it. "What exactly did someone tell you?"

"This, ma'am." I play the fake tip even though I don't know if I believe it. Maybe if she sees what we're up against, she'll start talking.

"I am not an attorney, but that seems very circumstantial and general," Dean Northrop says. "I suppose it's possible Chloe ran an errand in the area, but it's equally possible someone else caused that tie-up downtown."

I nod. "There's another possibility. Could be Ellie and Chloe had a mutual enemy, one who saw an opportunity to frame Chloe for the murder. Is there anyone here on campus she has problems with?"

Dean Northrop shakes her head slightly. She takes off her glasses for a second time and cleans them with a wipe she takes from a desk drawer before she says, quietly, "I am going to entrust you with something. This is not to be shared with other students and certainly not to be put into any broadcast about these tragic events."

These tragic events. Not the murder of a student on her campus. Something distant, far away, that she only knows cause she read it in the news. "Yes, ma'am," I say quietly, too eager for info to cross her.

"I am considering having you sign an NDA," Dean Northrop says. "Don't make me regret that I'm not." She crosses her arms. "Several years ago, Chloe was arrested for a string of burglaries around campus. She was an impressionable teenager who had fallen into the trap of drug addiction, you see. The judge understood that she was not a true criminal and required her to get the help she needed to get clean. I've kept it to myself so that she would not be judged harshly. But I know that some of her victims felt she deserved more than a slap on the wrist, so I suppose it's possible that someone is seeking revenge by framing her for this murder."

"Any names in particular?" I ask.

Dean Northrop shakes her head. "Most of them were students who have long since graduated. I don't remember their names. Although I believe one of them is that Mexican girl who was dating Ellie. What's her name... something Gomez."

"Jessica?" My voice is flat so that I won't give away that I know this is a pile of BS.

"That's it. You might want to investigate her more closely if you haven't already." Dean Northrop's coffee mug clangs as she puts it down on her desk. "Now, if you'll excuse me, I have work to do and I'm sure you have an interview to prepare for. Please do not forget to get me that proposal before you meet with Dr. Armstrong."

"Yes, ma'am," I say. "I'll let him know I need to put off our meeting."

I shake hands with her as if nothing's wrong, but my thoughts are racing. She's the third person who's tried to convince me that Jessica killed Ellie since I got proof Jessica's innocent. That ain't a coincidence.

Someone decided to make Jessica their scapegoat. So if I want Ellie's killer, I have to find out who started this rumor that Jessica did it.

twenty-seven

I TEXT EVERYONE on the way to the coffee shop. We need to meet ASAP so we can figure out our next move, but I ain't got time now cause I don't want to be late to meet someone who was so skittish about talking in the first place.

Dani texts me back as I pass the boarded-up restaurant two doors down from the coffee shop:

> Sure you don't want me to flirt my way into answers? I'm SURE Sarah knows more than she's letting on from what you said she was like today!

I shake my head ruefully and put my phone up before entering the coffee shop. I'll get her in line after I finish this interview.

The coffee shop's surprisingly empty for this time of day. There's one woman sitting at a table by herself in a corner, reading one of those paperbacks that looks like the kind you can buy in the airport. She's older than I expected, closer to my parents' age than my own, with an oval face and green eyes. Some of her dark hair's tied back into a loose ponytail and the rest hangs down to the middle of her neck. I make a point of saying my name loud when I order my coffee to see how she reacts; she looks up slightly and nods, then goes back to her book. I set up my mic while I'm waiting, then approach her as soon as I have my coffee.

"Lisa?"

She puts the book aside. "Sorry for insisting on secrecy. It's just that if my boss knew what I was about to say, I'd lose my job." She grabs her coffee and gulps it. "See, I told her something was off about the guy Ellie was with, but she basically shut me down. So if he hurt Ellie, it's on her."

"This guy, you mean?" I show her a photo of Mark I downloaded from the neuroscience website.

Lisa face contorts as she looks at the photo. "Yeah, that's him. Can you put that away, please, before I throw up?"

"Sorry. I had to be sure." I check my phone's still recording after I close the photo. "What exactly is it about him that upset you that night?"

"What he did to Ellie, that's what. That girl was always a ray of sunshine that brightened the place up. But that last night... unhappy doesn't even begin to cover it. She seemed worn down, defeated. No light at all. He killed it. And then he killed her, didn't he?"

"I can't say for sure." I pat Lisa's hand. "You have any idea what he said to her that made her so upset?"

Lisa hesitates. "I don't like to repeat what I heard. It was so horrible."

"Please tell me." My voice is as soft as I can make it. "I know it's ugly, but the only way we can get Ellie justice is if we know the truth."

"Right. Okay." Lisa takes a deep breath. "I heard him say, 'Your baby brother'll think you're a whore, you want that?' How dare he call that beautiful girl a word like that!" Lisa's eyes narrow and on top of the table, her hands curl into fists.

My throat tightens too. I'm pretty sure I know exactly

what that was about, and that makes it worse. "Poor Ellie," I say. "How'd she take it?"

"About how you'd think. She just crumpled, like she wanted to melt into a puddle on the floor. Stammered something too about how she didn't want that. I tell you, being too sweet is what got her killed. She should have told him where he could go if he was gonna talk to her like that." She shakes her head. "His phone rang and he said he had better things to do than keep talking about this and then he just walked out and left her there with the bill. And that sweet angel's face just crumpled and it broke my heart, seeing her dissolve into a puddle of tears. So I go over there, right, and I says, 'He's not worth it, angel. You forget him and find you a man who treats you as good as you deserve,' but all I get from her is these big tears rolling down her face."

"Just sad, or did she seem like she was scared of him too?"

Lisa shakes her head. "Just heartbroken far as I could tell. I told her not to worry about the bill but she wouldn't listen. She paid it and then some. Look at the last thing that angel did for us before God called her home." She takes a folded paper out of her pocket.

I unfold it. It's a copy of the receipt. Ellie had given a 100% tip and written on it:

Please share with all the waitresses. You are all so wonderful and kind and I hope you never let anyone make you forget it. ♡ Ellie

Tears roll down Lisa's face as I stare at it, a dark thought coming to mind.

Maybe I'm wrong, and I hope to God I am, but that note looks like a suicide note to me. Did Ellie's killer beat her to it?

I swallow hard, pushing that horrible thought aside. "You

reckon anyone else eating here heard what happened between the two of them?" I'm hoping there were other witnesses who'll come forward if I ask so I can get more of an idea of whether Mark was threatening Ellie or just being an asshole.

"Oh, everyone did. He wanted to humiliate her. And you know what the worst thing is? She ran past a full house when she left, sobbing her heart out, and not one person cared enough to stop and ask her if she was okay. Not one. I couldn't get away cause I had other tables to work, but maybe I should have. Maybe if I had she'd still be here with us." Lisa's face trembles.

"It wasn't your fault," I say softly. "The only one to blame is whoever stole her life after she left here. And I intend to find out who that was and make them pay."

"Good," Lisa says, "cause they'd better pray it's you or the cops and not me or there's gonna be a second killing around here. Eye for an eye, that's what it says in the Bible."

I pat her hand. "Did Ellie ever come in with this girl?" I ask, showing her a photo of Chloe.

Lisa leans forward and looks. "Not that I can recall."

I nod. "What about this one?" I ask her, showing her a photo of Sarah.

Lisa's eyes widen, then narrow. "Only in a big group once. That little girl was as gracious as anything but I could tell it was fake, like she didn't want to be here one bit."

"Was it the big group or just she didn't like Ellie?".

Lisa shrugs again. "Had to be the group. How could anyone not like our sweet angel?" She dabs at her eyes with her napkin.

"We're almost done," I promise her. "Let me ask you this. I heard there was a car double parked outside just as Ellie left. Did you happen to notice it?"

The waitress nodded. "Didn't see it cause I was too busy but we got complaints. Manager had Melinda— that's the hostess on duty that night—announce that if anyone had a silver car double-parked out front, they needed to move it in the next two minutes or it was getting towed. But whoever it belonged to wasn't even in the restaurant cause no one moved. Damn selfish idiot, whoever it was."

I nod. "So you didn't see the car leave, then?"

"Nope, but..." Lisa's eyes widen. "Now that you mention it, I heard a car start as Ellie was running out the door. Wait... you think... that bastard double parked so he could grab her when she came out, didn't he?"

"I don't know, ma'am." I keep my voice soft. "Do you happen to know which way she went after she left?"

"Toward the apartments. Too bad that bakery next door was closed already; she could have used something sweet to soothe herself and maybe then she'd still be with us." Lisa crosses herself, shaking her head sadly.

I thank her for her time and give her my card in case she thinks of anything else. She asks me if I know where she can send flowers so Ellie's family will know how much the wait staff loved her. I give her the lab's address, in care of Jessica. In my opinion, she deserves them far more than Ellie's father does.

Talking to Lisa leaves me feeling down in a way I haven't since finding Ellie's body. I can't stop thinking about that note Ellie left the waitresses and wondering if she'd felt hopeless enough thanks to Mark that she wanted to end it all and whether she would have taken her own life if someone hadn't done it for her.

I can't prove it and we'll never know, but it leaves a bitter taste in my mouth. Still, the only thing I can do now is move forward with the investigation. I spend the bus ride back to campus flipping through my notes about the murder and making sure the digital whiteboard's updated, trying to concentrate on putting everything together instead of on how crushed Ellie must have felt by Mark's words. There were times after I escaped my kidnapper I regretted not letting him take my life along with everything else he stole from me. The feeling that it would have been best for everyone if I'd been killed had faded over time, but it never really left me til I came up here to go to school cause here, no one knew what had been done to me.

Ellie didn't get that chance. The best I can hope for is that the pain faded some as she walked home that fatal night and that by the time her killer put their fingers around her neck, she had enough will to live left to fight with all she had to survive.

Jessica texts, pulling me out of my dark thoughts, and asks me if I can meet her in the garden behind the science building cause she's found something she wants to discuss with me. Good. Hopefully the fresh air'll help clear my head. I text the others to come meet us if they can and pull the string to request a stop and run out of the bus soon as it does, not stopping til I get to the garden.

Jessica's sitting alone on the bench where Ellie made her final video, her head in her hands. She looks up as I come down the path.

"What's up?" I ask, sitting down next to her.

Jessica blinks hard. "I was going through Ellie's research and I found something I did not want to find." She lets her breath out slowly. "The others are coming or just you?"

I check my phone. "Alicia's busy but Hailey and Dani are on their way and Ken said we can get him on video whenever we're ready." I put my hand on her shoulder. "Do you want to wait for them?"

"No need," Hailey says. "We're here. We booked it as fast

as we could when we got your message." She takes out her tablet and sets it up for Ken. "What'd you find, Jessica?"

"As I was saying, something I wished I didn't." Jessica sighed. "Ellie had been collecting research surveys from potential participants in her study. I cannot share the details even now but in the folder for rejected applicants, I found a form that Chloe had filled out." She bites her lip. "Maybe this means nothing. But Chloe poured her heart to Ellie. She told her all about the accident that took her father's life and how it has shaped her and it felt as if she was grasping at a straw, at the only chance she had to get it all out of her system. And Ellie did not accept her into her study after she made herself so vulnerable. This leaves me wondering if it is possible that the rejection sent Chloe over an edge."

"Maybe," Dani said, "but maybe not. Maybe just getting it all out helped her feel better. Why did Ellie not accept her?"

"She marked it as unable to be objective because she knew the subject personally," Jessica says. "I hope it was not a fatal decision." She shakes her head slightly. "I did not want to believe that Chloe could hurt Ellie after the love Ellie showered her with. Ellie did not see her as only the Dean's daughter or as someone to be pitied, and I am certain this meant a lot to her. But this piece of evidence suggests that she repaid Ellie's kindness with violence."

I bite my lip, aware of the need to tread lightly so that Jessica won't feel any worse than she already does. "Remember what Ellie taught you?" I say. "Could be there's other explanations for all of this." But I ain't sure I believe myself. Sighing deeply, I say, "We need to talk to Chloe. So far she ain't willing to meet with me, but we've got a pile of circumstantial evidence against her and we need answers. And we have to do it without Dean Northrop finding out cause as it is, she's throwing her weight around and I can guarantee she ain't gonna like it if she learns her daughter's one of our top suspects."

"What?" Dani says.

I play the recording of my meeting with the Dean. "The Dean's trying to censor my podcast. I had to email Chloe to tell her that I need to put off Armstrong's interview."

"That's probably a good thing," Ken says. "If he's the killer, I don't trust him not to do something while you're alone in a sound booth with him."

"That would be dumb," I say, "but we do need a strategy."

"I will get Chloe to talk to me," Jessica says, "and this time if she says she is sick I will go to her house and have the conversation there."

"You have a mic?" I ask her.

Jessica swallows hard. "She does not trust easily. If she finds out I am secretly recording her words she will feel so betrayed."

"I know, but how else are we going to find out what happened to Ellie? Chloe knows something. I'm sure of it."

Jessica sighs. "I will have her meet me in a place where it makes sense for you to be so you can listen from the next table."

I reckon that's fair enough. "Make it at a time when Ken's free so he and I can make a date out of it. We ain't had an official one yet."

Ken says, "That's not exactly how I envisioned our first date, but I'd never say no to coffee with you."

"You guys are so sickeningly cute," Hailey says, smiling slightly.

My cheeks get hot. Dani says, "Maybe you two should follow it up with a date at the Burger Bistro tomorrow night, cause that's where I'm gonna take Sarah to get what she knows out of her."

"Dani..." I say.

"What? Everyone else can wear a wire to question someone and I can't?" Dani crosses her arms. "Back me up, Hailey."

Hailey's eyes narrow. "I-I think you need to be careful," she stammers. "If she's hung up on scum like Armstrong she might not be in the best headspace."

"Don't worry," Dani says. "I'll be totally sober, so she won't be able to get anything over on me. Who has her number?"

There's a long pause before Hailey says, "I do. Here." She hands Dani her phone.

I can feel tension in the air that I don't quite understand. Needing to hear the sound of my own voice to break it up, I say, "That's two suspects covered, then. That leaves Mark."

"And Armstrong," Jessica adds, "but if you can get Dean Northrop to cooperate, maybe you can get something out of him that no one else can." She crosses her arms. "Mark will be the problem case. I suspect he is the origin of the rumors that I had reasons to hurt Ellie."

"What's his problem?" I ask. "Did he want her job?"

Jessica shakes her head. "He has never had interest in the lab, only in the teaching assistant position. But maybe the lie he told about how Ellie wanted him but he did not want her is a backwards truth. I think he had a crush on her and resented that I was in the way."

"Could be," I say, "but if he did hurt her that night, it's more likely because she wouldn't stop trying to expose Armstrong." I hesitate, not wanting to hurt her further, but she needs to know the truth, so I tell her that Lisa overheard him say something horrible to Ellie and then tell her what it was. "I reckon it was a last-ditch effort to stop her from exposing Armstrong."

Jessica shakes her head slightly."I told her this was a bad

idea and that her next step should have been to contact a lawyer but she would not listen."

"What did she think she would get out of Mark?"

Jessica sighs. "She saw that Armstrong could be harsh with him, and so she thought he would be eager to help her expose him so that he could free himself. That was Ellie. She had too much faith in other people."

"Okay," I say. "It's obvious we need to get him to talk, and without Armstrong interfering, either. But how? He knows Alicia's investigating with us so that bridge is burned and no one else is in his class."

Jessica says, "I will confront him about what he said to Ellie the day she died. Him I don't mind recording in secret. He deserves it." She stands. "In fact, I will do it right now."

Her phone buzzes. She glances at it, making a face. "But first, Chloe says there are flowers delivered to the lab for me. I am not in the mood. Maybe I will tell her to wait."

"No, don't," I say. "I'll go with you to get them. It's high time I meet Chloe and see what she's all about."

twenty-eight

CHLOE MEETS US in the conference room, holding a vase containing purple lilies and white daisies. She's taller than I expected her to be from her photo, with long, skinny arms and small hands. She'd be pretty except she's got these huge brown eyes that take up far too much of her face, which is too thin.

"They're in memory of Ellie," she tells Jessica, pushing her hair away from her ear. "I hope you don't mind that I looked at the card, but I was curious."

"That solves one mystery, though not the more important one of why Ellie is only a memory now," Jessica says, taking the flowers. "Who are they from?"

"I reckon it's the wait staff at the Burnt Olive," I say. "The waitress asked me where to send some."

Chloe flinches. "Oh. I didn't realize you had someone with you." She turns toward me. "I wasn't deliberately rude to you, I promise."

"I'm sure you didn't mean to be." I introduce myself while Jessica looks at the card ."I've been trying to get ahold of you to talk to you about Dr. Armstrong for my show, so I reckoned now was as good a time as ever."

Chloe stiffens. "Oh. Right. Um, maybe we can do that via email? He doesn't like me to be away from the office for long."

"Wait, Chloe," Jessica says, putting the card down. "Are you sure you are all right since Ellie's death? She was your friend."

Chloe's face trembles. "I wish I'd gotten home in time to save her that night." She turns away. "I don't like to think about it, but I was, um, running an errand and I didn't get back til 8:15. Dr. Armstrong said that there wasn't anything I could do for her but I still feel horrible."

"Dr. Armstrong told you this?" Jessica asks.

Chloe's eyes widen and she goes slightly pale as she nods. "He doesn't want me to beat myself up." She frowns as she stares at the flowers over Jessica's shoulder. "Don't let that mouse eat your flowers. They're so pretty and it would be a shame to ruin them."

I raise my eyebrows as Jessica says quietly, "Chloe. The mouse is not one that I can see."

Chloe's cheeks go bright red. "I-I know. I saw her in Mom's office the other morning too. But don't worry. Mom took me to see Dr. Dixon to get my meds adjusted, so..." She turns toward me. "And now you know too that I see things. It doesn't mean I killed Ellie, all right?" Her face is trembling and she's breathing hard.

I nod, not sure what else to do. I'm walking a real fine line here cause if I push Chloe too hard, she'll clam up and worse, she'll tell her mother and that'll be the end of my freedom to investigate. But it's clear something's going on with her and I reckon she knows something that she ain't telling.

"I understand that," I say. "Let me ask you this, though. You didn't open a social media account under your doctor's name, did you?"

Chloe's eyes narrow. "Of course not. Why would I do that?"

"No idea, but someone did." I show it to her. "They've gone to great lengths to make us think it's you. See their profile photo?"

Chloe jumps back as I show her the photo. "They weren't lying," she says under her breath.

"Pardon?"

"Nothing." Chloe swallows hard. "I don't know anything about that account, but it kind of freaks me out that someone would use my psychiatrist's name and a drawing of me as their profile photo. It makes me feel like I have a stalker."

"This is understandable," Jessica says. "We think this person wants to frame you for Ellie's murder."

"They do." Chloe's voice is flat. She fidgets with a plastic ring on her middle finger. "T-they know no one will believe I'm innocent because of my schizoaffective disorder."

"We believe you," I say. It ain't a total lie. What Chloe's saying fits with the AI generation and everything else. "But do you know who's behind it?"

Chloe stiffens. "Of course not," she stammers, then lets her breath out slowly. "I really do have to get back to work. If I'm not there when Dr. Armstrong wants me, there'll be hell to pay."

"Chloe, wait," Jessica says. She reaches for Chloe's hands.

Chloe pulls away. "I can't stay, Jessica! Don't you understand that?"

"I do." Jessica's voice is soft. "But can we at least make up that coffee you missed when you were with Dr. Dixon?"

Chloe blinks hard. "Oh. I'll text you, okay?" She turns toward me. "And I'll answer the email you sent as soon as I find out from Dr. Armstrong what he wants me to say." She turned and hurries out of the room.

Jessica stares at the door as it closes, shaking her head sadly. "I hope the errand she was running the night of the murder was not a relapse into illegal drug use. This could be very dangerous to mix with her prescribed medications."

"You reckon that's why she's so paranoid?" I ask.

"It is possible. But the way she said she was being framed was so matter of fact that my hypothesis is instead that someone threatened to make her look guilty if she tells what she knows."

I turn away from her, thinking. "That would answer the question of why she'd leave us a phony tip implicating herself."

Jessica nods. "This, and the fact that I cannot imagine her knowing how to use AI to create a realistic voice note. She was unhappy that Dr. Armstrong wanted the lab photos taken with a digital camera as she rarely uses one, so how can this be the same person who is comfortable with advanced technology?"

"Right." I cross my arms. "So we're looking for someone who hates both you and Chloe. They reckoned we'd think the tip involves your silver car and focus on proving you killed Ellie, but they framed Chloe for sending it."

Jessica hesitates. "There is a flaw in your logic. It assumes malicious intent. In my case it is possible." She lets her breath out slowly. "There are men like Mark who see me as too quick to judge them as misogynists while also resenting me for achieving a high position in what was once a male-dominated field. But people have no reason to hate Chloe."

"Some think that she got off too easy after she robbed those houses," I say. "Dean Northrop said so this morning."

"Her word does not mean much when she is always on Armstrong's side." Jessica crosses her arms. "But even if that is true, the point is, Chloe might have been in the wrong place at the wrong time and this is why they are pressuring her to stay silent."

I nod slowly as I think about it. "She said she got home

too late to save Ellie. Could be she found her dead and the killer nearby."

"Yes," Jessica says, "this hypothesis makes sense. Then the killer makes this fake account to look like her, as a warning that if she doesn't keep quiet about what she saw, the police will get this phony evidence that she killed Ellie." She crosses her arms. "And there is only one person I know who will make these types of threats. The same snake who Ellie threatened to expose."

I ain't sure about that, but I know one thing: Things are falling into place now and it won't be long til we have the answers we seek. "I reckon Dani's idea to seduce Sarah into telling her what she knows is a good one after all," I say, "cause if anyone's close enough to Armstrong to know what really happened that night, it's Sarah."

twenty-nine

"SO WHAT EXACTLY DO WE need to get out of Sarah?" Dani asks me as she puts her hair up later that evening. She's already gotten Sarah's number off of Hailey, who's come over to help her get ready, and texted her to make plans for their date at the Burger Bistro.

I've coordinated with Ken so we can have our first date at the same time so we can keep an eye on her—too bad it ain't really just us having a good time together.

"Anything we can, I reckon." I rub my temples; this ain't the time for a headache. "For one thing, I want to know if this infatuation she's got with him is one-sided or if he's taking advantage of her."

"That's a weird thing to ask on a date," Hailey interjects. "Tell me about some other person you might be sleeping with."

"Yeah," Dani says. "I don't know how I'll get that out of her without her getting suspicious." She pulls down the front of her shirt. "I guess I can talk to her as if I'm the party girl everyone thinks I am. You know, get drunk, hook up, move on."

"That's so not you," Hailey says. Her voice is soft and her head's tilted up at Dani. "You know that, right?"

"Course. I'm just playing a part so we can get justice." Dani turns toward us. "Do I look right for it?" She's put on the purple crop top and tight jeans she was wearing the last time she got drunk and put her hair back.

Hailey's eyes stay on Dani's exposed belly for a second too long before she says, "Perfect. Let's get you made up."

As Dani sits down backward on her vanity bench so Hailey can help her with her makeup, she says, "You guys didn't really answer my question. Besides her bedroom habits, what am I looking for?"

"Anything she knows about complaints against Armstrong," I say, "cause if there's others he made go away, Ellie taking the next step would be a huge threat to him."

"There's a ratings site," Hailey says as she mixes two colors of eyeshadow together for Dani. "Rate Your CU Professor Dot Cedarwood Dot Edu. It's school-owned, but still. When things like this happen, people flock to those kinds of sites to warn others that the prof is pervy."

I write that down. "I'll check that out while y'all finish getting ready," I say. "Thanks." As I open my phone, I add, "Seems to me she likes him so much there ain't anything she won't do for him, so if you can get her talking about what she did do, that'll help. And I want to know her real feelings toward Ellie. That waitress said she seemed uncomfortable when they had a party for the lab at the Burnt Olive."

Hailey frowns. "Are you thinking she did it? Shy little Sarah from my AI Tech class?"

"We can't rule anyone out," I say, "but I'm leaning more toward thinking he did it and she's helping him cover it up. Scared, quiet girls are the type predators like him go for cause they ain't gonna fight too hard when he crosses a line."

"Could be." Hailey puts the eyeshadow brush down and picks up eyeliner. "If she thinks he returns her feelings, she'd probably do just about anything he asks. Bastard."

"Even make that fake account to frame Chloe?" I ask. "We were assuming the killer did it but maybe we're looking at it wrong and he's got an accomplice."

"It's hard to say who did what," Hailey says, "but she'd have the skills to pull off making that account. I just told you, we're taking a class in AI applications together. Not that voice generation is that hard. Whoever did it would just have to plug what they wanted to say and what type of voice they wanted into one of a dozen apps. And the image is even easier cause there are apps now where you can upload a photo and ask for it to be converted to a drawing."

"Still," Dani says. "I can't imagine Dr. Armstrong doing that himself. He'd be afraid of it being traced back to him." She frowns. "Wait. Can you trace it, Hailey?"

"Yes and no," Hailey says. "There's apps that can tell you which AI app was used to create a voice, but they're not fool-proof. We already have an IP address for the phone used to send the voice clip, so there's that, even if it did trace back to a fake name." She picks up a tube of lip gloss. "Here, Dani, you want me to do your lips or you want to do it yourself?"

They're sitting very close together as Dani opens her eyes. "Um, I got it," she says nervously, blushing hard. Hailey hands her the lip gloss and their knuckles collide for a second. Dani swallows hard and looks away as she takes the tube of lip gloss.

Hailey says, "Um, I'm gonna go, okay? Believe it or not, I do have work besides the stuff I'm doing for you guys, and since you're busy tonight it's a good time to get caught up."

"Wait," Dani says. "Don't you want to see my reaction to you making me over?"

Hailey hesitates. "I do," she says, "but I hate that we're

going to all this trouble for some girl who you're not really into." She blinks hard. "Be careful, okay? You know what happened to Ellie after Jessica helped her get ready for some other thing disguised as a date and I can't stand the thought it might happen to you too."

"I'm always careful," Dani says. "I learned a long time ago I can't be good, so…" She smiles, but I can tell it's forced and that she's nervous as hell.

"Right." Hailey lets her breath out slowly. "Take a photo for Insta," she says, "and call me when you're done to let me know how you make out." She turns and hurries away, letting the door slam behind her.

Dani sighs deeply. "Is it just me, or is she a little jealous?"

"More than a little," I say, "but we ain't got time for that right now." I pat her hand. "Maybe when this is all over, you and Hailey can go on a real date."

"You and Ken too," Dani says. "I'm sorry yours has to be ruined cause of this case." She looks in the mirror at the lavender glittery eyeshadow and eyeliner that makes her eyes pop. "Hailey did a great job. I look more like I'm ready for anything than when I used to party for real." She sighs. "I really wish she was coming to watch my back."

"You still got me and Ken." I bite my lip. It should be the four of us double dating, not all this subterfuge that's clearly got Hailey upset.

"Yeah, I know." Dani puts on her lip gloss. "Listen, if he shows up before the next 10 minutes, don't leave yet. I don't want it to look like we all came together."

"I'm aware." It's the tenth time Dani's told me this, but I do my best to cut her some slack cause I know her nerves have to be even higher than mine.

After Dani goes, I put on one of the shirts I borrowed from Ken and a pair of black dress slacks and shoes. Done. I can't help remembering getting ready for my horrible senior prom back home. I wasn't out to anyone but my parents, who didn't fully understand but who warned me to keep my feelings to myself so I couldn't get hurt, and I went with a girl who wasn't out as bi either. I'd let her make me up and told myself it was worth it cause she would get to feel like she was dating a girl, but the whole night, I was miserable, and after fifteen minutes she wandered off to make out with some random person in the parking lot—I don't even recall if it was a girl or a guy—so it was all for nothing.

I shake my head to get rid of that memory. It's better than thinking about my abduction, but not by much, and I'd appreciate it if my brain would stay in the present.

I open the site Hailey gave me, as much to pass the time as anything else.

The first two pages are all glowing reviews. Those have to be fake; there's no way everyone loves any teacher that much, especially not one that preys on female students. The reviews are all anonymous and there are page after page of them with no way to jump to the bottom.

I'm about to give up when I finally hit pay dirt on page 10:

This site is a bad joke! The same school that can't be bothered to do anything about our complaints of freaking sexual MISCONDUCT sure gets busy making sure no one sees them. Since no one'll see this post either, I feel comfortable telling those who need it to DM me on my Social Strands account for a group where you will be heard. IYKYK. And if you don't know... then please, don't take this professor's class so you won't have to find out...

Unlike the positive reviewers, this one's not anonymous. Her name is Meghan Wilcox and I find her on Social Strands, but it doesn't say anything on her profile about whatever it was she was talking about.

I swallow hard. I ain't a survivor, not of him, anyway, so asking her for an invite to her group would be intruding on people's pain. But I need to know.

It takes me forever to write a DM cause I keep writing and erasing, but finally I come up with something good:

> Hi Meghan, I think Joshua Armstrong may have killed a student to keep her from telling what he did to her & I want to get justice... can we talk? - CJ

Just that short message takes a lot out of me. My body's heavy and my eyes burn, and if Ken wasn't on his way, I'd crawl under the covers and stay there. Instead, I sit there hugging myself and trying not to let my mind go places it ain't got any business going. I keep imagining Ellie getting into her killer's silver car and having to remind myself that witnesses saw her walking home. I'm getting what happened to her mixed up with what happened to me and I have to cut it out before Ken gets here cause I ain't gonna be any use to anyone if I can't get out of this mood. I make myself breathe deeply and count my breaths.

In...1...out. In...2...out...

Ken knocks on the door. He's wearing a gray suit and black tie that make me shiver. I stare into his eyes, letting myself get lost in them.

"You okay?" he says.

I nod. "Just nervous is all." It's only half true but I tell myself I'll explain the rest in the car.

I spent the first half of the ride staring out the window and watching the world zoom by too fast to recognize while I try to find the words to say what I need to say.

Ken pulls over to the side of the road and I jerk up. "There ain't something wrong with the car, is there?"

"No, and we're not getting pulled by the cops either." Ken pats my hand. "But I can tell something's off. It's like you're not all the way there, like when Vicki's looking right at you but her mind's a million miles away. What's up?"

I swallow hard. "Armstrong doing what he does without consequences is getting to me. Right before you came over I saw something that upset me." I show him the message Meghan had on the Rate Your CU Professor site.

Ken reads it. "What a bastard," he says, "and Northrop too, burying complaints under bullshit positive reviews." He puts his hands over mine. "We'll get him. That's a promise."

"Hope so." I swallow hard. "There's something else. I don't know how to say this."

Ken puts his hand on my shoulder. "Hey. There's nothing I'm gonna judge you for. Not even if you like those stupid reality shows where you gotta eat worms and shit." He grins, making me shiver all over again.

"I know. It's just hard cause... well, something happened to me when I wasn't much bigger than Vicki and I suppose Armstrong being how he is got me all stirred up about it all over again."

Ken's smile fades. "What happened?" he asks gently.

My heart pounds. "I was kidnapped," I say, my voice shaking. "The cops said it was my fault cause I sneaked out of the house to meet him a-and..."

Ken's eyes widen. "The cops were full of shit. Whatever he did to you, you didn't deserve it even if you did take a risk." He rubs my shoulders. "Wanna tell me about it?"

I nod. "I'm just looking for the right words." I let my breath out slowly. "Okay. So this guy, he was, um, a predator, I reckon, like Armstrong. And I was thought I was a freak cause I didn't feel like a girl and that's what everyone said I was. So he got on my social media, or maybe it was my email, I can't remember which, anyway, he pretended he was a sixteen-year-old boy who liked me and he let me pour my heart out to him more than once. He kept pushing me to run away with him til he wore me down and I sneaked out my window late at night to meet up in some woods. When I got there, I saw this man my daddy's age leaning on a tree, lighting up a cigarette and something felt wrong so I tried to go back the way I came but... "

My breath knocked out of me. The smell of leather. A hand pressed over my mouth. Dragged backward, arms pinned to my sides. Thrown in the back seat of a Jeep. Warned what'll happen if I don't lay still...

I blink hard. "He tied me up so tight the plastic cut into my wrists and then he rolled me over and pulled down my jeans and he... he..." A sob escapes and I can't go on.

"Shit." Ken hugs me tight. "I am so sorry, CJ." He strokes my hair. "And the cops didn't do anything?"

I shake my head. "I reckon that's why I've been so on fire since I learned what happened to Ellie. I wasn't about to let anyone take justice from her the way the cops did to me."

"That and you know if you hadn't managed to get away we wouldn't be having this conversation cause that man would have done the same to you when he was done with you." Ken's voice is thick. "I worry about it happening to Vicki sometimes. She knows not to talk to strangers but if she got catfished like that..." He shakes his head.

Fear shoots through me. "There ain't any chance she's talking to strangers online, is there?"

"Social media's blocked on her computer and Mom and Dad watch everything she does on it, but she's not gonna be eleven forever." Ken smiles ruefully as he takes tissues out of the glove box for me. "End PSA. You'll be all right and so will she. Right now let's focus on getting Armstrong. That'll be one less asshole able to mess people's lives up once we do." He flicks his signal hard as he gets ready to pull back onto the road.

I watch Ken carefully as we drive to the restaurant, hoping against hope he doesn't see me any differently than he did before he knew.

thirty

THE BURGER BISTRO is a step down from the Burnt Olive. It ain't fast food—it's still a sit-down restaurant that's got a bar near the front, but it's less fancy and instead of a hostess there's a sign inviting you to take a table wherever you'd like. The bar's pretty crowded and so's the restaurant; it's smack in between the college and Cedarwood General Hospital, so there's a steady stream of people coming from both.

Ken puts his arm around me as we walk in. There's a table in a quiet corner that no one's taken and I ache for this whole thing to be over so he and I can sit there, but Dani and Sarah are all the way at the other end of the room so we have to pass it by.

"I sure hope we can find a table we can see everything from," Ken says under his breath while I wish we had the sophisticated equipment cops have on the TV so we could watch from a monitor in a van in between kisses.

It doesn't look like we're gonna have any luck, but then someone throws some bills down on a table across from Dani's and walks off. The table's in need of cleaning, but it'll do the job, so we take it.

Dani's leaning forward, looking Sarah in the eye. "You really do it all," she says. "The lab on top of working for Dean Northrop and taking a full courseload. Wow."

I bend over the menu, pretending to be poring over the choices. "She's sure laying it on thick," I whisper.

Ken says, "I wouldn't mind getting to look in your eyes some tonight." He reaches for my hand.

I take it, only half paying attention cause I'm trying to keep my ear out in case Sarah spills something useful. So far she's bragging about how she's taking some accelerated program that'll let her get an advanced degree and her BA at the same time, which I don't care about unless Armstrong's the one who got her in it.

A waitress comes by and takes the dirty plates out of the way, blocking my view of Dani and making too much noise. When she goes, me and Ken can barely hold in our giggles. This whole thing is ridiculous and it probably ain't even gonna work.

Ken says, "Hey, you ever tried bison? I heard they make it good here."

"I was hoping for lamb," I say, "but I'd wager it's the most expensive thing on the menu."

"It's all right. I'd pay any price to make you smile." Ken brushes my cheek with the back of his hand.

My ears perk up cause I heard Armstrong's name. "Hold that thought," I whisper. Ken's eyes narrow with disappointment as he drops his hand. I reach across the table for it, aware I'm only giving him but a consolation prize.

"I'm that obvious, huh?" Sarah says. She dips a fry into ranch dressing and chews it before she goes on, "Look, I know he's three times my age, but he gets me. N-not that we're anything. I mean, he's my professor so we can't be. Not yet, anyway."

Dani makes her eyes narrow as she bites into a black bean

burger. "So why exactly did you ask me out if you're so into him?"

Sarah goes deep red. "It's not like I don't like you too. Y-you're not my plan B, I promise."

"But?" Dani asks.

"But the heat's on Josh... um, Dr. Armstrong. Your friend was in the Dean's office asking questions about that bogus complaint Ellie made and she wanted to know if there were others. And I had to think fast and it was really uncomfortable." Sarah takes another bite. "There's nothing there, Dani, I promise. I mean sure, there were some complaints and stuff, but nothing ever stuck because it was all jealous bitches lying about him. But if I told the truth, your friend would think that he killed Ellie because she wouldn't let it go."

"You're sure he didn't?" Dani's playing it cool in a way I never could in her place.

Sarah's eyes narrow. She nods. "It had to be Chloe. I don't know why, but that girl's not exactly stable, so... maybe she was delusional enough to think he was into her and she got jealous when she found out Ellie actually slept with him."

"I guess." Dani's face is neutral. "Though my friend Hailey says someone else made a fake account and tried to frame Chloe."

Sarah's eyes widen. "Do you think it was Jessica?"

(I whisper to Ken, "You reckon any of this is real, or is she just making up whatever pops into her head?"

Ken's jaw tightens. "No telling. I think we should order.")

"I wish you knew Ellie better," Dani says. "She sounds like she was surrounded by all this drama and I'd love to be able to tell CJ who to focus on." She reaches for Sarah's hand. "If you know something, don't be afraid to tell me, okay?"

Sarah swallows hard. "I need a drink first." She opens her pocketbook and rummages through it. "Shit. I left my drink-buying ID at home. Can you..."

Ken and I exchange glances. This smells like a set-up to me. I hope I'm wrong.

Dani says, "Oh. I don't like to use mine except at places where I already know they're not going to make a big deal out of it."

"I know, but I can't deal with Ellie without a drink. Please? You can get whatever you like and sneak some to me."

Dani pushes her hair behind her ear. "I could go for a rum and Coke, I guess."

Shit. Is she really giving into temptation or just playing along to make Sarah trust her? Either way, this seems like bad news.

I can't see what happens next cause our waitress comes over again. By the time we're finished ordering, Dani's putting her ID away, so I suppose she must have ordered alcohol while we were distracted.

"So while we're waiting," Dani says, "tell me a little about Ellie, just enough to tease me."

"Fine," Sarah says. "She was like, this rockstar in the lab's eyes, but —"

A woman wearing a white pantsuit and a black bow tie comes over to Dani's table, along with a waitress. "This the young lady who ordered a rum and Coke?" she asks.

The waitress nods slightly. The woman takes something out of her pocket. I see a flash of silver.

A cop's badge. Shit.

("I knew it," I whisper to Ken. "What the hell is wrong with Dani? Why did she give in so quick to this?"

Ken puts his finger on his lips. "All we can do is let it play out now." He takes out his phone and when I glance over, he's got the video camera up.)

As Ken records, the cop says to Dani, "We know that ID you gave this waitress here was fake. How old are you, really?"

Dani looks down at the table. "Nineteen. Look, I'm sorry.

My friend wanted a drink and forgot her ID, but since you caught me, can't we just forget it and take a regular Coke?"

"It doesn't work that way," the cop says. "Using a fake ID is a serious crime." The cop takes out a pair of handcuffs from a case on her belt. "You're under arrest. Stand up and put your hands behind your back."

Dani goes pale. As she stands, she says, "Please... can't you confiscate my fake ID so I can't use it again and write me a ticket or something?"

"Sorry." The cop adjusts the cuffs. "This isn't the sort of thing you can be let off with a warning for. Now put your hands behind your back or you're getting charged with resisting arrest."

Dani's eyes flash as she does what she's told. I watch Sarah's face as the cop clicks the cuffs closed around Dani's wrists and informs her that she's being arrested on one count of possessing a fake ID and one count of attempting to use it to purchase alcohol. Sarah's head is bowed like she's upset, but I can't tell if it's real or fake. I'm too busy fighting tears myself.

My best friend is about to spend the weekend behind bars, and it's all cause of me. I'd told her twice not to do this, but I'd relented cause I was so eager to get info from Sarah. And now we hadn't got a single thing that made it worth it, unless you count Sarah admitting she has a crush on Armstrong.

The cop pulls on latex gloves and asks Dani if she has anything dangerous on her.

"N-no." Dani's voice shakes but she stops just short of a sob.

The cop begins patting her down. I hold my breath, aware of what they're about to find. She pulls out the clip-on mic with two fingers. "What's this for?"

Sarah's head jerks up. "A MICROPHONE?" she says. "Were you recording me?" She blinks hard, and now I know it's fake cause she says, "Dr. Armstrong warned me to be careful. People are always trying to set him up, but I thought you were different."

"Like you weren't trying to set me up," Dani says. "You're the one who should be in cuffs."

"That's enough, both of you," the cop says. She grabs Dani's elbow and puts her other hand on her shoulder. "I don't know what this is all about, but it's not looking good. You'd better hope the DA doesn't decide to charge you with anything in relation to this mic." She turns Dani around. "Let's go."

"Worst first date ever." Dani holds her head up high but I can tell how hard she's fighting tears. The cop takes her the other way, toward the bar in front, so I can't even catch her eye to tell her that Ken's fixin' to call his mom to get her a lawyer and that she just needs to keep her mouth shut til then.

The cop says loudly as she marches Dani away, "This is what happens when you use a fake ID in this restaurant, so if anyone else is thinking about it, think again."

Sarah slides down in her seat like she's embarrassed. A waiter passes by, blocking my view, and when he moves, she's gone.

"Bitch," I say under my breath. "Bet you anything she did that on orders from Armstrong."

Ken nods slightly. "I'm gonna call my mom," he says, "and we'll take it from there." He reaches for my hand. "She'll be all right."

"She's spending the weekend in jail."

"I know. But at least it's not for murder. They'll probably let her go after court Monday." Ken swallows hard as he picks up his phone.

I reach for his hand, praying he'll let me take it. He does and I hold it tight, but after a sec he says he has to make his call and pulls away before walking off.

Our food comes in the meantime; I've got no appetite anymore but I pick at the bun while I'm waiting.

My phone buzzes.

It's a DM back from Meghan. I let my breath out slowly and make myself read it:

> I looked at your profile. Somehow you forgot to mention that you have a podcast through the school. Are you really interested in answers or are you yet another person trying to silence women who have been wronged by that piece of crap?

I glare at it, my thoughts racing so hard I can't put a sentence together. This is all I need right now. I put the phone up without saying anything.

Dani's in jail and my best lead won't talk to me.

Armstrong's won, ain't he?

thirty-one

KEN RUBS HIS hands together as he sits back down. "Food's here. Good."

I stare at him, unable to fathom how he can think of eating at a time like this. "Your mom's gonna help Dani out, right?"

He reaches for my hand across the table. "She's gonna be fine," he said. "Mom wasn't too happy but I got her to see that Dani wasn't actually drunk so she made the call." He stares down into his burger and fries. "I think she was probably relieved that it wasn't me that needed a lawyer this time. But we can't keep asking her firm to represent all of us. It doesn't look good for her."

"This better be the last time." I take a sip of my Coke. "Did she give you an indication of how bad this is?"

"Could get rough but she doubts it. I didn't understand all the details, but there's two versions of the fake ID law. One's a felony and the other's a misdemeanor, and she's 99% sure that they'll slap her with the misdemeanor since it's her first offense."

I nod without really understanding. "Are we talking jail time or what?"

"That I don't know." Ken frowns. "Aren't you gonna eat more than a few crumbs of bread?"

I push my plate away. "I'm sorry. I don't mean to waste your money. But how can I eat when Dani's behind bars where they probably won't give her much?"

"She got her burger in her before they arrested her," Ken says, "and anyway, you not eating isn't gonna change anything for her." I shrug and Ken says, "Tell you what. After we finish up, let's go for a walk and piece together what little we got out of this before the cops showed up. That way, it won't be a total waste."

"Being with you never is." My voice is flat even though I mean it. I hope Ken knows I ain't just saying things.

My stomach feels tight even though I ain't eaten all day, but I manage to force down a few bites. The meat's juicy and pink on the inside and the fries are steaming hot, just how I like them, but I might as well be eating cardboard cause I'm too upset to taste anything. Ken gobbles his down so fast I doubt he's got any more enjoyment out of it than I have. After a couple minutes, he calls the waitress over and asks her for a box for me and the bill.

"Case not eating catches up with you later," he says.

I reach for his hand. "I'm sorry I ruined what was supposed to be a good time together."

Ken shrugs. "This doesn't count as a first date. This was work. Though if Dani hadn't been stupid enough to take Sarah's bait, maybe things would have worked out different."

My throat tightens with anger at how Ken's blaming Dani when Sarah's the one who did something wrong, but I don't want to fight so I say nothing.

The waitress returns with the box. "Meal's on the house, guys," she says. "My manager feels bad that it got ruined by all that drama at the next table."

"Thanks." My heart pounds and I wonder if I should leave

it at that, but decide not to, for Dani's sake. "Have you had a lot of trouble like that?"

The waitress shakes her head slightly. "It happens sometimes cause we're so close to the college. I'm glad you guys had more sense than those two." She leans forward, lowering her voice. "But I had a feeling there was gonna be trouble as soon as those girls walked in."

I bite my lip so that I won't give away that I know Dani and that she ain't a troublemaker. "Why? Have they been here before?"

"Not the one who got arrested. But the other one's been in here a few times. She's tried that trick where she tells her companion that she forgot her ID before, but usually with someone old enough to drink. In fact, the other day she was in here with an older gentleman who ought to know better than to buy alcohol for her."

I raise my eyebrows. "Really." I open the photo of Armstrong that Chloe sent me. "Not to be nosey, but was it this man?"

The waitress nods. "That's him. Should have known he was a teacher cause he was so polite and apologetic when I called him on the alcohol thing. He said they'd had some bad news and he was trying to steady her nerves. "

"Did they say anything more specific?" If Sarah and Armstrong were talking about the murder, we've hit pay dirt.

The waitress shakes her head. "I didn't pry. Long as they weren't messing around with alcohol in here, it wasn't my business."

She says she has to get back to work before I can ask her anything else.

Our plan to go for a walk's foiled by the big signs in the parking lot saying that the parking lot's for patrons only and you're risking getting towed if you leave your vehicle here while you go somewhere else. That would be all we would need to round out the evening, so we slide into the car while I try not to think about Dani sitting on a hard bunk in a holding cell.

"Mind if we stop by the Burnt Olive?" Ken asks. "I still want to give you that walk I promised you. Besides, I want to take a look at where Chloe double parked. Maybe it'll spark something."

I shrug. "I ain't great company right now," I say, putting my hand over my stomach, "but if you reckon it'll help, go for it."

"I don't know what will help." Ken's voice is soft. "I know none of this is what we planned, and you've got to be heartbroken about Dani, but I'm lost as to what to do for you."

"Being with you helps. And finding proof Sarah set Dani up."

"Don't go getting sidetracked. Whatever role Sarah played in Dani's arrest, that's second in importance to what happened to Ellie."

"I know. But she's been interfering in the investigation since the beginning and I can't help thinking she pulled that trick with Dani to stop us from getting too close to the truth."

"Could be." Ken pulls into the lot at the Burnt Olive. "No leaving this lot either, but we're only going down the block and we can get back here before the tow truck if need be." He parks and gets out, holding out his hand for me to take.

Maybe I haven't totally ruined our date. I let my breath out slowly as I take Ken's hand.

We walk past the lot to the area where Chloe double-parked. It's a nice night, not too cold but not too hot, and you can see the half-moon clearly, hanging over the restaurant like something out of a painting. It would be romantic if we had the time to stop and stare at it. I squeeze Ken's hand tighter.

"So she was parked about here," Ken says, gesturing toward the red zone in front of the restaurant. "You think there's any truth to what the fake tipster said about her taking off at the same time as Ellie?"

"The waitress confirmed it," I say, "though I reckon it would take a few minutes to get out of here cause of the traffic jam she caused. I wouldn't be surprised if no one made space for her and that made everything take longer to clear up."

"Good observation," Ken says, and I smile slightly. "The tipster said she came from that way and got back in her car." He points.

I follow his finger toward that boarded-up restaurant. "If that's true, I reckon she was behind that restaurant, which means only one thing: she was up to no good. Even if she didn't do anything to Ellie, she was doing something she shouldn't have been."

Ken nods. "Like a drug deal, maybe. Think about it. She meets the guy back here, she gets the drugs, she comes back and gets her car." He lowers his voice. "Speak of the devil, look who's coming this way."

I turn. Chloe's walking slowly down the sidewalk, wearing a blue hoodie drawn as tight as possible around her face so that it squashes her hair. It doesn't do much for her; I can still see her face and I recognize her hand when she plays with the hoodie string. Her eyes dart everywhere, landing on me, then away, and I ain't sure she's seen me.

"Is she high now?" I whisper.

"Dunno. Never saw her before so I can't tell how this is different than sober." Ken gestures for me to make myself flat against the wall and I do.

At the boarded-up restaurant, Chloe turns and goes through the alley to the back of the building.

I tiptoe after her. Ken shakes his head and puts his hand

on my arm. "Don't. If it's what we think it is, it's too dangerous. They could see you and if the cops pass by…"

I pull away. "I have to," I whisper back. "It's our only chance to find out what she's mixed up in."

Ken's jaw tightens. "I wanna have your back, but two of us in the alley's asking for trouble." He hugs me, awkwardly. "If you're not back in ten minutes, I'm coming to get you out of there though, all right?"

I nod and hurry to the alley.

There ain't any lights back here; the only reason it's not pitch black is cause the moon's overhead. I look around for escape routes as I follow Chloe, There's a car parked at the southern end of the alley, blocking my exit that way, which is just as well cause I don't know where it leads. The only other way out's the way I came, and it feels like a long way away even though I've gone maybe 15 feet.

I hold my breath as I pass graffiti-tagged walls and a bunch of dumpsters that it would be real easy to shove someone in to get rid of them. I'm trying to be as quiet as Chloe, but both our footsteps bounce off the walls and crash into my ears while I bite my lip, trying to ignore the smell of days-old trash coming from next to me.

Chloe looks over her shoulder, breathing hard. I duck back, making myself flat against the opposite wall. She turns back around and quickens her pace.

Fuck. She knows she's being followed.

I slide along the wall as quiet as can be while she hurries toward the car. It's a dark-colored one, so we can rule out a third person having the same kind of car Chloe does, I reckon. Chloe tiptoes up to it, looking over her shoulder every few seconds, and knocks on the window.

I come as close as I dare. If Dani were here, she'd try to take photos, but it's so dark my phone screen looks like a big black rectangle.

I doubt even Hailey could do anything with something this dark. I give up that idea and grab my wireless mic out of my pocket instead, clipping it to my shirt collar and connecting it silently to my phone. Maybe it'll pick up something worthwhile.

The window rolls down a crack, just big enough to stick your hand through. The driver says, "Get in. We need to talk."

It's too dark to see anything through the window but my own reflection, but the voice is one I heard not an hour ago.

It's Sarah.

thirty-two

I BEND MY knees and lean forward, ready to spring into action if Sarah tries to force Chloe into the backseat.

Chloe grabs tight to the back door handle but doesn't open it. "How do I know this isn't a trick?"

Sarah whispers so low I barely catch it even with my ears strained to the max. All I get is, "helped...that night.... If you do what you're told..."

Does she know I'm here? Could be she's letting me hear the bits and pieces she wants. I make myself flatter against the wall while I order my brain to stop serving up these paranoid thoughts.

Chloe says, "I will. But please, not a car, not after—" She cuts herself off as surely as if she's been interrupted even though I don't hear anything.

"Fine. But if we're caught, you'll pay." Sarah lowers her voice again so I can't hear the rest. That has to be deliberate. Doesn't it?

Chloe stiffens at whatever it is Sarah just said. "I'll talk to my mother, all right. I'll tell her everything."

Sarah says, her voice soft and threatening, "Then you'll go

to jail. It's your word against ours, and she knows you're a liar."

Chloe's shoulders shake. "M-maybe that's best. I can't do this anymore. T-that reporter thinks I killed Ellie a-and I can't look Jessica in the eye cause she knows I know something. A-and every day at work, I have to —"

Sarah turns up her music, drowning out the rest. Chloe jumps back a step while I try to make myself even flatter. Sarah turns the music off and hisses, "Point made, I hope? Look, I told you before: if you want to stay out of jail, we have to stick together."

My phone beeps. Shit. My battery's low.

I'm hoping it's quiet enough no one heard, but Sarah stiffens and says, "You'd better not have let that reporter follow you."

My heart pounds even before I start running. Sarah calls loudly, "I know you're out there somewhere, bitch! Didn't you learn anything from your girlfriend getting arrested?"

So I was right. She set Dani up.

I make myself keep running even though I don't want to.

Another car pulls into the alley, getting right in my path. I jump aside, looking over my shoulder.

Sarah's still blocking the alley at the other end and this car's got this exit covered.

I'm trapped.

thirty-three

I GRAB MY keys and hold them straight out while I make myself flat against the wall. They ain't much of a weapon, but they're the best I have, and I'm not about to let myself get kidnapped twice.

The driver of the car closest to me rolls down the window. "You getting in or what?"

It's Ken. What the hell is wrong with me that I forgot he said he was coming back for me?

I throw my keys into my pocket and hurry to get into the car. My brain insists on playing a movie over and over of Sarah speeding toward us, but when I look over my shoulder, her car's gone, probably backed out the other way.

"Sorry," I say as I slam the door shut. "I got freaked out by what was going on."

"I got that. What were you gonna do, stab my tires with the keys to stop me from running over?" Ken grins.

I glare at him, not appreciating being laughed at. "My stupid phone started dying and Sarah heard it beep." I check the phone. 10% battery; maybe it'll play the recording, but maybe it won't.

Ken lends me a car charger while I stab at the record button, cutting it off before it drains my battery altogether. "Sarah, huh?" he says. "So she's in deeper than we thought?"

"I suppose." I shove the charging cord hard into my phone. "Can we get out of here, please?"

"You got it. But chill with the cord. You'll break your charging port."

I know Ken's right, but I can't help thinking he's talking to me like I'm Vicki's age as he backs out of the alley. I take a couple minutes to compose myself before asking him if he wants to get coffee so we can go over what I heard in the alley.

Ken's grip tightens on the steering wheel. "I think we'd better call it a night. I don't like keeping the car out too late in case my parents need it for something."

My stomach sinks. Ken's had enough of me for one night, and maybe forever. "I reckon I need to tell the others that Dani's in jail," I say awkwardly. "They ought to know."

Ken nods but says nothing. I open my phone to text the group; my combined text and DM app's still open to Meghan's DM. "Dani's not the only reason I'm out of sorts tonight." I show him my screen. "It hurt my feelings that she thinks I'm on Armstrong's side when I'm a survivor too."

"So tell her," Ken says. "She doesn't know you so how can she understand if you don't?"

I can't tell if his voice is colder than usual or my imagination. "I suppose. The rest of the group first, though." I start a new text and take my time composing it, mostly so I don't have to look at Ken.

Hailey's the first to text back:

Oh no!!! I knew something like this was going to happen! EMERGENCY MEETING? Please?

I text her back that I'll let her know when I'm home and ask Ken if it's okay if I loop him in.

"Not if we're talking about Dani getting arrested," he says. "I lived through it, I don't need to hear it. But if it's about the case, sure."

"K." I let my breath out slowly. "I'll want to discuss that. Sarah and Chloe are both involved somehow. From what little I heard, I'm guessing Chloe's the killer, but that doesn't make a whole lot of sense. I can see Sarah covering for Armstrong since she's crushing on him so hard, but what's Chloe to her?"

"Maybe Armstrong's the link between them." Ken flicks his turn signal. "If he's calling the shots…"

"Could be. You reckon he killed Ellie? But what do the other two have to do with it?"

"Don't know. You sure the girls didn't give you a single clue?"

I stare out the window, trying to think. "Seemed like Sarah knew something that Chloe was scared of her knowing. She said something about Chloe going to jail if she didn't keep her mouth shut."

"Blackmail." Ken's voice is heavy. "But why?"

My phone buzzes, throwing me off my train of thought. The display says CEDARWOOD PD.

My heart pounds as I answer.

"It's me, Dani. I'm allowed three phone calls so I thought…" Dani sighs deeply as I mouth her name to Ken and put it on speaker so he can hear. "I'm so, so sorry. I should have known better than to try to pass off that fake ID just because Sarah wanted me to."

"Don't say another word about it," Ken says. "They could use it against you."

Dani's quiet for a second. Then she says, "My case is mostly settled anyway. Thanks for the lawyer, by the way. She made some deal with the DA. I have to plead guilty Monday morning and then I can come home."

"Guilty to what?" My heart pounds even though I'm glad that Dani's gonna get out soon.

"I forget the exact words. It's, um, not a felony, the other thing."

"Misdemeanor?" Ken says.

"Yeah, that's it. Sorry, my brain's not working. Anyway, I'm being taken to court first thing Monday morning and if the judge accepts my plea that'll be the end of it. The lawyer said I'll probably be sentenced to probation and community service."

"What time's the arraignment?" I ask. "I'll come down to support you."

"No, don't." Dani's voice shakes slightly. "I... the lawyer said I'll be in handcuffs and the uniform I have to wear is so ugly. I don't want you to see me like that."

I blink back tears. "Are you sure?"

"It's just a formality anyway," Dani says. "When I come home I'll tell you all the details, I promise. Just don't let me being an idiot derail the investigation, okay? Focus on that til I get out of here."

"Dani —"

There's a beep. "Shit. I only have 30 seconds to say good night. I'll see you guys Monday. Sorry again I ruined everything."

Dani hangs up.

I blink back tears as Ken pulls up in front of my dorm. He says, "Well, at least she's coming home and you know she'll be all right." He stares at his reflection in the rearview mirror. "Not like me if they decide I'm the one who killed Ellie."

"They won't," I say, "cause we have too much evidence pointing to other people. All we have to do is untangle it."

"If you say so." Ken swallows hard. "Well, I guess this is it for now." He holds out his arms for a hug.

I hug him and he strokes my hair, but when I attempt to kiss him, he pulls away and kisses me on the cheek.

My eyes burn with tears that I don't dare shed. "Oh. Sorry. I thought you wanted..."

"I do, believe me. But after what happened tonight... it's not a good idea, Ceej."

My throat stings as I swallow. "I ruined our evening."

"It's not that." Ken strokes my cheek. "I don't want you to think it's anything you did. I mean, yeah, I'd have rather you weren't focused so hard on work that I felt like a second thought, but I get it. The case comes first, and it's not like I didn't know that going in."

"Then why..."

"Cause." Ken sighs deeply. "The way you're crying over Dani... that's just a tiny little taste of how it's gonna be if they arrest me, and I don't want to do that to you."

"I told you, they ain't locking you up. And if they did, I would still stand by you. I'd work twice as hard to clear your name and I'd visit as much as I could in the meantime."

"I know you would. That's the problem." Ken looks away from me. "I love you for wanting to stand by me and I want nothing more but for us to be together. But it's not fair to you. I'm walking around with this shadow cast over me cause I know the cops are after me and it's just a matter of time before they dig up enough dirt to put me away for something I didn't do. And if I am arrested, it's gonna mean more than a couple nights in county jail. They want me for murder. That means no bail and me getting sent to Rikers."

I breathe in sharply. "That can't happen. Rikers ain't no place for you." I'm not even from here, but I know a place like that will chew up a man like Ken and spit him out half-broken. It'll be a miracle if he survives his first night there.

"Course not. But if they charge me with killing Ellie, that's where I'm headed. I can't let you hang onto me if that happens, can't let you be consumed with getting me out and praying I don't get killed before you can." Ken sighs again. "Maybe when all this is over, we can focus on each other. But for right now… I think it's best we just stay friends."

My eyes fill with tears. "Please don't do this…"

"I wouldn't if I had a choice." Ken looks away. "I'd better go. I feel bad enough about hurting you without sitting here watching you cry."

I can't help thinking there's more to him breaking up with me than being afraid of going to jail, but if there is, he ain't saying, and he's making it real clear we're done before we really began. I bite my lip hard, trying to stop the tears. I don't want to cry in front of him any more than he wants to see it.

"If that's what you want," I say uncertainly.

"Like I said, it's not my choice," Ken says. "It's just the way it is."

I don't know if I'm supposed to hug him goodbye now or what. I open the door without a word and get out, trying to hold my head up high and walk as if everything's normal.

I make it as far as the elevator before I burst into tears.

Going into my room makes it twice as bad. It's quiet hours, so no one's around and there's no noise coming through the walls. I know that's normal for this time of night, but it makes me feel like I'm walking through those secluded woods I was taken from all over again. When I open my door, it hits me twice as hard that I'm alone tonight. There's been plenty of times I've come in and Dani ain't been here, but I've known she'll come back sooner or later, and this time it won't be til Monday—and that's only if the judge accepts the plea deal.

I throw myself on my bed and sob my heart out.

My phone buzzes. I don't feel like looking at it, but I make myself lift my head and check out the screen.

It's Hailey, asking if I'm home yet.

I sniff hard, making myself stop crying. I can't give in to despair now, not when Dani and Ken and most of all Ellie need me. I've got to get this all under control.

I text Hailey and the others to set up our group meeting, hoping that someone can make heads or tails out of what I saw in the alley.

thirty-four

WHEN WE GET ONLINE, Alicia thinks I look horrible and insists that we all come over to have the meeting in person in her dorm. "You're sleeping here tonight," she says, "so that you won't be alone. Everyone else too, if they want."

Jessica says it ain't appropriate for her to sleep over at Alicia's when she's supposed to be her mentor, but Hailey and I agree to come over soon as we've packed our overnight things.

Half an hour later, we're both in Alicia's room, eating cold pizza left over from the other night. I fill them all in on Dani right away and Hailey says, "Y-you're sure she's coming home Monday?"

"That's what she said," I tell her, "and she won't let me go to her arraignment."

"She's probably embarrassed," Alicia says. She takes a sip of water. "Anyway, this is small potatoes, trust me. She's far from the first college student to try to get her hands on alcohol at a local restaurant, and it's not like she has a history of causing trouble. She'll get a slap on the wrist for sure."

"I'm going anyway," Hailey says quietly. "I don't care how embarrassed she is. I won't let her face the judge alone."

"You tell her we all love her." I let my breath out slowly. "Question. How well do you know Sarah?"

"We don't hang outside of class. Why?"

I tell her to hold on a sec while I text Ken to see if he wants in, biting my lip so no one'll notice the tears that well up in my eyes.

Ken texts back:

> It's been a long night & I need to unplug from all this shit. Fill me in tomorrow, k?

My stomach sinks. Is he avoiding me now?

Swallowing hard to push my disappointment down, I explain what I overheard in the alley. "I ain't sure how Sarah and Chloe are connected, but obviously they're both involved somehow."

Alicia frowns. "If Sarah's blackmailing Chloe..." Her eyes widen. "Wait. Sarah sent the fake tip, but Chloe really was double parked at the Burnt Olive, right? So how did Sarah know that? Unless... maybe she followed Ellie home."

I stare at her as the words sink in. "Could be. But if Sarah killed Ellie, what's Chloe got to do with it?"

Alicia shrugs. "Wrong place, wrong time? She lives there so maybe she walked in on the murder."

"Could be." I get up and look out the window, suddenly too restless to sit still. "Couple things still ain't adding up, though. How'd that necklace end up in Chloe's car? And what's Sarah got on Chloe?"

"And how does Armstrong play into this?" Hailey says. "I refuse to believe that sleazeball's innocent."

"We have to keep an open mind, though," Alicia says. "Remember Ellie's rule. Three possibilities. One has to be that Sarah's the killer and that somehow she's blackmailing Chloe into keeping her mouth shut."

"Nah," Hailey says. "I think Armstrong's the killer and

Sarah'll do anything to cover for him. He has motive cause Ellie was gonna expose him and wouldn't be talked out of it, and so far, we don't know where he was that night."

"We know he was at the podcast studio around 9," I say. "Vicki swears she saw him messing with Ken's car."

"Which tracks," Hailey says, "cause if he killed Ellie, after he dumped the body he needed to get rid of her clothes or maybe find someone to frame. So he sees a car in an empty lot and figures he'll pin the murder on the driver."

"That's awfully complicated," I say. "Besides, if the necklace was in Chloe's car, chances are that's how Ellie's body got to the park."

"And at the very least, Sarah was at the Burnt Olive when Chloe bought the drugs," Alicia adds, "cause otherwise, how did she know Chloe was double-parked or when she drove off?"

"Armstrong could have told her," Hailey says.

"You're getting too stuck on one idea," Alicia says. "Stop finding an answer for everything and just look at the facts."

Hailey's eyes narrow.

I say, "Don't fight, y'all, that won't help. We have to all stick together." I freeze. "Wait. Sarah said that to Chloe tonight." I check out the recording on my phone, but it's muffled and hard to hear. Damn it.

"Give me that," Hailey says. "Maybe I can do something with the audio."

I text her the recording and she plugs her phone into her laptop and gets to work.

"I say, "I ain't remembering exactly, but I think Chloe said something about not wanting to do this anymore and Sarah talked her out of it."

"Yep," Hailey says. "It's right here." She clicks a button and her computer plays it:

Look, I told you before: if you want to stay out of jail, we have to stick together.

"See?" Alicia says. "Sarah knows something that could get Chloe arrested, but Chloe also knows something that could get Sarah in trouble."

"Right," I say. "Wait, go back, Hailey, I want to hear again what Sarah said right before that."

Hailey does, and we hear again Chloe's desperation to get out of this and Sarah replying that it would be her word against theirs.

"That's it," I say. "Your word against 'ours.' Not against 'mine.' There's a third person involved in this mess, and I'd wager almost anything it's Dr. Armstrong."

"So we're both right, then," Alicia says. "Sarah and Armstrong are both involved somehow. The only question is who did what."

I nod. "That's the thing we were missing. It ain't one killer we're looking at. It's one and two accomplices. I reckon Chloe dumped the body and that's why Ellie's necklace is in her car."

"And that's why Sarah sent that tip," Hailey says. "We thought it was to mislead us, but that was only part of it. It was a threat to keep Chloe in line. She made it clear that she and Armstrong could easily pin the murder on Chloe if she doesn't do what they want."

"Wow," Alicia says. "The rot is deep. But why would Chloe even involve herself in this? Jessica said she and Ellie were friends. You don't think Chloe was sleeping with him too, do you?"

I shudder. "Gosh, I hope not. But it's real clear what we have to do now. We know there are three people with dirty hands in this thing, so we need to get someone to break and tell on the others. And the one most likely to do that's Chloe."

"Jesicca already said she'd talk to her," Alicia says. "But I'll call her and see if she's arranged it yet." She dials Jessica's number and walks off, speaking rapidly in Spanish.

"Hope this works," I say quietly to Hailey.

"Me too," Hailey says. "But maybe by the time Dani comes home, the killer'll be in jail."

I doubt it'll be that fast, but I'm pretty sure it's gonna happen soon. "A couple hours ago, I thought Armstrong won cause Sarah got Dani carted off to jail," I say, "but now that we've put our heads together, I'm starting to see light at the end of the tunnel."

"Of course there is," Hailey says. "You were always meant to solve this."

My cheeks get hot. "I appreciate you saying so. But deduction ain't my strong skill. I've got the reporting part down more than the investigating."

"Then you're halfway there." Hailey smiles slightly. "You'll get the rest. Just give yourself credit."

Later, after Alicia comes back to tell us that Jessica'll try again to have coffee with Chloe tomorrow and I'm lying on the floor in my sleeping bag, Hailey's words echo in my ears.

It's not just that I don't give myself enough credit. It's that my judgment keeps getting clouded by my feelings, especially when something rubs up against my memories of my kidnapping.

I need to cut that out. If I stay in the present and look at all the possibilities, I'll solve this thing much easier than if I'm mixing up what's going on here with what another predator did to me.

When I check my phone, it's after midnight, but I grab it and DM Meghan back anyway, cause the first step is to talk about what happened to me, and the second's to find out if Armstrong's gone beyond being a pervert to being a killer.

I write and erase, over and over, my heart pounding hard. Finally, I have something workable:

I didn't mention the podcast bc I wasn't even thinking about it, tbh. I just want to know if Armstrong killed Ellie, that's all, and to get her justice bc I didn't get any after I was kidnapped by a pedophile a few years back.

I stare at it, thinking. I want to go into more details but I don't, and besides they don't matter. The point is that I ain't a stranger who wants to know Ellie's story for no reason. I'm a survivor too, even if the predator I crossed paths with wasn't the same one who most likely took Ellie's life.

It takes me a long time to hit SEND after I decide that message is good enough. I sit there staring at the button for what feels like hours before I finally go for it.

The act wears me out and I flop back in my sleeping bag, my body screaming for sleep. But I ain't depressed for once. On the contrary, I'm filled with hope. We're real close to getting Ellie's killer, and we're gonna make it past the finish line soon as Jessica gets Chloe to crack. I can feel it.

thirty-five

THE NEXT MORNING, I wake up to a DM from Meghan. She still doesn't trust me and says she wants us to hop on Zoom so she can question me to make sure I'm for real.

I stare at the text awhile, wondering if this is even worth it. If Meghan ever agrees to talk to me, she could give me insight into how many girls Armstrong's messed with and whether Ellie was part of her anti-Armstrong group. But is that gonna get us any closer to proving he killed Ellie or is it just gonna make me feel sick?

Alicia's bedroom door is closed when I look over my shoulder. My body aches for Dani or Ken and I ain't sure which one of them I miss more. All I know is they wouldn't be mad if I woke them to help me figure out what to do, and I don't have that with Alicia.

Hailey's up, but she's tiptoeing around making coffee and after I reassure her that she didn't wake me, she says, "I'm going to my parents' for the day. My mom, um... she's not well and missing a Sunday with her..."

"Course," I say, hugging her. "You still planning to go to Dani's arraignment tomorrow?"

Hailey nods. "She's not going to push me away that easily."

I look away, feeling like I ain't a good enough friend cause I'm not insisting on going too. But Alicia comes out a few minutes later to tell me Jessica's fixin' to meet Chloe in half an hour if I want to come.

"This is giving me an awful sense of deja vu," I whisper as Jessica sits down at a table across from ours. "Sure wish we had better things to do than listen to other people's conversations."

"Hopefully it'll be the last time." Alicia sips her coffee. "At least you got a date with Ken out of last night."

I swallow hard, hoping Alicia won't see how close I am to tears. I slept good last night, but Ken breaking up with me's as raw as it was when it happened.

Alicia frowns. "Ceej? Did things go badly between you and Ken?"

I don't want to talk about it, but my head bobs up and down of its own accord. "He said it ain't our time," I say, my voice shaking. I force air into my lungs and a smile across my face. "It's all right, though. We just have to wait til after we catch Ellie's killer, that's all."

"That's bull," Alicia says.

Chloe waves to Jessica and hurries across to meet her. Thank God. I put my finger on my lips and check my mic to make sure it's set up right.

We have time cause Jessica says she'll get them coffee. But Chloe pushes her hair behind her ear and says, "I-I don't think coffee's a great idea for me today, thanks. My anxiety's acting up, you know, like it does right before I get manic."

Jessica's already halfway on her feet, but she sinks back into her chair. "Are you sure this is what it is?"

Chloe reddens. "I wish it was something else," she says, staring down at the table, "but I know my mood swings so…" She swallows hard. "Why? What else could it be?"

"We are all jumpy since Ellie died," Jessica says, "and I have noticed how bad it is for you." Chloe's eyes widen; Jessica's got her good. "Talk to me," Jessica says. "If you are on edge it is not good to hold it in."

Chloe's eyes dart all over the place. They land on me for a second; terror shoots through me and I double over in my seat, praying she didn't recognize me. We only met once, so there's a chance she wouldn't. When I feel her eyes leave me, I sit back up.

"I-I don't want to bother you," Chloe says. "I know how heartbroken you are since Ellie a-and I wish I'd gotten home just a few minutes earlier so I could have saved her."

Jessica raises her eyebrows while Alicia and I exchange glances. Jessica says, "You said this yesterday. How do you know when she died?"

"I don't, I swear. I'm just guessing based on what I read in the paper about it."

Jessica leans forward, looking Chloe in the eye. "Chloe. I know this is not true."

Chloe goes pale. "Why would I lie? There was nothing I could do to save Ellie, I swear."

I make sure the volume's up on my mic. Chloe's confessing without saying so. I'm sure of it.

Jessica says, gently, "This part I believe but the part about you guessing when she died is a different story. We know someone else was there with you twhen you found her because whoever made that fake account knew details of your movements that night."

Chloe freezes in the middle of twisting her hair around her fingers. "I didn't kill Ellie. You know that, don't you?"

"I do know it. But I think you came home in time to see

Ellie dead on the ground but the killer threatened to make it appear you did it if you didn't pretend you had never seen any such thing. Is my hypothesis the correct one?"

Chloe bites her lip. "Close, but no cigar."

"Then what did happen?" Jessica leans forward and takes Chloe's hands. "I am not angry with you. But I need to know what happened to Ellie. You know how I felt about her. And I know you loved her too. So you owe it to her to tell me the truth."

"I-I can't," Chloe's eyes are darting everywhere and she can't seem to sit still. Her leg is shaking and she's fidgeting with her hands. "Please... it's bad enough it happened."

Jessica sighs. "Listen to me," she says, grabbing Chloe's hand. "You are giving Ellie's killer too much power. As long as you allow them to blackmail you, you will be forced to do more and more things that go against your nature. You have already been told to betray Ellie by keeping secret what you saw that night and every time you listen to them and act to hide their culpability, you betray her again. There is only one way out of this trap. You must stop listening to them and do the opposite of what they want. You must tell the truth about the night Ellie died."

Chloe whimpers. "I can't! I want to but if I do I'll go to jail." Her voice breaks. "You don't understand what they made me do that night."

"Then make me understand." Jessica's voice is calm and even but there's pain in her eyes. How could there not be when someone killed the love of her life and Chloe's protecting the killer instead of helping get justice?

Chloe sniffs. "All I can say is that after what they made me do, I never want to get in my car again. Ever." She rubs her temples. "There. I didn't break my promise to them so they can't get me. But if you figure it out from what I said, that's not my fault."

My phone rings before Jessica can respond. I sure hope it doesn't cut off the recording as I glance at the display.

Shit. It's Dean Northrop's office calling.

On a Sunday, when she ain't supposed to be in the office? This can't be good.

I don't want to take it, but what choice do I have? I walk away for privacy.

Dean Northrop's crisp tone comes loud and clear through the phone. "Given last night's events, I thought it wise to arrange a meeting despite the Office of Student Affairs being closed. We need to talk about the circumstances surrounding your friend's arrest and what this means for the report I hired you to complete."

My stomach sinks. Dean Northrop's about to try to shut me down, ain't she? Well, I'm just going to have to find a way to go on behind her back if she does, cause I ain't giving up when we're this close to proving her daughter's involved in Ellie's murder.

I agree to meet her in her office in half an hour.

When I knock on Dean Northrop's door, she's filling out paperwork of some sort and it's a good 30 seconds before she bothers to acknowledge me. "Close the door," she says curtly, even though no one else is in the office. "This is not for everyone's ears."

"Yes, ma'am." I pull the door closed.

Dean Northrop crosses her arms. "The situation last night is quite unfortunate for many reasons, not the least of which is that I question your judgment in how you are approaching this investigation. If you thought my assistant had any valuable information, why would you engage in this type of subterfuge instead of being honest with her about what you wanted to know, especially since you chose to employ someone who would so easily give in to the temptation to acquire alcohol?"

I stare at her, unable to believe what I'm hearing. "With all due respect, ma'am, Sarah has demonstrated over and over that she has something to hide, and that's why going to extremes was necessary. Have you noticed any changes in her behavior since the murder?"

Dean Northrop's eyes narrow, but she says, "I did not call you in here to gossip about Sarah. She is not our concern right now. Your friend's behavior is. You may recall that when I agreed to let you investigate this tragic death, I told you that it was important you do so in a way that protected the reputation of the university. I am not convinced that this incident did so, especially not when it resulted in the arrest of a student for use of a fake ID." She pulls a big book off the shelf behind her. "This is the Student Code of Conduct—I trust you have read it before?"

I haven't, but I ain't about to say so. "Of course, ma'am."

"Good. Then you know that any student who is arrested for an alcohol-related offense is in violation of the code and that the consequences can, at my discretion, include suspension pending the outcome of an expulsion hearing."

My throat tightens with anger. "You'd really ruin Dani's future over this, ma'am? Sarah purposely encouraged her to break the law. The waitress said she's been caught trying to get others to buy her alcohol before, including Dr. Armstrong a few weeks ago."

Dean Northrop's face goes pale, or at least I think it does. It's hard to tell in this light. She rubs her temples and says, quietly, "I told you, we are not here to discuss Sarah. Whether or not she encouraged poor behavior is irrelevant. Your friend is the one who chose to go along with Sarah's request, yes?"

I have to admit she has me there. "Yes, ma'am," I mumble.

"But don't you think it would be cruel to go to this extreme when Dani ain't ever been in trouble before?"

"You do have a point," Dean Northrop says. "I haven't made up my mind yet. There are many factors that go into a decision like this." She leans back in her chair, making it squeak. "My daughter told me last night that she feels like you are under the mistaken impression that she is involved in this terrible crime. Is that true?"

I hesitate, not sure how much to admit. Chloe needs help, but Dean Northrop ain't gonna believe me if I tell her, and I doubt she'll stand for me playing her the recording of Sarah threatening Chloe, either. "Not exactly, ma'am. We have reason to believe she witnessed something that she's afraid to come forward about."

"I can assure you that if she saw anything, she would have told you. Regardless, too much stress will exacerbate her mental health issues, so I need you to back off her." Dean Northrop leans forward. "If you will do that for me, I will forget what Sarah told me about your friend getting arrested in front of her. Do you understand what I'm telling you?"

My eyes dart around the room, looking for a way out. They land on Dean Northrop's diploma from Los Angeles University. May 12, 1999. I stare at the date, unable to believe I never noticed it before.

1999. The same year Armstrong quit cause he got a student pregnant. And if that student kept her baby...

I swallow hard. "With all due respect, ma'am, I'm trying to help Chloe." I open my phone. "Someone made a fake social media account and they did it for the purpose of framing her for this murder."

Dean Northrop holds up her hand. "You're telling me that you know she had nothing to do with the crime, then."

"No, ma'am. I'm telling you she's a witness and the killer is threatening to make it look like she did it if she doesn't keep her mouth shut."

"I see." Dean Northrop's jaw is very tight. "Even if this preposterous theory was true—which, for the record, I don't believe for a moment—we are in agreement that Chloe is innocent and that she's unwilling to come forward about anything she may or may not have seen. Therefore, it is not a productive use of your time to bother her further about this. So please, cooperate with my request for everyone's sake. Your friend will get to continue her studies, my daughter will get to move on with her life in peace, and you will be free to investigate more likely suspects. So do we have a deal?"

My heart pounds and I know I should just say 'Yes,' for Dani's sake if for no other reason. But I have to know if what I just deduced is at all correct cause if it is, then Chloe's got a real motive to kill Ellie.

"I'll leave Chloe alone if you answer me this one question," I say slowly. "Does she know that Dr. Armstrong is her father?"

thirty-six

DEAN NORTHROP'S EYES WIDEN. She laughs nervously before she says, "Of course not, because it's not true. Where on Earth did you get such a ridiculous idea?"

"Your diploma, ma'am. You graduated from Los Angeles University the same year Dr. Armstrong resigned after being accused of impregnating a student. I did the math and Chloe's the right age to be that baby."

"I see." Dean Northrop twists a mother-of-pearl bracelet she's wearing on her right wrist. "I would suggest you base this investigation on solid facts and not gossip and innuendo. If Dr. Armstrong did impregnate anyone, which it does not appear has been proven, it was not me. I did not even know him in those days. And in any case, Chloe's father was my late husband. I implore you never to bring up his death or this ridiculous theory to my daughter; she was in the car with my husband when he had his fatal accident, and as you can imagine, it has left deep marks on her psyche that she may never overcome." The Dean's voice is soft and I can almost hear tears. Whatever lies she's telling now, I have no doubt of how much she loves Chloe and hates that such a tragedy befell her.

"How old was she when he died?" I ask gently.

"Eight. And that's all I'm going to say about it. Now I have answered your question, silly as it was, so I hope you are willing to do what I have asked of you."

"Yes, ma'am," I say. "I won't pressure Chloe to answer any more questions."

Dean Northrop nods. "I will trust you to honor your word. In the future, please make sure you keep the school's reputation in the front of your mind while you continue your investigation." She stands, which I reckon means this conversation is over. "One more thing. Don't forget to send me your proposal if you still want Dr. Armstrong to appear on your podcast."

"I won't, ma'am," I promise, and hightail it out of there.

My thoughts chase themselves around my head as I hurry into the hall. I don't have any intention of backing off Chloe, but it's clear I'm going to have to get the info I need some other way besides questioning her, cause I can't risk Dean Northrop kicking Dani out or shutting me down.

I have no doubt she was lying about who Chloe's father was, either, but I don't know why. It doesn't make sense for her to be the girl Armstrong once abused cause if she is, she knows what he's all about. So why would she let Chloe work closely with him, never mind hire him at this university or bury all the complaints against him? And does any of this have a single thing to do with who killed Ellie or why?

I rub the back of my neck, feeling a headache coming on, and then grab my phone to text Meghan back and agree to let her interview me to see she can trust me. I want to get her to tell me what she knows about Armstrong, and Chloe too, cause that's the only way I'm gonna make headway in any of this without the Dean catching me.

.   .   .

Meghan texts back that she wants to meet at noon, which only gives me an hour to get ready, and Hailey's already gone so I don't have anyone to help me with my Zoom link and have to set it up myself. Dani has a ring light on her side of the room and I feel funny using it without her permission, but my video looks grainy when I try to get by without it, so I set up on her side of the dorm and hope she ain't too mad when she comes home.

That's settled with 20 minutes to go, which gives me time to take notes on everything that happened this morning. It seems like Chloe's up to her neck in this one way or another, cause Sarah's blackmail threat ain't coming from nowhere any more than Dean Northrop's against us is. Reminding myself of the rule Jessica said Ellie made, I try out different possibilities, but nothing adds up. If Chloe's the killer, there's no reason for Sarah to be at the scene of the murder or to blackmail her—they could just tell the cops what they know and they'd come out looking like the heroes that solved the case, even if Dean Northrop would be mad as hell. But if Sarah were the killer, how'd Ellie's necklace end up in Chloe's car? And then there's the third person on the scene, who's most likely Armstrong. If he's the killer, I could see him planting the necklace in Chloe's car and Sarah covering for him, but how could Chloe possibly keep it together on the job if she knew her boss murdered her friend?

Then there's the side issue of Armstrong's past and the possibility that Chloe's his daughter. Either Northrop's lying about that or she ain't, but does it matter? My mind keeps being pulled back to it but the only reason I can see for caring about it right now is that if Chloe knew, she might take up for him against Ellie, giving her a motive to kill.

My email beeps while I go round and round in circles about all of this. It's a message from Zoom.

Meghan's signed on. It's time to let her into the Zoom room and convince her to talk to me.

thirty-seven

MEGHAN IS ON audio-only but I ask her to cut her camera on. "It's only fair," I say. "We both ought to know who we're talking to."

"Right. Give me a sec." Meghan sighs deeply. Her camera blinks on; she's sitting cross-legged on a bed not too different from this one, wearing teddy bear pajamas that make her look like a little girl. Her blonde hair hangs limply down and she ain't got any color in her pale white cheeks, or any makeup on at all for that matter. "I should have been more ready," she says, "but I'm in California where's it's barely 9 AM and I overslept this morning."

I raise my eyebrows. "You ain't here at Cedarwood University?"

"Not anymore. I came home to start over." Meghan swallows hard. "I'm turning my camera back off, okay? I can't stand how I look right now."

I nod even though I know she doesn't need my permission. Meghan goes back on audio; her Zoom profile photo's much prettier cause she's all put together, wearing eye makeup that makes her blue eyes pop, a high ponytail, and a wide smile. She says, "That's better. Now, let's talk about you. How did you find out about me, exactly?"

My heart pounds. I don't like being on this side of the interview table, especially when it feels more like an interrogation. "I scrolled past all those fake positive reviews looking for the truth about Dr. Armstrong," I explain, hoping my voice sounds strong enough to make her believe me. "I got reason to believe he's involved in the death of a student, or at the very least that he messed with her when she was alive."

"Good luck with that," Meghan says, her voice flat. "I hope you don't get shut down before you get to the truth." She sighs again. "You're a podcaster, though, right? Sanctioned by the school?"

I hesitate, aware of what she's getting at. "The school and I are at cross purposes at the moment," I say carefully, "cause I want the truth and certain people want the school to look good." I cross my arms. "I reckon you know something about that?"

"No comment." Meghan's clicking in the background, typing notes maybe. "I don't understand why you care so much. I looked into you. You're a freshman, right? You wouldn't have even had anything to do with a graduate student."

"She still died and she shouldn't have, and I saw her video about what Armstrong was doing to her." My voice rises of its own accord; I breathe in sharply, ordering myself to cut that out. It won't do to seem defensive. "Look," I say quietly, "she ain't here to speak for herself and all I've found so far is a tight little knot of people busy protecting each other so I can't tell what's what. So if there's any light you can shed on any of this, I'd appreciate it if you'd help me out."

Meghan is quiet for a long time except for the clicking. After a minute it hits me that she ain't tapping; she's opening and closing one of those pens that's got a button on top.

Finally, she says, "It's not that I don't want to help. I'm just not sure legally how much I'm allowed to say." My phone buzzes the next second and it's a DM from her:

Pause the recording.

It's a weird request, but off the record's better than nothing, I reckon, so I do it.

Meghan thanks me and says, "The thing is, I signed an NDA, and I'm not sure I can even tell you why." She clicks her pen some more before she goes on. "This is entirely off the record and if you ever repeat it I'll deny I said it, but I sued the school, Dr. Armstrong, and Dean Northrop and the best my lawyer could do was get me a lot of money in exchange for my silence about what he did to me."

"I'm sure you wouldn't want to relive the details anyway," I say. "I didn't want to tell you much about what happened to me for the same reason." I look away, my cheeks growing hot, then back at the camera. "But he did do something that makes you think Ellie was telling the truth?"

"I know she was. I saw her video the night she died and reached out to her, but she never got to read the message." Meghan sighs deeply. "Before we go back on record, can you tell me a little more about what happened to you? I'm not being nosey, I swear. I just want to help."

A high-pitched ringing starts up in my ears. I'm light-headed but not dizzy as I grab onto the edge of Dani's desk as tight as I can, letting it hold me up. "There ain't much worth telling," I say. "Short version is when I was fourteen I got catfished by a pedophile who kidnapped me and... well, you can guess the rest. Anyway, the cops didn't care about anything but the fact that I was out of my house without leave so nothing happened to him til he tried to do it again to some girl in another town."

"Just like nothing ever happens to Armstrong," Meghan says softly. "Can I ask you something? Did you move up to New York to get away from the place it happened at? Cause that's why I decided to continue my education in California, to get as far away from where I was taken advantage of as I possibly could."

I swallow hard. "I ain't ever thought of it that way, but I suppose. Here's a place where no one knows me so I can be myself." I let my breath out slowly. "You ain't studying at Los Angeles University, are you?"

"No, why?"

"Cause," I say heavily, "I found out Armstrong was forced to resign from there in 1999 after he got someone pregnant and I was hoping you could help me look into who it was and whatever happened to them."

"Shit," Meghan shakes her head. "There's no getting away from him, is there?"

"Not til we nail him for this. Listen, is there anything you can tell me that'll shed light on whether he actually killed Ellie?"

Meghan's clicking her pen as she answers. "On the one hand, I can't put anything past a man who pretends he wants to mentor female students so he can take advantage of them sexually. But honestly, he has no reason to kill her. He's gotten away with doing this crap for years and years because he knows that the school will bury any complaints and if anyone takes it further, he's got the best lawyers money can buy and they'll use the legal system to buy victims' silence. That's what he did to me, so it stands to reason it's what he would have done to Ellie if she wouldn't drop this. Hang on til she signed an NDA and move on to the next girl."

My stomach sinks. What Meghan's saying makes a lot of sense, but there goes one of my theories. "Did you ever meet Dean Northrop's daughter?" I ask.

"Chloe?" Meghan's voice holds a note of surprise. "She's still around?"

I ain't sure how much to tell Meghan, but I got a feeling she knows something big, so I take a risk, saying, "She works for Armstrong now, and we're trying to work out if she's just a witness to Ellie's death or involved in a worse way."

"Holy crap," Meghan says. "That mother of hers really does have unlimited power. I just hope Armstrong's not abusing her daughter, even if it would be karma for all the complaints she's buried." Her breath echoes on her microphone as she lets it out. "That girl's got problems. I don't want to gossip about her, that would be mean. But my lawyer thought one of the reasons they were in such a hurry to settle with me was because of the trouble she got herself in. The same week I filed my lawsuit, Chloe was arrested for a string of burglaries on campus, and if news had broken that the school was being sued at the same time, that would have been the end of Dean Northrop's career. So they offered me a pile of money in exchange for an NDA and my lawyer encouraged me to take it, and one problem went away. And after that, I guess Dean Northrop did her thing to make the other disappear too."

"I reckon so." I write down this new development. I ain't sure where it fits in, but I don't want to forget it either. "You suppose Chloe could have killed Ellie?"

"Gosh, I hope not. I never actually met her, so this is all coming from what my lawyer told me. I mean, I guess Chloe could have wanted to silence Ellie to protect her mom, but if she was going to do that, why didn't she ever come after me?"

She has a point there, but still, something doesn't add up. "Anything else you can tell me that might be helpful?"

Meghan chews her lip. "Is Mark Anderson still TA-ing for him?"

I sit up straighter. "You reckon he's involved with this?"

"Maybe. He's a piece of crap, that's for sure." Meghan

sighs. "I probably shouldn't tell you this, but he doesn't just assist Armstrong with teaching. He's like, his wingman." She gulps water; the sound of it echoes on her mic. "I met him at an open house for all the labs and the next day he called and said he'd spoken to Armstrong about me and Armstrong wanted to get to know me better. And other women who Armstrong messed with told me the same thing."

I raise my eyebrows. "So you're saying Mark scouts out likely targets?"

"Yep." Meghan's voice is heavy. "You don't sound surprised."

"He was the last to see Ellie alive," I tell her, "but he won't tell us where he went after and every word he said, first he looked at Armstrong for approval."

"Huh. I never thought of him as a murderer, but anything's possible. If Ellie exposed Armstrong, he'd probably get in trouble too, so..."

"Right" My heart is pounding as I reach for my tablet to update the digital whiteboard. "One more thing. There's a girl working part-time as the Dean's assistant and she seems to have a big ol' crush on Armstrong. Her name's Sarah Buchanan—you ever heard anything about her?"

"She hasn't reached out. What's she like otherwise?"

"My friend said she was shy and quiet, but since the murder she seems willing to do anything to interfere with me looking into things, so I reckon she's covering for him somehow."

"Shy and quiet is his type." Meghan sighs deeply. "If she's that in love with him, she's in a lot of trouble. He's a master manipulator." She clicks her pen a few more times, clearly unnerved by this conversation. "Turn on your recorder so we can say goodbye—as far as the world knows, I didn't tell you anything at all because of my NDA, okay?"

"Sure thing," I agree, and turn on the recorder so I can

thank her for her time. We hang up and I lean back in my chair, more confused than ever. If Meghan's right, we're on the completely wrong track, but the evidence all points to one of the people she doesn't think could possibly have killed Ellie. What am I missing here?

There's a knock on the door. I turn off the ring light before I answer.

It's Alicia and Jessica.

"We thought maybe you do not need to be alone," Jessica says, "and anyway I have a news you will want to hear."

thirty-eight

THE ROOM SUDDENLY seems far too small, but I don't feel like going out anywhere so I invite them in anyway, and hurry to pick up the blanket that's been on the floor since before Dani was arrested.

Everyone sits down cross-legged on the floor, leaning against the bed, so I reckon I should have left it. Jessica says, "Every Sunday there is a meeting for Dr. Armstrong's RAs and TAs. Today's was all about damage control and not talking to press."

"Me, they mean," I say, rolling my eyes.

"And other press, too, I'm sure," Alicia says, "but that's not what Jessica wanted to tell you."

I apologize and Jessica goes on, "The important thing is it was an opportunity for me to corner Mark. He went to the TA office to do some work afterward and I used the mic you gave me." She hits play so I can listen.

Jessica: It is only you and me in the room, Mark. Dr. Armstrong is not here to save you. So you will have to tell me the truth. Why are you spreading this rumor that I killed Ellie?

Mark: I'm sorry, but I don't know what you're talking about. You mean... it's not true you killed your ex-girlfriend because you were jealous that she asked me out?

Jessica: We both know the real reason Ellie met with you that night. So let us review the evidence. You were late to meet her, you threatened to make Bobby ashamed of her if she did not drop her plan to expose the snake you work for, and you left in a huff. Minutes later, she is dead, and soon after rumors and false evidence against me appear. The most likely hypothesis is that you killed her and are trying to put blame on me to save yourself.

Mark (laughs nervously): You are desperate, aren't you? You are right about one thing. If that bitch had known what was good for her, she'd have kept her mouth shut. But you can tell those little girls you hang around with that they suck at playing detective. The cops already questioned me and they already cleared me. I do not need to explain why or how to the likes of you.

Jessica: Where were you when Ellie was killed, then? An innocent person would share their alibi.

Mark: Oh, you are bad at this, aren't you? I'm not going to make it that easy for you losers. But I will say this. Ask your friend Chloe where I was... if she is even coherent enough to put a sentence together. I heard she's back to putting poison up her nose.

Jessica says angrily, "He was baiting me. But it is clear he hated Ellie."

I nod. "That and he's in deep with Armstrong." I tell Jessica what Meghan said about him.

Jessica's jaw tightens. "It is true he is Armstrong's top recruiter," she says. "I found the lab independently but Mark invited Ellie."

"Right," I say. "So if she told on Armstrong, chances were

Mark was going down too." I open the digital whiteboard. "Don't forget to upload that so we can..." My voice trails off as my eyes light on Mark's column.

It's grayed out and marked INNOCENT, and a quick check tells me Ken did that. What the hell?

I text him to ask what's up with that and he texts back that he'll hop on video real quick to explain. When he does, he says, "Everything else adds up, but physically, Mark couldn't have killed Ellie. Look." He turns the camera to show Vicki standing in front of a tall lamp and goes and stands next to her.

"Vicki's shorter than Mark," he says, "but the principle's still the same."

Vicki says, "How about if I stand on my tiptoes?" She's sniffling and sounds congested, but Ken doesn't seem worried so I reckon it's nothing.

Ken puts his hand on her head. "Beside the point. Let's do this." He turns toward us. "The lamp's about as tall as Ellie was," he says. "So I'm gonna put my hands right here like I was strangling her." He does and then says to Vicki, "Now you put your hands where you'd put them if you were doing it."

"This is only pretend," Vicki says, as if she thinks any of us would believe she's actually a killer. She takes a deep breath and reaches up, but her hands don't nearly touch Ken's.

"See?" Ken says triumphantly. "A shorter person can't make those bruises in the same place."

"He could if he stood on a box or something," Vicki says, "but Ken said that was very unlikely."

"It is," Ken says. "That'd draw too much attention to them. So I'm sorry, Ceej, but it's back to the drawing board. There's no way Mark could have killed Ellie."

I sink into my bed, annoyed. If Dani were here she'd see what I'm not seeing, I'm sure of it. "Put that in the notes so Dani can see when she gets back," I tell Ken. I put my head in my hands, thinking, but I can't find a way to make it work that Mark's the killer even though he's got a strong motive and is busy framing Jessica without realizing we already know she's innocent.

Jessica suggests that maybe Mark helped kill Ellie without actually doing it. I reckon she's right, but how are we ever going to find out who did murder her when everyone who seems likely keeps turning out to be nothing but an accomplice?

There doesn't seem to be anything else to say, so I let Ken get back to his Sunday afternoon and sit staring into space, trying to figure out what I'm missing.

thirty-nine

I **SPEND** ALL of my Statistics for Journalists class the next morning wondering how Dani's doing in court and wishing I'd gone with Hailey. I've got my phone on vibrate in case Hailey texts me, but it's quiet the whole class period, which drags on and on while I fight with myself over whether Dani's really coming home and if she can help me figure out what's what with Mark.

Hailey's text finally comes right after class is dismissed, while I'm weighing whether to text Ken to meet for lunch or leave him alone. She says that Dani's signing her release papers and asks me to come down to help take her home.

I jump on my bike and head downtown, where I find Hailey pacing back and forth on the sidewalk in front of the courthouse. The building's smaller than I expected; it doesn't look much different than the post office, with American flags and steps on the outside and a banner on top of the door that reads CEDARWOOD COMMUNITY COURTHOUSE.

"Security wouldn't let me wait in front of the door," Hailey says, shoving her hands into her pockets, "so we have to hang out down here and hope she doesn't slip past us when she comes out. I texted her too, but for all I know, her phone could be dead."

"She's coming home, that's the important thing." I don't know Hailey well enough to put my hand on her shoulder so I just take a step closer toward her. "You okay?"

"Yeah. I just... I get why she didn't want us here, cause seeing them escort her into the court in cuffs was a lot." Hailey swallows hard. "Sarah deserves to rot in hell for getting Dani arrested on purpose."

I nod. "I'd like to know how she fits into this whole thing. And Mark too." I open the digital whiteboard and show Hailey how the clues add up to Mark but his size rules him out.

Hailey puts her hand to her chin, thinking. "You're right, things aren't adding up. But like you said the other day, we're not looking for one killer. We're looking at a conspiracy. So maybe Mark helped the killer somehow."

I nod. "All roads lead to Armstrong, if you ask me. Could be he ordered Ellie killed or did it himself."

"And the others all helped cover it up. Yeah. So we need to figure out who did what, and I think the best way to do that is to focus on Chloe."

I cross my arms. "We have to be careful. If Dean Northrop finds out —"

"Dani!" Hailey calls, and gestures toward the courthouse steps

Dani's standing at the top, blinking hard. Her hands are scrunched into her pockets and she's wearing the same purple crop top and tight jeans she was arrested in. Her hair's in a loose ponytail that looks ready to fall out any second and she's got dark circles under her eyes; I reckon she didn't get a single wink in all weekend.

Dani sighs so deeply her entire body shakes before she comes slowly down the steps toward us.

"You guys really didn't need to be here," she says flatly. "I could have taken the bus home."

"We're your friends," Hailey says, "and as far as we're concerned, you're a sight for sore eyes." She puts her hand on Dani's shoulder. "How about we get some sugar in you? The bakery's open."

Dani shakes her head slightly. "I really don't want anyone to see me til I've washed the stink of that stupid jail off me." She turns toward me. "Did you at least get something good out of me getting myself arrested?"

"Depends," I say casually. "You think Sarah blackmailing Chloe qualifies?"

Dani's eyes widen. Hailey says, "CJ's learned a lot since you were... away. If you let us take you to breakfast, we'll catch you up."

Dani bites her lip. "How about we order in?"

Hailey and I exchange concerned glances. "Pancakes'n'-More?" I suggest. "Or Ice Cream Kitchen?"

"Whichever." Dani pushes past us, toward the bus stop. "Let's just get out of here."

It's obvious she ain't in any shape to help us with the case, but I still want to pick her brain so I fold up my bike and take it on the bus with her and Hailey. Dani puts her earbuds in soon as we get on the bus and doesn't take them out til we get home. I'm worried, but Hailey whispers she can't blame Dani for wanting to shut out the world after spending the weekend behind bars, and I can't say I blame her.

Soon as we get back to campus, I suggest we ask Alicia if she minds hosting so we can all eat together, but Dani says, "I'm not promising anything til after I shower." She throws her stuff into her shower caddy and hurries to the bathroom. It ain't like her to go to the shower fully dressed instead of in her robe; she's usually grossed out by the idea of her clothes being in a communal bathroom.

I sink into my bed. "I wanted to tell her about Dean Northrop's threat, but now I ain't sure she can handle it."

"It's not fair to her if we don't, but I don't know..." Hailey sighs. "She seems really rough right now. Being locked up obviously did a number on her and on top of that, the stupid judge treated her like a serious criminal, lecturing her about making better choices or paying the price. So she gets a record and a lecture while no one does anything to Sarah even though she tricks people into buying her drinks all the time. What kind of bullshit is that?" Hailey slams her phone down. "Let's look at the digital whiteboard again. Maybe figuring this crap out'll get my mind off of how Dani's being treated."

"Good idea," I say, "cause there's more than one person who needs to learn they ain't getting away with what they do to people anymore." I sign into the whiteboard too.

Hailey scrolls through the suspect list. "We forgot someone. Don't you think Dean Northrop belongs on this list?"

I can't help scoffing even though I feel bad. "Sorry," I say. "It's just that I can't fathom her putting those perfectly manicured fingers around Ellie's neck. Besides, she wouldn't implicate her own daughter."

"Point." Hailey flips the page. "Let's look at all the clues again. Maybe something'll jump out at us."

As we flip through clues, I stare at the photo of Ken's trunk all scratched up. "Here's something. We know Armstrong was in the podcast studio lot at 9 cause Vicki saw him. And that night, it looked like Ken's trunk was broken into. So logically, he was the one who did it. But why? And what's it got to do with the murder?"

"That's a good question. Maybe you should see if Ken'll let you take a look at his trunk."

I sigh. "That means calling him and after the last couple days, I don't know. He wants his space and disrespecting that's gonna make everything worse."

"It's going to be a question mark until you do, though," Hailey says softly. "Besides, you shouldn't give up so easily." Dani's key turns in the lock as Hailey goes on, "This business of breaking up with you in case he gets arrested is bullshit and if I were you, I'd tell him to his face."

"Ken broke up with you?" Dani says as she comes in. She rubs her temples. "What the hell happened?"

I look away. "He said seeing me in tears over you being locked up made him think I ain't gonna survive if they go ahead and pin Ellie's murder on him."

"Shit." Dani sinks into my bed. "So it was cause of me."

"No," Hailey says firmly. "It's cause he's being an idiot. But it'll change, cause CJ is going to find the courage to call him on his BS and make him see he's throwing away the best thing that ever happened to him."

"Good." Dani rubs the back of her neck. "I can't decide if I need food or sleep more. But I think food. That way maybe I can turn human enough to help."

Hailey and I exchange glances. "We'll order something in a minute," I say, "but first we need to tell you something." I take her hand and say, gently, "Dean Northrop made it real clear if she catches us questioning Chloe, she'll use you getting arrested as an excuse to kick you out of school."

"Course she did." Dani's voice is flat. "So the chances that Chloe's involved just skyrocketed, cause there'd be no need for threats if we weren't going to find anything."

"Maybe," I say. "I was fixin' to keep looking into her behind the Dean's back but if you think it's too risky I'll back off."

Dani swallows hard, but she makes herself smile and says, "I don't want to let her push us around. Besides, if Chloe killed Ellie, she needs to pay for it." She rubs the back of her neck. "As soon as I get rid of this headache, I want everything you know about her."

"Where we eating from?" I ask as I open my DoorDash account.

"Burnt Olive," Dani says. "Let's honor Ellie's memory while we're getting justice for her. And call Ken and tell him to get his butt over here. No reason you should be eating alone."

Things still don't feel right with Dani, but I reckon she has a point so I text Ken and ask him if he wants to come over to discuss the case and that we'll order a gyro and fries for him if he does. I don't know what to make out of it when he says yes.

Half an hour later, we're sitting on the mat we got for when we get takeout so that we won't get food on the floor, eating gyros and fries and taking another look at the evidence. "Dani reckons there's more to Chloe's story than meets the eye since Dean Northrop's so gung-ho about keeping us away from her."

"She's used to throwing her weight around, that's for damn sure," Ken says. "And that makes more sense than Mark. She's tall enough to have done it." He zooms in on his phone so he's looking just at Chloe's column. "Wait... no it doesn't, not if this photo is accurate."

What now? I cross my arms and wait for Ken to explain.

"Look," he says, holding out his hands. "See how big my hands are? Now look at this photo you have here of Chloe." His fingers move smoothly across the screen while I watch out of the corner of my eye, trying to pretend it ain't doing anything for me to look at them.

Ken enlarges the photo so we can see Chloe's hands better. They're folded over a chair arm. Her arms are as skinny as Jessica always says, but more important than that, her hands aren't but a third of the size of Ken's.

"Same problem as Mark," he says. "Those tiny hands couldn't have made marks that match my fingers."

I stare at the photo. "But if she didn't kill Ellie, how'd that necklace chain end up in her back seat?"

"Beats me. I guess someone could have planted it."

"No," Hailey says. "She told Jessica she's never using the car again and she made it clear it was a cryptic hint about something she's scared to say. Something happened."

Hailey's words echo in my ears. "What if two things are true?" I ask slowly. "What if... someone else killed Ellie, but Chloe dumped her body in the park?"

I look around, waiting for Ken to tell me again I'm offbase. But all that happens is he says, "That could be."

"Yeah," Hailey says. "You were just saying we're looking at a conspiracy. That necklace chain is proof you're right."

Dnai crosses her arms. "But why would she do that? Wasn't Ellie one of her only friends?"

"Dunno." I lean forward, thinking.

"Let's walk through it," Hailey says. "So Mr. or Ms. X kills Ellie at, say 8:10 PM while Chloe is on her way home."

"She's got a baggie of speed in her pocket," I add. "I ain't ever done anything like that, but I reckon that would make her nervous cause if she gets caught..."

"Her butt goes to jail and probably violates some sort of probation," Dani says flatly. "That's one of the terms the judge emphasized this morning; if I get caught with drugs or alcohol while my case is still open, that's at least three months behind bars."

"Which you won't do," Hailey says, "but she might have. And when you have something on you that nobody can find out about..."

"It leaves you open to blackmail." I pace back and forth. "Which we know Sarah's doing to her. So, all right. She comes home, she gets caught with the drugs, and she gets told either dump Ellie's body for us or you're going to spend some time with the cops."

"That's dumb, though," Ken says. "Dumping the body'll

get her in way worse trouble. At least with drugs she could maybe get rehab."

"Not necessarily," I say. "She already had court-ordered rehab once so the judge might not be too willing to do it again. Besides, I reckon she wasn't thinking clearly. She saw Ellie's body. She knew if she refused, jail was the least of her problems cause they could kill her too to keep her quiet."

"It was a genius plan in a way," Hailey says, "cause soon as she gave in, now they can make her do whatever. If she ever says no to anything, no matter how crazy, they send anonymous proof to the cops she moved the body and she goes down for the murder too."

"Right," I say. "And we know Sarah's one of the people involved cause she made Chloe tell her mom we're harassing her when we ain't." I cross my arms. "Sure looks like Sarah's guilty as sin. Only question is, how do we prove it?"

forty

KEN WARNS ME not to jump to conclusions, but everyone agrees that Sarah should be on the top of our list.

Except Hailey, who stares at her feet but says nothing.

When I ask her what's up, she shakes her head. "I don't know Sarah very well, okay, but I can't believe this girl I did a project with turned out to be this monster. She's quiet but... not monsterish." She blinks hard. "I guess you never know how people really are, huh?"

"Amrstrong messed her up," I say, "not that's an excuse for all the shit she's done since. But she thinks he's in love with her and he's letting her think it so that she'll do what he wants." My eyes widen. "Wait... we all know she'll do anything to cover for him, but you reckon he'd do the same for her?"

Dani rubs the back of her neck. "I'm not following. Sorry."

"I mean, come at him like we think he can help clear something up and ask him if he knows where she was. I'd bet anything he'd throw her under the bus, and maybe let something slip cause he thinks he's pulled the wool over our eyes."

"Let's do it," Dani says. She rubs her temples. "But not right now. My head's still killing me."

"You probably slept wrong on that jailhouse bunk," Hailey says.

"I didn't sleep much at all," Dani says. "They questioned me pretty hard about what I was trying to do with that recording and even after the lawyer made them leave me alone, they kept moving me from one cell to another and after they finally left me alone, I was lying there worrying I'd be sent to Rikers for this stupidity so…" She sighs. "I don't want to sleep but I think I'd better."

I frown. "I can handle Armstrong myself, I guess."

"No," Ken says. "You know how he is one-on-one. I say wait til Dani can go with you. You need witnesses."

"There's plenty we can do in the meantime," Hailey holds up her phone. "I'm still friends with Sarah on social media, so I'll take a look through her posts. Maybe that'll get us somewhere."

"Good idea," Ken says. "Maybe you can dig more into Armstrong's past so you can be ready to confront him."

"I guess." I sigh. "I just can't help feeling like we're running out of time and you're gonna end up in the cops' crosshairs."

Ken stiffens, but he says, "That's what my lawyer's for. Look, you only get one chance with a guy like Armstrong. Don't burn it rushing in too fast." His phone beeps. "Crap," he says, glancing at it. "It's the middle school." He answers the phone, his voice tense. Turns out it's the school nurse. Vicki's got a fever so she's being sent home sick.

"I gotta bounce, I guess," he says, "and looks like I'm not gonna be around for a while." His shoulders slump.

"I'll walk you out," I say, then turn away, my cheeks reddening. "I-if that's okay."

"Yeah, of course." Ken lets his breath out slowly. "I sure hope this isn't anything but a cold."

I want to reach for his hand, but I don't dare. I follow him out silently.

At the car, I say to him, "I know this ain't the right time, but, um, I... wish you'd give us a chance romantically."

Ken's face trembles, but he says, "Right now my mind's not in the right place. All I can think is that if I get arrested while Vicki's sick..."

"I know." I hold my arms out. "Let me comfort you. Please."

Ken lets me hug him. I hold him for as long as I dare and then I say, "One thing you can do that'll help all this is check your trunk. That night Ellie died I noticed a bunch of scratches and I think Armstrong put them there. I want to know what else he did."

"If you say so," Ken says. "I'm short on time but if it makes you happy..." He presses a button on his keys to pop the trunk.

I hold my breath, prepared for anything. But Ken's trunk is empty.

"Told you," Ken said. "Maybe that wasn't Armstrong. We live close enough to downtown that you never know when some idiot's gonna try their luck."

I stare at it. "I don't understand..."

"Whatever Armstrong was doing, it wasn't that, that's all," Ken says. "Maybe the asshole went for a run to clear his mind after taking Ellie's life and he really was just catching his breath. Don't stress about it, k?" He slams the trunk closed...

... and as he does, a tiny piece of paper falls out of the lock.

"What the heck?" Ken says as I bend down to pick it up.

It ain't paper. It's some sort of silky material with writing on it. A part of a label from a piece of clothing, maybe. The whole brand name ain't on there, but what is there is a fancy capital S interlocked with a fancy capital R, suggesting it came off an expensive brand.

"This could be his," I say.

"Could be, but I don't have time to worry about it," Ken says. "I gotta bounce, okay?" He climbs into the car. "If Vicki gets better enough, maybe I can have everyone over for dinner one day soon so we can figure this out." He waves to me as he starts the car and I back up so he can get going.

I don't care what Ken says. I know this came off Armstrong's clothing.

The only question is how it fits in with everything else we know.

forty-one

WHEN I SHOW Hailey the fabric, she doesn't think it means much of anything.

"That could belong to anyone," she says. "And even if it is Armstrong's, what does it prove?" She crosses her arms. "From what little I know of this creep, I wouldn't be surprised if the whole point of him messing with Ken's trunk was to distract us with a side issue that doesn't mean shit."

My stomach sinks. I suppose she's right, but I ain't willing to admit it. "He was up to something," I say. "Even if it was just a distraction, he's in the center of this thing."

"Maybe." Hailey crosses her arms. "But I'll have something more useful soon. I just downloaded a language analyzer app. Nothing fancy, but it'll compare the language Sarah uses in her social media posts to the transcript of that fake voice clip and any posts she made on the April Dixon account. If we can prove definitively she made that phony tip, we'll have something real to confront her with."

"K." I play with my phone. "Add this, too. The night you and Dani went to the party, someone texted me a threat."

Hailey's eyes widen as I show it to her. "Thank God I was

there. Dani was so out of it." She lets her breath out slowly. "Forward me that too, okay?"

I do, but then I say, "Any way we can compare this fabric to brand labels so we can prove it belonged to Armstrong, long as we're finding things to confront people with?"

Hailey bites her lip. "If you take a photo and do a reverse image search, maybe you'll find something. But I still say this isn't important."

I ignore her. I ain't gonna waste time arguing when we're this close. When I do the reverse image search, I find out that the letters on the fabric match a brand called Sebastian Bellini, which makes luxury ties.

"Still doesn't prove it's his," Hailey says, "and anyway I think I'm right cause if he was really breaking into the trunk, whatever tool he was using would have been in the lock, not a piece of his tie."

My throat tightens with anger, although I have a sneaking suspicion she could be right. "I still want to know what he knows and this could be the key to finding out."

Hailey sighs. "CJ, please... from everything we've seen, this guy is grandmaster level when it comes to mind games. You can't go at him all upset. It'll blow up in your face."

I make myself breathe. "Someone's gotta stop him," I say weakly. "I'm sick and tired of him getting away with one thing after another. All the things he's done to women are bad enough but now Ellie's dead. I can't kick this can down the road, not when there's no telling what he might do next, and we all know there ain't anything he could do that's so bad the Dean'll put her foot down about it."

"That doesn't make it your responsibility." Hailey's voice is soft.

"I'm the one who's been digging up the truth about him while the cops are busy trying to put my friends in jail." My voice shakes. "Look, if Dani didn't need her sleep I'd ask her to go with me but as it is, I have to do it alone, cause I can't wait a second more."

Hailey's shoulders slump. "There's no talking you out of this, is there?" I shake my head slightly and she says, "At least let me go with you, then."

That feels weird. Hailey's always in the background, doing computer stuff, never on the front lines like me and Dani. But if she's offering, I ain't gonna refuse so I say, "Okay."

Nobody's in Armstrong's office when we arrive. The front door's open, but Chloe's desk is empty and all the lights are off.

"Weird that he'd leave the front door unlocked," I say, walking slowly around the room. I try his office door and it opens even though he ain't inside. "You reckon he left in a hurry?"

"What I think is that we should get out of here," Hailey says nervously. "Something feels off, like way off. Armstrong's not the kind of person who forgets to lock up." She crosses her arms. "I told you. Master mind game player."

I hesitate, my hand on the doorknob. "Let's beat him at his own game, then. I'm going in."

"And what if he comes back and catches you?"

I hesitate. "You stay out here. Maybe you can find something on Chloe's desk while you're playing lookout."

Hailey's jaw tightens. "I really wish you wouldn't do this. I'm 99 percent sure this is a trap."

"Maybe. Or could be that's what he wants us to think so we don't look too hard." My heart pounds as I slip inside and I'm almost certain Hailey's right, but something in me won't let me walk away anyway.

It's pitch black in Armstrong's office. I turn my phone flashlight on and tiptoe forward, holding my breath and trying to shake the feeling that Armstrong's fixin' to jump out of the shadows and grab me from behind like my kidnapper did.

His desk is even neater than Dani's usually is, which isn't what I'd expect from a busy professor. His computer's password-protected so there ain't any way I'm getting in there and all that's on his desk is a folder marked ATTENDANCE ROSTERS. I open it and I find printouts of class lists, held together with a paper clip. The top list has some names circled. They're hard to read in the dark, but one of the names is Sarah's. All the names circled seem to be women's.

When I slide my phone light down far enough, I find Alicia's name circled too.

I swallow hard, staring at it. Either he left this out cause he wanted me to see it, in which case he's threatening Alicia, or he didn't and he just has her on his list of girls he wants to mess with.

I take a photo for Hailey to enhance later and hurry to close the folder.

Next, I check out his desk drawers. There are two: a small one on top and a bottom one underneath it that's got a lock on it. I open the top drawer first. It's got all sorts of electronics in it: earbuds, computer wires, and a flash drive that may or may not be important. I pocket it just in case.

I squat to check out the lock, wishing Dani was here. She probably would have a hairpin or something to break into the drawer with. As is, best I can do is grab that paper clip off his list of potential victims and hope he doesn't notice it's missing.

I unbend the paper clip and stick it in the lock. I got no idea what I'm doing but I reckon if I jiggle it enough it'll open the lock.

There's a click and I grin as I pull the paper clip out. I open the drawer and catch a glimpse of a file folder...

...but an alarm goes off, making siren noises like one of

those car alarms that always keeps people up at night back home.

Shit.

I slam the drawer closed and run out of the room, pulling the door closed behind me. Hailey's already crouched behind the desk. She whispers, "Turn on the lights. He's coming."

I do. Hailey hurries around to the front of the desk and grabs a pen out of her purse, crouching over like she's leaving a note on Chloe's desk.

The door opens and Armstrong comes in. "Well, what have we here?" he says. "It seems two little fishies are caught in my net." He laughs as he takes out his phone. "You have two minutes to explain to me why I should not call Campus Security to report two students breaking into my office. And I suggest you keep your hands visible so that I am not forced to restrain you for my safety."

forty-two

HAILEY'S EYES WIDEN as she slowly puts the pen down and raises her hands into the air. "You have it wrong," she says. "We just got here, didn't we, CJ?"

My arms are already aching but I don't dare put my hands down. "That's right," I say, hoping Armstrong doesn't hear the slight tremble in my voice even though the chances are less than zero that he misses it. "We wanted to ask you something but you weren't here so we were fixin' to write you a note when you came in."

Armstrong laughs again. "While an alarm is ringing in my office loud enough to awaken the entire campus? Surely you don't expect me to believe that." He points his phone toward us. "What will I do with you? Hmm... perhaps I should call Campus Security after all. But it might be more fun to post a photo on social media of the two of you caught red-handed, hands raised in surrender like the criminals you are." He presses a button on his phone; I've no doubt he's taking a blackmail photo.

I stare back at him, refusing to allow him to intimidate me. "Karma's a bitch, ain't it? We have proof you tried to break into my boyfriend's trunk the night Ellie died."

Armstrong's jaw tightens, but then he laughs again. "No one will believe that. But all right, I'll play along. What proof do you ladies think you have?"

"Your tie got caught, for one thing," I say. "Could be you knew that, could be you didn't. But I don't know anyone else who wears ties from Sebastian Bellini and anyway, an eyewitness places you in the lot at the right time."

"Does she, now?" Armstrong smirks. "I'm afraid you'll have to do better than that. I went for my nightly run around that time, you see. I did notice a child staring at me from a vehicle—you really should tell your boyfriend that leaving a young girl unattended in a darkened parking lot is very dangerous, by the way—and so I jogged around the back of the car so as not to scare her. My tie must have rubbed against the trunk, that's all."

My throat tightens at the implied threat. I won't let him hurt Vicki. I won't.

Hailey says, "Didn't I tell you that piece of fabric was irrelevant?" She turns toward Armstrong. Her eyes are wide and I can tell she's terrified of him, but you'd never guess it from how calm her voice is. "We came here to ask you whether you knew anything about where your girlfriend was at the time of the murder."

"My girlfriend?" Armstrong laughs. "I'm afraid that whoever you're talking about has misled you. I've been happily single for years." His jaw tightens. "But there is no reason to discuss that any further, or anything other than —"

"Does Sarah Buchanan know she's not your girlfriend?" I interject. "She seems awful sweet on you, and she's made it clear she'd do anything to protect you."

Armstrong's jaw tightens. "Do not interrupt me again or it will be a holding cell in the security office for you. And this time, I doubt the Dean of Students will dismiss it as the typical hijinks of an immature student."

"You can't hold us here," Hailey says, her eyes flashing. "That's false imprisonment. Either call the cops or let us go."

I breathe in sharply. Pressing him to call the cops on us seems like a bad move.

Armstrong smiles slightly. "It's called a citizen's arrest, my dear." He sighs. "I suppose I don't have any real proof that you two broke into my office, just like there is no real proof that a certain Kenneth Hansen was involved in the murder." He turns toward me. "I know that he means a lot to you. It would be a shame if he spent time behind bars, wouldn't it?"

I can't help stiffening slightly but I look him in the eye anyway. "My boyfriend's innocent. What about your girlfriend? Or imaginary girlfriend, I suppose. Any idea where she was?"

"Oh, of course." Dr. Armstrong's tone is light "She was busy killing Ellie." He snickers. "For a moment there you thought I would throw her under the bus, didn't you? The truth is, I have no idea where she was or what she was doing. Nor do I know why she chose to claim she and I are involved. But there is one thing I do know." He leans forward. "You two will never be able to prove who did what that night. Maybe you're right and you've stumbled onto a killer. Maybe you're wrong, and poor, sweet Sarah is harboring murderous impulses. And maybe you are completely off base and it's someone else altogether, someone who had a stronger reason than petty jealousy to want Ellie dead. Best leave this one to the police, because you are both in way over your head." Armstrong turns and pulls the outer door open. "Get out of here, ladies, and be quick about it before I change my mind about letting you off the hook for this unfortunate incident." He laughs to himself. "Oh, and Ms. Jennings? I'm afraid I can no longer appear on your podcast."

Hailey and I don't have to be asked twice. We hurry out of

the office and don't look back til we're safely out of the science building.

"You okay?" I ask Hailey when we pause for breath in the garden.

"I will be." Hailey crosses her arms. "I told you we should go as soon as we saw he wasn't there! We're lucky we're not sitting in the back of a police car right now!"

"He wasn't ever gonna call the cops. He was messing with us." I rub my wrists anyway, suddenly feeling the weight of the plastic cuffs my kidnapper used to restrain me. "Anyway, it wasn't a complete waste. I did get this." I pull the flash drive out of my pocket.

"Yeah, if it's not full of viruses," Hailey says, rolling her eyes. "I'll text you a link to a scanner app. Use it before you try to open anything on that flash drive."

"You ain't coming back with me?"

Hailey shakes her head. "I need my space to cool off after what just happened. Don't worry. We're still friends. But don't ever ask me to do anything this stupid again." She turns and walks away, moving fast.

I rub the bridge of my nose, wondering what I've just done.

I tell Dani the whole story as soon as she gets up. I expect her to be upset at me, but she just says that Hailey ain't used to being on the front lines and that she'll get over this quicker than I think.

"You think you got anything useful out of him for your trouble?" she asks me after she finishes reassuring me.

"This," I say, taking out the flash drive, "if it ain't full of viruses. Plus, clearly he was spooked by what we're looking into cause looking back, I'm pretty sure he wanted to get out of us what we knew."

"Which means that no matter what he said about how you'll never find out who did it, he let something slip."

I nod. "There was something he said when he was trying to convince us he and Sarah were about to slip through our fingers, but I can't quite remember." I toss the flash drive on my desk. "Hailey ain't sent me the virus scan app yet so we're stuck til she cools down."

"Not really. Hailey installed virus protection on my laptop a long time ago. So if you want to see what's on there, I can make sure it's safe."

"K." I hand Dani the flash drive. "I was fixin' to have Hailey enhance this too. Maybe she'll do it for you." I show her the photo I managed to get before I got caught and explain what was on it.

Dani swallows hard. "That's his idea of a hotness list or something? Gross."

"Yeah, that's what I'm thinking. Alicia was on it and I sure hope he ain't planning on going any further than circling her name."

"He's not," Dani says. "I'm pretty sure that anything you found, he wanted you to find. It's more intimidation bull-shit." She puts the flash drive in her laptop and opens the virus scanner. "Let's see... Virus check, malware check, adware check..." She clicks things off on her options before she runs the checker. "We'll know soon if it's safe."

It feels like forever before the virus scan's ready. While we're waiting, Dani asks, "So did you at least make headway with Ken before this all happened?"

"Not really." My voice is flat. "He was in a rush cause of Vicki being sick. Best I got out of him was that he'll have us all over for supper once she's well again."

"That's actually a good thing, believe it or not." Dani squeezes my shoulder. "I bet he's so into you that he doesn't trust himself to stay broken up if he's alone with you all night. So he wants us all there as a buffer."

"If you say so. Still seems like there's something more bothering him about me than he lets on."

"That's just you being insecure." Dani's computer beeps. "Okay. We're all clear. Let's see what's on this." She double-clicks and finds a video and a PDF. "What do you think he's up to?"

"Only one way to find out," I say. "Let's start with the document."

Dani opens it. I read over her shoulder:

Dear Barbara:

I know we agreed many years ago to keep certain things to ourselves, for the sake of our daughter. I am not ordinarily a man who goes back on my word, as you are undoubtedly aware, but recent events have made me reconsider. Perhaps if Chloe had known all along that I was her father, she would not have been driven to such destructive behavior.

I have tried to be her father from afar as she struggled with drug addiction. I understood the neurobiology behind it and suspected the trauma of the earlier automobile accident had changed her brain chemistry in significant ways, though I knew that her belief she had inherited Eugene's addictive tendencies was mistaken.

I truly did have faith that the treatment I had paid for would take effect and she would live a proper life. However, now that my best researcher is dead and she is responsible, I can no longer remain silent.

So, we are at a crossroads. For now, I will keep to myself that Chloe is responsible for Ellie's death, on one condition: you allow me to tell her the truth and relieve her of the burden of her guilt over her supposed father's death. I think you will agree it is best for everyone if I do so. It is up to you what to tell her about why we lied to her all these years, but I strongly recommend that you admit you loved me until the world insisted otherwise. I know I certainly shall tell her that if she asks.

Yours always,
Joshua

I stare at the letter, unable to believe what I'm reading.

Dani says, "I thought we proved Chloe didn't kill Ellie."

"We did." I cross my arms. "He wanted us to see this so we'd believe Chloe's the killer. If it's true she's his daughter, which I ain't sold on cause the whole rest of this letter is a bunch of lies, he's no kind of father, cause he wants to trade her freedom for his own." A pulse starts up behind my eye. "I almost don't want to know, but what's the video?"

"Something incriminating Chloe, no doubt," Dani says. "We'll need Hailey to chill out fast cause she knows how to analyze it to see if it's a deepfake." She double-clicks the video.

It's grainy, like security footage, and it keeps bouncing up and down. In the background, someone's breathing hard, and footsteps hit the ground in time with the bounces.

From what I can tell, the video's the park at night. The camera follows Chloe as she walks with Ellie's body. She's got her arm around Ellie like she's helping a drunk person walk as she drags her toward the bushes. She's struggling some under Ellie's weight, but she manages to get her across the park.

I cover my eyes with my arm out of respect for Ellie. "I've seen enough. Turn it off. Please."

"Yeah." Dani clicks with the mouse. "You can open your eyes now. It's gone." I drop my arm, breathing hard, and Dani says, "Obviously Armstrong's invested in making us think Chloe killed Ellie. But I guess he doesn't realize that we know it's impossible so for once, we're a step ahead of him."

"Two steps," I say. "He told me and Hailey the reason he

was in the studio lot was he was going for his nightly run. That's BS cause obviously, he was running in the park while he filmed this."

"Right." Dani swirls the mouse around and around. "So… we have proof he was involved in the murder, except he never appears on camera and I don't think the cops will be impressed by us claiming that's his breathing and his footsteps. So the question is, what's our next move?"

forty-three

THE NEXT MORNING, I run into Ken in the cafeteria while Dani and I are heading toward Hailey's table. He's putting his breakfast into a to-go box, I reckon for Vicki cause she ain't with him, and he's got one of those N-95 masks on we all ditched a long time ago.

"Vicki has her appetite back, huh?" I say, going up to him.

"Yeah." Ken grabs three slices of bacon with a pair of plastic tongs and tosses them into the box. "She's real congested and her temperature creeps up every time the ibuprofen wears off, but she's the same old Vicki. We had to do everything but lock her in the room to convince her she wasn't coming down to get her own breakfast this morning." He grabs eggs for her, adding, "We're still waiting on the COVID test. The doctor said she doubts that's what it is but Mom insisted on it just in case."

"Oh. That's why that mask's hiding your handsome face."

"Yeah. Better safe than sorry, right?" Ken sighs deeply.

"You okay?" What I really want to know is whether we're okay, but I don't dare ask, especially when he's clearly stressed out.

"I had enough problems before Vicki took sick," Ken says,

"but I'll be all right." He closes the box. "I'd better get back before she gets any more stir-crazy. But hey. I'll check with Mom whether it's okay with her to have the team over as long as we stay in the yard so we're not exposed to Vicki's germs. If it is, I'll text you and you guys can head over, okay?"

I make myself smile even though I want so badly for him to be willing to spend time one-on-one that my chest aches. "Sure thing."

My shoulders shake as I hurry to get my food before heading back to the table. The whole cafeteria probably can see I'm crying, but I don't care. Best to get it out now so I can concentrate on what Hailey has for me. I sure hope she's over yesterday, cause I don't think I can take her being ice cold to me on top of how Ken's being.

I hold my head up as I walk back to the table, but as soon as I slide into my seat, Dani pats my hand and says, "Ken drama getting you down?"

"No. Just me being a baby. He said he's checking with his mom about us all coming over to discuss the case but it's like we're nothing to each other anymore."

Hailey says, "Some people shut down when they're scared. It's easier than being vulnerable." She fidgets, twisting her hands toward her chest and back again. "Speaking of which, I'm not mad anymore and I hope you're not either."

"I ain't," I promise. "I never was. I just felt bad I dragged you into something you didn't want to be in." I stab at my eggs with my fork. "Anyway, we don't have time for petty jealousy..." I trail off, something hitting me. "That's it. That's what Armstrong said to us that's been nagging me."

"I remember that too," Hailey says. "Given the video and stuff, he wanted to plant a seed in our minds that Chloe killed Ellie. But still, he talked like he knew something, didn't he?"

I nod. "You reckon he was telling us that's why Ellie was killed?"

"Maybe. Or he wanted us to deduce that when it's nonsense." Hailey takes her glasses off and rubs them on her shirt bottom, cleaning the lenses. "Trying to figure out his games gives me a headache. I'd rather stick to tech stuff."

"Speaking of," Dani says, "tell CJ what you told me while we were waiting."

"Right." Hailey takes out her laptop. "The video isn't a deep fake, which isn't really surprising because we pretty much figured out that Chloe moved Ellie's body. But this isn't raw footage either." She opens the video; I look away cause I don't want to see it but she says, "This is important. See how it sort of blips?" I lean forward and look closely, and I can see what Hailey's saying. The video jumps from Chloe having her right arm around Ellie to Ellie being on her other side, and Armstrong breathes out twice without breathing in.

"It's edited?" I ask.

Hailey nods as she closes her laptop. "He wanted to make it look like Chloe was the only one at the park. He kept himself off camera, though he forgot to mute his mic so we know he was going for a run while filming this, but I bet there was someone else helping Ellie move the body." She closes her laptop, triumphantly.

I cross my arms. "I'd wager it was Sarah. She knows what Chloe was up to that night. The fake account proves that. You get any proof that's her, by the way?"

"Oh yeah. That's the other thing I meant to tell you. I ran that language analyzer I told you about. This isn't foolproof, okay, but there's a 95 percent match. She sent that voice clip and she also texted that threat."

"So she's involved in what happened to Ellie for sure, then." I reach for my phone. "Let's get Jessica and Alicia and see what we can do to find out exactly how."

. . .

Jessica wants us to meet her in the garden but nobody feels comfortable talking there when Armstrong could pop in any minute. So she says since her car's parked right down the hill, she'll take us all downtown to the coffee shop. The last thing I need is coffee and I'm overfull from breakfast, but it'll be quiet there so I agree and we all pile into her car.

It's a tight squeeze with three of us in the back. Hailey and Dani are both taller than me and I end up in the middle, squashed between them. I bite my lip, glad it's a short trip cause the lack of space makes me feel as trapped as I did when I was kidnapped.

"So what is the news?" Jessica asks as she starts the car.

"We'll show you when we get there," Hailey says, "but we have proof Armstrong's trying to frame Chloe."

Dani adds, "But Chloe isn't 100% innocent either. She didn't kill Ellie but she did dump her in the park."

Jessica's hands tighten around the steering wheel. "Armstrong made her do this thing to Ellie?"

"We believe so," I say. "The thing is —"

Suddenly, police sirens blare behind us and the cops order through the megaphone, "Pull your vehicle over to the side of the road. Everyone sit still and keep your hands where we can see them."

What the fuck? I turn my head, trying to see over Dani's shoulder, and catch a glimpse of a bunch of police cars with their lights on, at least five or six.

They mean business. It looks like we're all going to jail and I don't know why.

forty-four

TOO MANY COPS TO count jump out of their cars and surround ours, their guns drawn.

My eyes dart to Dani, then away. Her eyes are wide and she's biting her lip as the cops rap on Jessica's window and bark orders at us, telling us to all get out of the car.

"My probation...," Dani whispers, tears in her voice. My ears are ringing so hard I can barely hear her, or what I'm being told to do. Jessica's saying something, trying to explain that this ain't Chloe's car, so I reckon that's why they stopped us, but the cops won't listen.

"We'll see," a cop says. "Out of the car, now! All of you!"

My heart pounds as I do what I'm told. A cop barks at me to get down on one knee, then on both, then to flop down on my stomach and spread my arms and legs. I obey, helplessness washing over me as I lie flat, the gravel poking into the skin on my hands.

I breathe in deeply, pushing away the memories of my abduction. For some reason, the thought pops into my head that Ellie must have felt this helpless when the killer pinned her against the wall and began to strangle her.

My breath catches in my throat as a cop throws herself on top of me and pats me down.

The marks on Ellie's neck... the bruises on the back of her head and her legs...

Ken had said the cops thought he grabbed her around the neck so hard that it knocked her against the wall. But what if they had it backward? What if the killer pushed her down and strangled her on the ground while she tried to fight back?

I bite my lip as the cop cuffs my hands behind my back, trying desperately to hold onto that thought despite the memories threatening to overtake me.

"Please," I force out of my too-dry mouth as the cops help me sit up. "What charges am I being arrested on?"

"Nothing yet," the cop says. "You're being cuffed for everyone's safety right now. Though if I were you, I'd tell us where Chloe Lancaster is cause she's wanted for murder and the last thing you want is to be associated with what she did."

Fear shoots through me. They ain't gonna listen if I tell them what we know, and there's no use arguing anyway, not when they've already got me in cuffs. "T-this ain't her car," I stammer. "It's my friend Jessica's." My eyes dart back and forth. All five of us are handcuffed now and being questioned by different cops. Hailey and Dani both have tears in their eyes, which makes me feel lower than low.

The cop crosses her arms. "But you know Chloe?"

"Not really." I hesitate, not sure how much to say. I don't want to get Chloe in trouble when I don't know the whole story, but I ain't about to go to jail for her either. "I've been helping the Dean of Students look into what happened to that girl who died, so I know Chloe's her daughter and that Ellie was her neighbor."

The cop nods. "Cassandra Jennings," she says, reading my ID card. "You're the one who had that podcast the kid called into." She pats my shoulder. "Doing a podcast on the murder?"

"Hoping to, ma'am." I stare straight ahead.

The cop gestures to someone else and says, "Take her to a squad car til we're done. I don't want her overhearing anything that ends up on her podcast."

My heart pounds even harder as I'm escorted away. A cop sits with me in the back of the squad car and tries to tell me that I need to do the right thing while I worry about where they're going to put me if they take me to jail. I don't say a word cause I'm so worried about being housed with women even though that's likely safer for me than being locked up with men.

The cop's walkie-talkie goes off with a bunch of police codes and she answers in kind. Then she says, "Okay. Looks like you were right and we got the wrong car." She removes the cuffs and tells me I'm free to go.

I rub my wrists as I get out of the car, anger rising in my throat that I didn't get an apology and neither did anyone else.

I hurry back to Jessica's car and slide into my seat. Dani and Hailey ain't back yet but after a minute a cop makes a big show of escorting Hailey back to the car like they think she's fixin' to go anywhere else.

Hailey's eyes flash as she closes the door. "Do not ask me if I'm all right." Her shoulders slump. "Just tell me one thing. Was this Armstrong getting revenge for yesterday?"

"I reckon not." I cross my arms. "I think we scared him enough he called the cops on Chloe. Could be they got the same video we did."

Hailey's head bobs slightly. "So now what?" she says. "T-they aren't going to take Dani in, are they?"

"Nope," Dani says, getting in the car. "They know if they did they'd get sued. They had no reason to stop us in the first place since this isn't Chloe's car."

Alicia comes back and says, "It'll be a minute. Idiot cop insists on verifying Jessica's immigration status before letting her go. She's legal, don't worry, but they're full of BS today."

No one says anything while we're waiting for Jessica. I want to tell them what I realized while I was down on the ground, but no one seems in the mood for talking. Besides, Jessica should be here for that.

When Jessica finally comes back, she slams her door shut and says, "Everyone ensure you have a seatbelt on in case the idiots are still watching."

I click my seatbelt into place. "Still want to get coffee?"

The engine roars to life, startling me, as Jessica turns the key. "What I want is for them to go so I can contact Chloe," she says. "It is time for her to tell us exactly what she knows so that we can end this."

Chloe doesn't answer her phone when Jessica calls and Alicia tells her in Spanish to leave it alone til we get to the coffee shop. No one says a word the whole ride, making five minutes feel longer than the 12 hours my parents spent driving me up to school from home last August.

Jessica stays quiet til we're sitting at the corner table where I interviewed Lisa that long ago day. Then she says, "You have proof the snake is behind this all?"

Hailey pushes her hair behind her ear. "Y-yeah," she says. "Um…"

"I'll get you something to drink," Dani says quickly.

"And the wifi password?" Hailey asks. "I need it so I can show Jessica what I showed you guys."

"You got it," Dani says. "You want to come with?"

Hailey shakes her head slightly but doesn't speak.

I know how she's feeling cause I'm still shaking on the inside too about the cops, but I don't know what to say, so I turn to Jessica instead. "One good thing came out of this," I say, forcing a smile as Dani returns, holding a caramel iced coffee and a receipt that has the Wifi password. "I think I know —"

Hailey smiles slightly. "You sure know how to cheer a girl up." Her smile fades as she opens her laptop and gets to work. "This video's very disturbing," she warns Jessica, and Alicia reaches for Jessica's hand. "It shows Ellie after... you know."

"I understand," Jessica says thickly. "I still want to know."

"It's edited," Hailey says as she turns her screen around. "There was another person there. I'll explain why if you want."

Jessica's eyes widen. "She dumps her with no clothes. The snake's last act was to humiliate her after death." Alicia rubs her shoulders but Jessica pulls away. "If Chloe does not answer her phone this time, I will go to her apartment and drag her out of her bed. She needs to explain why she did this thing."

"Sure hope you can get answers out of her," I add, "cause I got a good idea who actually killed Ellie, but I ain't got proof yet."

"What?" Dani says.

Jessica's phone buzzes before I can explain. She says, "It is her. Finally."

She opens it, then frowns and says something to Alicia in Spanish. Alicia rubs Jessica's back.

Jessica says, "Chloe has texted that she has decided to go to the police station and allow herself to be arrested. She is contacting us to tell us that her lawyer has already advised her not to speak to us about the night Ellie was killed."

Crap. Sarah's gotten to Chloe, and now she's about to confess to a murder we all know she didn't commit.

forty-five

I **WANT** TO go to the police station right away, but no one else does and Dani's worried about Northrop expelling her in retaliation. The two of us head off to try to convince the Dean otherwise while everyone else goes home to chill out.

Sarah's on the phone when we walk up. Her eyes dart from me to Dani and she hurries to end the call.

"Dani," she says before I can ask her who she was talking to. She twists a lock of her hair. "They let you out. I mean, obviously they did. Um... are you okay?"

"Fine, not that you care." Dani crosses her arms. "Whatever fake apology you have for me, save your breath. You set me up, Sarah, and there's nothing you can do to take it back."

Sarah blinks back tears. "I know you'll never believe me, but I didn't want you to go to jail. I thought you'd just get a ticket or something."

"Maybe there is something she can do to redeem herself," I say to Dani. Turning back to Sarah, I say, "Who put you up to it?"

Sarah shakes her head slightly. "You're not going to trick me twice."

"Sarah." My voice is soft. "Dr. Armstrong ain't worth

what you're doing. You already messed up a date with someone you really like cause you didn't want us to look too hard at him, and this whole time he's never cared one bit about you. Yesterday he told me and Hailey that you ain't his girlfriend and that he thought chances are you killed Ellie."

Sarah goes pale, but she says, "He was obviously joking. You don't get his humor." She twists a lock of hair around two fingers. Lowering her voice, she says, "Anyway, Chloe was arrested half an hour ago so that's that." Aloud, she says, "If you're here to see the Dean, you'll have to come back later. She's busy with Chloe's situation and doesn't want to be disturbed.

"Yeah... no," Dani says. "We have proof Chloe didn't kill Ellie that she'll want to pass on to her lawyer."

Sarah breathes in sharply enough we can hear it. "Really? That's great news if it's true. W-what proof?"

"That's between us and Dean Northrop," Dani says. "If she thinks you're trustworthy, we'll tell you."

Sarah's face crumples. "I told you, I didn't want you to go to jail!" she calls as we walk toward Dean Northrop's office. "Even if you did deserve it for trying to set me up."

We ignore her, knocking on the Dean's office door.

"Who is there?" The Dean's voice is slowed down and cracks a little. I almost feel sorry for her, but then I think of all the women she let down and my sympathy fades to nothing.

"CJ Jennings, ma'am," I say. "We need to talk."

I don't expect her to answer, but she shuffles to the door and opens it. "This must be Ms. Olsen," she says, glancing at Dani. "I suppose you two have come to do damage control."

Dani locks eyes with her. "We had nothing to do with Chloe's arrest. But maybe we should talk about it in your office, away from eavesdroppers."

The Dean sighs deeply. "Very well. Come in. But I am

expecting a call from Chloe's lawyer, and when she contacts me, that is the end of this conversation."

"We understand, ma'am," I say. "We ain't gonna take up too much of your time." I cross my arms as Dani closes the door behind us. "First things first. Expelling Dani ain't gonna do any good. It won't get Chloe out of this mess. The only thing that will is if you give up what you know about the night Ellie died."

"Me?" Dean Northrop laughs bitterly. "Surely you don't expect me to sit here and entertain accusations that I killed a student."

"Not you," I say, "but we reckon you know more about who did than you let on." I cross my arms. "Chloe has the same size hands you do. Those hands ain't big enough to strangle the life out of Ellie. But we're guessing that at some point Dr. Armstrong let slip what he made Chloe do that night. What'd he demand in return for his silence?"

Dean Northrop's lips are a thin line. She checks her phone. "I do not know yet what I can and cannot say without bringing further trouble to my daughter or to myself. I'm sorry. All I can tell you is that the police think my daughter was jealous of Ellie's success, and they are wrong."

"Course they are," I say. "We just told you, Chloe ain't guilty of murder. But someone else is, and we reckon you can probably help us put him away."

Dean Northrop taps the phone against her palm, thinking. "The best I can offer you is that I will bring up the matter to my attorney. If she gives me the green light to talk to you, I will do so." She stands, indicating the conversation is over. "Please excuse me so I can make that call."

Dani says, "As long as you aren't starting expulsion proceedings for no reason, we'll go."

Dean Northrop nods slightly. "Help my daughter," she

says, "and maybe you will make a better impression on me than your police report did."

Dani thinks we should go right to the cops after the meeting with Dean Northrop. At the very least, we can convince them that Chloe couldn't have killed Ellie.

We stop at home first cause I want to get all my ducks in a row. I check the digital whiteboard, highlighting the notes Ken added about the killer having to have hands his size and the bruises elsewhere on Ellie's body. While I'm at it, I add to Sarah's column that she made a prank call to the station right after the murder and that she's also been interfering with the investigation every way she can. While I'm at it, I change the status of a couple suspects so that the cops won't think someone's guilty who's not or vice versa.

I read through everything, thinking about what likely happened that night and if it all fits. A smile spreads slowly across my face as I check everything one last time.

It won't be long now before Ellie gets justice, at least not if the cops listen to me for once.

forty-six

THE DESK SERGEANT doesn't want to let us through to see Detective Cooper, but when I say I have proof that the suspect in custody didn't kill Ellie, she calls him.

The whiteboard for Ellie's murder is gone when we sit down in Cooper's office. I ask him if that means the case is closed, but he says he can't comment on an ongoing investigation.

Ongoing. Good. Then he hasn't charged Chloe yet.

"The thing is, sir," I say slowly, "Chloe Lancaster ain't your killer."

Cooper's head jerks up. "Between you and me, I don't believe so either. But — and this is not to go any further than this room under any circumstances — she made a full confession."

"That confession was coerced," Dani says as my stomach drops.

"Coerced?" Cooper asks. "Please explain."

I hold out my hands, aware I only I have one chance to convince him. "Ain't... I mean, haven't you noticed how small her hands are? Mine are bigger than hers and so are Ken's. You reckoned he did it for a long while cause they matched up with the bruises, remember? So someone with tiny hands and short stubby fingers ain't gonna fit those marks."

Cooper's eyes widen. "I suppose you could have a point. I'll have forensics run some tests to confirm your theory." He crosses his arms. "She went to great lengths to convince us that she was the killer. You say she was coerced to do so?"

"Yes, sir," I say. I hesitate, thinking about what to say that's least likely to get Chloe in worse trouble. "We reckon she had drugs on her that night and that she walked in on the murder in progress."

"And the killer threatened to turn her in for the drugs if she didn't commit a worse crime. She should have known better." Cooper sighs. "I don't suppose you have any proof of any of this?"

"Not exactly," I say, "but we do have a recording of a suspect blackmailing her again on a later date." I play the recording of Sarah threatening Chloe. "The way I see it, three people know what happened that night, not counting Ellie herself: Chloe, Sarah, and the killer."

Cooper rubs his temples. "Forward me that recording and I'll have our forensics team analyze it. If it does turn out to be Sarah Buchanan's voice on that tape, I will talk to the DA about arresting her for extortion. But beyond that, I cannot promise anything." He jots something on a yellow pad. "Do you have a theory as to who the killer is?"

"Yes, sir." I tell Cooper everything I've figured out, showing him the evidence on the digital whiteboard.

Cooper's eyes widen as he stares at it. "I have to say I'm impressed. However, you need to let us take it from here. Please do not try to confront the killer yourself."

I promise I won't, but in the back of my mind, I ain't sure I can keep that promise.

forty-seven

TWO WEEKS FLY by with nothing happening except Dean Northrop sending me a curt voicemail saying that Chloe has been denied bail on charges of obstructing justice. She ain't being charged with murder, at least, but the cops are taking too damn long making their case, and I can't shake the feeling that certain people are fixin' to take off for spring break and not come back.

Vicki's tests come back negative for COVID and RSV and Ken tells me the doctor reckons she has bronchitis. When she's past being contagious, he invites everyone over for a barbecue. He's outside playing basketball with Vicki when I get there; I stand and watch as he leaps up to grab the ball out of the sky as if it's nothing. If the cops ever make an arrest, maybe there's a future for him and me, but I got no business letting myself think it.

I'm about to make myself sit down at the picnic table when Vicki spies me and runs over to give me a hug. She's talking a mile a minute about how much she missed me and how the worst part about being sick was being stuck in the house with just Ken and her parents and I can't get a word in edgewise. After a while, Dani offers to show her how to spin the basketball on one finger to get her out of the way so Ken and I can talk.

"So the nightmare's almost over, huh?" Ken says, smiling at me. "My lawyer said I'm probably off the hook now."

"Yeah." We're standing close enough together I could easily brush his fingers with mine, but I don't dare. Instead, I stuff my hand in my pocket and say, "If the cops ever get their act together. I got half a mind to go confront a certain someone myself before he can run away."

Ken's smile fades. "Don't," he says. "I'm out of danger so there's no need for you to run headfirst into it."

My throat tightens with anger that I know ain't reasonable to feel. "Ellie still needs justice," I say. "Chloe shouldn't be the only one sitting in jail."

Ken slaps his hands against his thighs. "I gotta start the grill, I guess. But hey. Maybe after we eat, we can go for a walk?"

I nod, pretending my heart ain't breaking. There's no way we can get back to what we were. I'm sure of it.

I end up eating three hot dogs and a hamburger, which is far too much food, but the longer we sit eating, the more I can put off Ken taking me somewhere to let me down gently. By the time he's ready to go for a walk, the sides of my stomach are killing me and I can't tell if it's from overeating or nerves or what.

"S-so what's up?" I ask nervously, stuffing my hands deeper into my pockets.

"You tell me." Ken kicks at some grass coming out of a crack in the sidewalk. "I get that you want to get justice for Ellie. But you did your part, Ceej. Why can't you let the cops do theirs?"

I force air through my too-tight throat. "Cause they're talking too long and soon it's gonna be too late." I cross my arms. "It's spring break next week and I got the strongest feeling that if we don't get this wrapped up before then, we never will."

"Right." Ken sighs. "Look," he says, "I love you for being so committed to justice, and I get it's what'll make you a great reporter someday but the way you go about this stuff... it doesn't make us couple material."

"Why?" My voice shakes and tears spring to my eyes.

"Cause." Ken shoves his hands in his pockets. "You probably guessed it, but I wasn't exactly happy with our so-called date. Every time I tried to get romantic with you, your eyes were over there on what was going on with the case. And I figured it wasn't fair to bring it up cause I knew going in we were working, plus Dani getting arrested put a damper on things. But now that my name's clear and you're still putting work before everything else, even your own safety..." He shakes his head.

I bite my lip, thinking. Hailey had been so mad at me too, for the same reason. But what am I supposed to do when the cops ain't doing shit about catching a murderer? "This'll be the last time, I promise," I say.

"Famous last words." Ken pats my hand. "I wish things were different. I wanna be the kind of guy who has the stomach for being second place to a noble cause, but I'm just not. It seems like as much as we want to be together, it's just not in the cards for us."

I blink back tears. "That's not true. I just told you, this is the last time cause after that we can put Ellie to rest and...."

"And what if it's not? What if you don't catch him or someone else gets killed or some other kid calls in needing help?" Ken's voice rises. "I don't want to give up on us but I can't do this! I can't constantly be on edge, wondering if I'm gonna lose you, and on top of that never have you all to myself."

I cross my arms. "So you're saying I have to leave it alone or I'll lose you?"

"No. I'm not an asshole. I wouldn't tell you how to live your life, ever. I'm just saying... I'm not ready to be more than friends after all."

Everything's blurry. "Just so you know," I say, my voice so thick with tears I doubt he can understand me, "I hated that I had to split my attention that night. All I wanted was to be with you."

"But you couldn't," Ken says softly, "and that's not something to apologize for. It's just who you are." Ken pats my shoulder. "You're still my best friend, so it's not like that much has changed."

I make myself breathe, trying to stop the tears. I wish almost desperately I could be okay with what he's saying, but I can't. "At least we proved to the world that me being nonbinary's not a dealbreaker," I sniff, "but that doesn't mean my heart ain't broken right now." There ain't any point to trying to control the tears so I don't, letting my shoulders shake and big, ugly sobs come out of my mouth.

"I know. I'm so sorry." Ken reaches for me but I can't let him hug me. It'll just make things worse.

Dani thinks Ken'll come around. She spends half the night telling me so after we leave the barbecue, and she also adds that if he doesn't, it's his loss.

She's right, but that doesn't make it hurt any less. Neither does Dani offering to go with me tomorrow to confront Sarah and get the ball rolling on justice for Ellie, but Ken's right that it ain't safe to do this alone, so I let her.

We're about to get going the next morning when there's a soft knock on the door.

It's Hailey.

Dani says, "Oh. I'm not going to Computer Science this morning."

"I know," Hailey says. "I'm not either." She grins. "I want to help you guys. Besides, don't I always watch your back?"

My stomach tightens with envy for just a second, but I push that down. I ain't got time to be jealous that Dani's partner's coming around when mine ain't, not when we have a killer to catch.

On the way to the Dean's office, Dani pats my arm and says, "Don't worry. It's almost over and then Ken'll be so proud of you he'll have to come around."

"Yeah," Hailey says as we approach the automatic door to the Student Affairs Office. "He's scared of losing you, that's all, which I can understand, but —"

She cuts herself off as we go through the door and approach the desk for Dean Northrop's office.

Sarah's not sitting behind it. Mark is.

forty-eight

MARK LOOKS UP from the mail he's slicing open with a letter opener. "I didn't expect to see you ladies here," he says, emphasizing the word 'ladies' so I ain't got any doubt he's misgendering me on purpose. "And from the looks on your faces, you weren't expecting to see me either."

"You've got that right," I say thickly. "Where's Sarah?"

Mark smirks. "Dr. Armstrong was left in quite the bind when his assistant got arrested. A few times a week, he asks to borrow Sarah, and I can't blame the Dean for obliging. After all, she owes him since it's her daughter that put him in this position."

I cross my arms. "I don't see why you couldn't help him out so that she could be where she's supposed to be."

"You're awfully uptight about a girl you can't stand." Mark slices through the top of the next envelope. "What's the matter? Are you afraid she's going to get away with murder?" He laughs to himself.

"No," Dani says. "We're afraid you are."

Mark's face crumples as I put my hand on Dani's wrist. "Ignore her," I say quickly. "We're all wound up over —"

"It doesn't matter if you believe that tripe or not," Mark

says, his voice eerily calm. "We all know it's not true. Chloe is in jail for Ellie's murder. I'm sorry, ladies, but you failed as detectives. You didn't see the killer right under your noses."

Dani and I exchange glances. "Is that what Dean Northrop told you about her situation?" I ask carefully.

"What else would she be spending all this time behind bars for?" Mark's hand slips and he cuts the top of a letter instead of just the envelope. "Crap," he says. "You girls are distracting me too much. What is it you wanted, besides to whine about how you aren't as good as the cops at solving mysteries?"

I make myself breathe. He's trying to push all our buttons. I can't let him. "We needed to talk to Dean Northrop."

Mark's jaw tightens. "About what?"

"That's between us and her," Hailey says. "I'm sure she's expecting us, so if you could just let her know we're here..."

"I'm afraid the Dean is not available this morning." Mark double clicks the mouse; his hands are as large as Ken's despite his short size. "She had an emergency to attend to."

Fear shoots through me. "I suppose you won't have any problem with us going down the hall to see for ourselves." I gesture with my head for the others to follow me.

Mark jumps up from his seat so quickly it falls over, making the other receptionists turn their heads. "You can't do that. Leave or I will have to call Campus Security."

"Go for it," I say quietly. "I bet they'd be real interested in what we know about Ellie's death."

Mark goes pale. He points the letter opener toward my chest. "Stop wasting everyone's time with these false accusations. The police ruled me out months ago. I'm too short to have made those marks on Ellie's neck."

Hailey gasps, and I can't say my heart ain't pounding too, but it's not just fear on my part. It's excitement, cause we just got him. "And just how do you know what marks need to match up? That ain't public knowledge." I take a step toward him even though common sense dictates I back up. "The way I see it, you know cause you made them. You knocked her down first. That's why there were those hairs in the mud and those bruises on her head and back. Maybe you were fixin' to have your way with her, maybe you just wanted to pin her down so she couldn't fight back while you killed her. But in any case, you ripped her necklace off her and then you squeezed the life out of her."

Mark laughs. "Do you hear this?" he says to the other receptionists. "Crazy, right?" They ignore him; one picks up the phone and the other hunches over her computer like she's got to concentrate hard on what she's doing.

"If it's so crazy, then how do you know things you can't possibly know if you aren't the killer?" Dani says. "And why are you pointing that letter opener at us like you think it's a sword?"

Mark laughs again. "You'll have to do better than that. Obviously, Dean Northrop told me about the evidence against her daughter. And I mean you no harm, don't worry. But when crazy people start throwing around false accusations... well, I'd have to be an idiot not to defend myself."

He ain't as good a liar as Armstrong; his eyes are wide and there's beads of sweat on his forehead, giving away how nervous he is. But there ain't no point in goading him on, either, especially without the cops watching my back. "We'll ask Dean Northrop ourselves," I say, "and if your story checks out, we'll leave you alone." I turn and hurry down the corridor before he can stop me, hoping the others have the sense to follow me.

Dean Northrop's lights are on and her door opens when I turn the knob.

When I walk in, it's as bad as I feared. The Dean's phone is off its hook and the cord's missing; we find it easily enough when we trace the source of a muffled moan to the Dean. She's lying on her back next to the desk. Duct tape's been pressed over her mouth and her wrists have been bound over her head with the phone cord.

I squat by the Dean. "Help's on the way. It was Mark, wasn't it? Chloe told you the truth and he attacked you before you could call for help."

The Dean nods as I pull out my phone. "Only reason I ain't freeing you is the cops need to see what he did to you." But as I dial 911, something sharp and cold presses itself against my throat while a hand squeezes my shoulder.

Mark says, quietly, "I don't think so. Drop the phone or I'll cut you."

My abductor's hand presses so hard over my mouth I can barely breathe. I struggle as he drags me backward but he's too strong for me and he's got my arms pinned to my sides...

My heart pounds and I breathe in as hard as I can, pushing away the memory away. That was then, this is now, and if I have to remember anything from that terrible ordeal it better be that I got away from him even though he had my hands bound so tight behind me I could barely move.

I didn't let myself end up dead then and I sure as hell ain't gonna let my story end that way now.

I move as fast as I can, hitting send and the speaker button real fast before putting the phone on the floor and raising my hands into the air.

"That's right," Mark says, his voice drowning out the dispatcher asking what the emergency is. "Now if you two ladies don't want me to cut her throat, stay quiet and do what you're told. You—" out of the corner of my eye I see his fingers as he gestures toward Dani. "Get the duct tape off the desk and give it to me."

Dani does, tossing it to him. It bonks him on the head. I duck back, scared the letter opener'll slip and cut me, and grab his wrist, twisting to try to force his hand open.

Mark fights back, twisting his wrist the other way toward me. My arm stings suddenly; he's cut me. I can't worry about the pain now; I keep twisting, the buzzing in my ears mixing with the sound of sirens in the distance and the clatter of the letter opener as it falls to the floor. I can't tell if I really hear Dani say, "Now!" or I imagine it, but the floor shakes as she and Hailey rush Mark hard, knocking him to the ground.

"Two against one and we're both bigger than you," Dani says.

Mark's hands shoot up; he's fixin' to strangle her like he did Ellie. "No!" I shout, and Hailey grabs his wrists and pins them to the ground.

More footsteps pound and it feels as if the whole office is fixin' to collapse. My ears buzz as a voice shouts from behind me. "Campus Police! Nobody move!"

I look up. "He...held...a letter opener...to...my...throat," I gasp. "And he also... killed... Ellie Bishop."

Talking's so much effort it makes the room spin. Panic rises from my chest and then...

...I'm flat on my back, staring at the ceiling. A plastic clip pinches my index finger and there's a soft beeping somewhere as I'm being rolled away.

"There she is," an unfamiliar voice says, and as I turn my head, I meet an EMT's eyes. "See? Told you she'd come around."

"What happened?" I mumble as Dani hurries to keep up with the gurney.

"You fainted," Dani says, her voice shaking, "and I thought Mark killed you too." She turns toward the EMT. "Can I ride with CJ to the hospital? Please?"

The EMT says, "Okay with me if it's okay with her, but no getting her excited. She needs to relax."

"They," I say, my voice strained. "Um, is Mark..."

"He's in jail," Dani says, "and Hailey's been taken to the

hospital too to be treated for shock. She didn't want me to go with her because she thought it was more important I stay with you." She smoothes back my hair. "Want me to call Ken?"

I nod even though I only half understand her. "My arm?"

"They stitched it up."

"And the Dean?"

"Hospital." Dani squeezes my hand. "The EMTs are giving me side-eye, so we can't talk anymore right now, okay?" I bite my lip, annoyed but too lacking in energy to argue. "I'll explain later," Dani promises, "and what I don't, the cops will. Detective Cooper's already been bothering the EMTs about when he can take your statement."

I doubt I can sleep, but by the time I'm in the elevator down to where the ambulance is parked, my eyes are starting to close. As I drift off, I hope I'm cleared to talk to the cops soon cause I have just as many questions about what happened while I was out cold as they do about what Mark did to me.

forty-nine

I'M STILL HALF OUT of it when they set me up in an ER bed. I don't have my own space; the ER is full of beds separated by curtains thin enough to hear what doctors are saying to other patients, or would be if I could get rid of the sound of my heart pounding in my ears. I'm hooked up to all sorts of monitors, so I can't go to the bathroom by myself. When the nurse takes me, the trip down the hall makes me as out of breath as if I'd run all the way downtown from campus, and soon as I sit down on the commode the room starts spinning so bad I'm afraid I'll fall if I get up and need to let the nurse wash my hands for me and help me back to my bed.

A couple minutes later, a doctor who ain't any older than me comes to see me. He's almost as tall as Ken but his skin is more bronze than brown and he's got black-rimmed glasses. He introduces himself as Dr. Kaluga and explains that the dizziness and pounding in my ears is cause I lost a lot of blood after Mark cut me and am in need of a transfusion. I have to sign consent forms and then he takes more blood so he can double-check my blood type and see how low my red cell count is. They won't let me have visitors til they have he transfusion set up, and then only Dani.

"He got me good, huh?" I'm somehow able to talk normally even though I still feel out of breath from my trip to the restroom.

"Not as bad as it could have been," Dani says. "I hope throwing the tape at Mark isn't what got you hurt. W-when I saw him holding that letter opener to your throat, I knew I had to do something cause h-he was going to kill you sooner or later."

"I reckon that was the distraction we needed so I could escape," I say, patting her hand. "I just kept reminding myself I didn't let that pedophile take my life and I wasn't fixin' to let Mark do it either."

Dani leans in to hug me, but a nurse tells her not to cause she might dislodge the IV they're using for the transfusion. Her phone buzzes and she tells me it's Ken. "He wants to see you and you're only allowed one visitor at a time." She smoothes back my hair. "Hurry up and get better while I go check on Hailey."

"Hey," I say. "If you like her, go for it before it's too late."

Dani turns bright red. "Tell Ken that," she says, and hurries out of the room.

Ken's wearing his N95, making him look like one of the doctors instead of himself. I can't tell if the flip-flops my stomach's suddenly doing are cause he looks even more handsome than ever or cause I'm still messed up from the lack of blood.

I swallow hard as I mentally check whether the pounding in my ears is gone yet. It's less, but it's still there. "I reckon this was why you broke up with me," I say, my voice shaking slightly. "You were afraid of something like this or worse."

"I was afraid I'd be saying my final goodbyes down in the morgue," Ken says, "but never mind that. You're in one piece; that's all that matters." He sits down by the bed and takes my hand. "I know you're not in a place to have a serious conversation, but I just wanna say, when Dani called me and I heard how close we came to losing you…"

"I know. I'm sorry."

"No, don't. I'm the one who should apologize." Ken puts my hand between both of his. It warms me up, and for a split second, I have this crazy thought like his blood's healing me even though I know the transfusion's coming from the bag attached to the IV. "What I'm trying to say," Ken goes on, "is that when I learned how close we came to losing you, I realized how stupid I'd been. I-if you'd passed on I'd never get the chance to tell you that I love you or to do this." Ken takes a ring box out of his pocket and opens it.

"What's this?" I make myself smile. "You ain't proposing marriage, are you?"

"Not just yet," Ken says, "but it's tempting cause I don't ever wanna take it for granted again that there's gonna be a tomorrow for us. Like the Bible says, you never know what the day will bring. But what I do know is that I don't ever wanna let you go again. So if you'll let me, I wanna be your boyfriend and I wanna put this promise ring on your finger to show you I'm serious about you."

My eyes fill with tears. "I don't know if I can have jewelry just yet, but otherwise, yes."

"I checked with the nurse and she said it's all right as long as I don't jiggle the arm that's got a needle in it. So may I?"

I nod. Ken opens the box and shows me the ring. It's a black band with turquoise stones in it.

"My birthstone," I say. "I can't believe you remembered." My birthday's the day after Christmas, so I ain't used to anyone making a big deal out of it.

"Think I'd forget something like that?" Ken slips the ring onto my finger. "I tried my best to find something that's not only for girls."

"It's not that I won't wear anything that has the slightest

hint of girl," I say, "but the fact you thought of it makes me love it twice as much. And you."

I want to kiss Ken, but he won't take off his mask. He gives me a gentle hug and a promise of a first kiss soon as I'm healed.

I'm in and out for the next little bit. I can't sleep too well with an IV in my arm, especially cause the nurses keep coming in to check on me, and I keep staring at my ring, hardly able to believe Ken really put it on my finger. Flipping through channels on the TV helps to pass the time but I'm too lightheaded to concentrate much. Besides, I ain't in the mood for reruns of cop shows and I sure as hell don't want to watch the medical dramas while I'm living through one.

Time drags on til something starts beeping and a nurse comes in and says the IV bag is done. She draws some blood from my arm, which is counterproductive if you ask me, but she says the doctor needs to see where my numbers are at so he knows whether I need a second round. When she goes, it's silent in my room; something feels missing til I realize my heart ain't pounding in my ears anymore.

Dr. Kaluga comes by an hour later. After running through the list of the symptoms I came in with, he has the nurse take me to the restroom to double check that the dizziness and shortness of breath are gone. When I come back, he tells me that my blood's back in a safe range but that he wants to start me on an iron infusion to get it up to normal. He also checks my arm and says so far he doesn't see any sign of infection in the wound, which I reckon is good news even though he says I have to stay overnight for observation after the iron infusion's done.

No sooner does he leave than Detective Cooper and Detective Estrada, come in.

Cooper says, "I want you to know that the DA is hoping Mark will be denied bail tomorrow. We've already taken statements from your friends and from Dean Northrop, but I need to hear from you exactly what happened."

I tell him everything as best as I can remember, hoping it's good enough. By the time I'm done, my head aches and I'm ready for a nap.

Detective Estrada says, "So when he slipped up and told you he knew about the bruises on Ellie's neck, that was the final nail in the coffin for you?"

"Yes, ma'am." My arm's suddenly itchy where Mark cut me. "I pretty much knew already, but that sealed it for me." I bite my lip, trying to ignore the itching. "Sarah did a real good job of making herself look guilty, but there was one thing that didn't add up. She called minutes after Bobby did that night and complained Ellie was sleeping with her boyfriend. It only put suspicion on her along with the other stuff she did to try to make sure we didn't look too hard at Armstrong. But this time, it proved she wasn't at the park moving the body with Chloe cause the call came in right around the time Chloe was doing it. And it wasn't Armstrong, so that meant it had to be someone else alto-gether, and Mark was the only one of the suspects whose whereabouts were still unaccounted for."

"CJ surmised that perhaps Mark was so late to meet Ellie that fatal night because he and Armstrong were discussing what to do to keep her quiet," Cooper adds. "You didn't get proof of that by any chance, did you?"

I shake my head. "It would have been just the two of them," I say, "though I suppose Sarah might know. He had to loop her in at some point. I'm also 99 percent certain that when Mark got that phone call right before he left Ellie high and dry in the Burnt Olive, it was Chloe telling him she was here and ready to score some speed. And given everything that happened after, I'd wager that he's the one who told her he had something for her, just so he could make sure she was in the right place at the right time to get blackmailed into disposing of the body for him."

"Chloe confirmed all that," Cooper says. "She made a deal with the DA's office that I am not supposed to share with anyone. Off the record, I can tell you that she will be spending the next year in a halfway house for recovering addicts who also have a mental disorder."

I rub my temples while I try to decide how I feel about that. I reckon it'll end up being a good thing for Chloe, but I hate that she has this on her record when she's more a victim than anything else. "And Sarah and Dr. Armstrong? They're in jail too?"

Estrada nods. "Sarah tried to take all the blame in a last-ditch effort to rescue her so-called boyfriend. But we're hoping that some time behind bars without access to him will help her get her head on straight enough for her to realize that flipping on him's her best option."

I swallow hard. "There any way you can get him for what he did to Ellie and other women too? Jessica said that he would have fired Ellie if she didn't keep sleeping with him and she ain't the only one he messed with."

"DA's looking into it," Estrada says. "Can't promise you anything but she's doing her best to get justice for every woman whose life he ruined." She pats my pillow as she stands. "Get some rest, all right?"

I flop back on my pillow as the cops stand. Detective Cooper notices my ring and says, "That's from your boyfriend, isn't it?"

I can't help smiling slightly as I nod.

Cooper says, "I know this sounds like empty words, but I truly am sorry that we had to rule him out before we could take him off our suspect list."

"I appreciate that," I say, "but I reckon I ain't the one who has to forgive you for it."

"Of course," Cooper says. "I'll tell him the same thing. But I want you to know that it was nothing personal and that I was glad when I could finally close the file on him." He turns and walks slowly away. It ain't til he's gone that I realize I forgot to ask him about Dean Northrop.

It's not til I get out of the hospital that I get my answer. Ken's barely wheeled me out the hospital door to his car when Dr. Blanton texts asking me when I might be up to coming to see him. Ken wants me to take it easy the rest of the day and I don't want to get in a fight about me being overcommitted to work when we just got past the last one, so I listen to him and make an appointment for the following morning.

When I walk into Dr. Blanton's office, Dean Northrop's sitting in one of the extra chairs; she's moved it so it's next to his desk, facing out.

"Glad to see you looking well, ma'am," I say to her. "If you don't mind, what exactly happened?"

"Nothing you do not already know," Dean Northrop says. "As you surmised when you found me tied up on the floor, that morning I found Mark in Sarah's seat. Chloe had told me everything, so I went into my office to phone the police and he followed me. He hit me in the back of the head and stunned me badly enough that he could easily overpower me and, well... you know the rest because you found me in that embarrassing position."

"I'm glad we did," I say. "I was never happy with how you let Dr. Armstrong push you around, but I sure didn't want you to die."

"I appreciate that." Dean Northrop sighs deeply. "I wanted you to hear this from me first. The board of trustees and I have agreed that it is in the best interest of this university for me to submit my resignation."

I look away, unsure how to respond. I've no doubt I'm expected to say I'm sorry to hear it, but the truth is I ain't. She deserves that and then some. "I reckon that is for the best," I say, "though I wish I could say something different."

Dean Northrop plays with her pearls. "It is my own fault. But there is a silver lining for me. This development will give me more time to spend with Chloe when she is released next year and to visit her as much as I am allowed in the meantime."

"One of the reasons we're having this meeting in my office," Dr. Blanton adds, "is that Dean Northrop was kind enough to submit my name to the board as a candidate for the interim Dean they must appoint, and they have offered me the position."

"And you're accepting, I reckon?"

Dr. Blanton nods. "It will most likely only be temporary, and I will make sure to find a replacement academic advisor for you who meets your needs." He crosses his arms. "The other reason Dean Northrop wanted to meet with us is to ask you if you would be willing to grant her an exclusive interview about the mistakes she's made that have led to this result."

"I know we did not get off on the right foot," Dean Northrop adds, "which is mostly my fault because my priority was to protect Dr. Armstrong at all costs. But you are the only one I would trust with this story. You see, you were correct that Chloe is the product of what he did to me, and I have betrayed both her and myself for years. But I know you will not depict me as the evil, heartless villain that many of the women whose complaints I ignored probably make me out to be."

My heart pounds. "I will do my best to be fair," I say. "But before I get to your story, I want to do Ellie's justice." I turn toward Dr. Blanton. "I'm fixin' to put together a podcast detailing everything we know about her death and the events leading up to it."

"That would be fine," Dr. Blanton says. "Please talk to your contacts in the police department to ensure that you do not broadcast anything they want to keep to themselves."

When this started, I would have objected to being censored like this, but now I get that the cops need to have some privacy so that they can make sure the charges stick. "Yes, sir," I say. "I was also hoping that this could be the start of a new podcast series. I want to leave CJ's Mysteries behind and create a platform for people who have survived predators like Armstrong to tell their stories."

Dr. Blanton smiles. "Nothing would make me prouder," he said, "and as soon as I am officially the Dean I will approve this project." He glances at Dean Northrop. "Is there anything else you would like to say?"

"Only that I'm sorry. Everything I did was to protect Chloe, starting with pretending my late husband was her father. Dr. Armstrong used our daughter against me from the moment my husband died. I'm sure you can fill in some of those blanks yourself, and I will sit down and tell you the rest after the dust has settled."

I shake hands with her for the second time. This time I'm looking forward to talking with her. Even though I'm still upset that she let Armstrong call the shots when she shouldn't have, something tells me she's yet another one of his victims and I hope to be able to tell that story.

That evening, I meet up with my friends at Ice Cream Kitchen to celebrate getting justice for Ellie. I'd have rather gone to The Burnt Olive, but Vicki's coming with us and Ken doubts there's anything there she'd be willing to eat.

Dani gets there before everyone else. She admires my ring

for about the fifteenth time; she hasn't said anything about Hailey since we both got out of the hospital, so I take a deep breath and ask her what's happening there.

Dani stares down into her Coke. "Nothing," she says. "We're, um... I was too late. She met someone like two days before. I guess even almost getting killed with us didn't change her mind."

My stomach sinks. She and Hailey seemed so perfect for each other. "I'm so sorry. But maybe she'll come around."

"Maybe. But whatever. She has a girlfriend, and I'm not going to be like Sarah and act like an idiot over a one-sided crush." Dani gulps her soda.

Ken and Vicki come in.

Vicki runs to give me a hug. "I'm glad you weren't killed." She tugs at her pigtail. "Can I see your ring? I was so mad Ken didn't wait til I could be there to see him put it on you."

"You were the only one," Ken says, grinning. "I wanted to be alone with CJ."

Vicki gets her angry smile on, but she relaxes when I show her the ring. "Ooh, pretty," she says, sliding into her seat across from me. "Can I have an ice cream sundae from the adult menu with five scoops and five types of candy?"

"We're not discussing dessert til you got your dinner in you," Ken says, which I reckon is his way of telling her no without prompting a silent tantrum.

Everyone else comes in all at once. Dani looks away when Hailey walks in with some girl none of us has seen before. The new girl's tall, with jet black hair that's probably dyed that color and an egg-shaped face. Her arm is around Hailey's back.

"This is Scarlett," Hailey says. "I hope you don't mind that I brought her. I wanted her to meet all my friends."

I force myself to smile even though I don't think this is right. Scarlett wasn't with us when we were trying to get justice for Ellie, so why should she be here now? But

Hailey's clearly happy enough with her to want to show her off to her friends, so who am I to complain about that? "Course," I say, and introduce myself to Scarlett. I hold my breath while Dani does the same. Dani's polite even though her jaw's tight and her eyes are so narrow they're practically slits.

Alicia says, "Let's get sodas to toast to Ellie with."

"And a five-scoop sundae?" Vicki asks.

"Not yet," Ken tells her. "But you can get a milkshake if you want, how's that?"

The waitress comes over. Ken orders a strawberry milkshake for Vicki and a root beer for himself. After the rest of us order drinks, Scarlett double-checks with the waitress that the sodas aren't anywhere near anything made with peanuts before she gets a root beer too. Dani buries herself in her menu while Scarlett's apologizing to us all for being a pain and explaining she's careful cause she's got an allergy. The waitress goes away and comes back with our drinks.

Ken tells Vicki, "I'll let you have a sip for the toast, but then you have to wait til you get your food."

"Don't worry," Vicki says. "I don't want to ruin my appetite before I get my sundae. Besides, I've been craving that hot dog and fries all week."

Everyone laughs. I say to Jessica, "You want to do the honors?"

Jessica nods. She lifts her glass and says, "To getting Ellie the justice she deserves. It will never be enough to know she is resting in peace, but I'm grateful for it."

"Ellie will not have died in vain," I say. "She's the catalyst for my new podcast. Survivors of all sorts of predators are going to get to tell their stories on the air so that what happened to her doesn't happen to them."

"I got one," Ken says. "To living our lives openly, all of us. No one should have to hide who they are like Ellie did."

"All of this," Jessica agrees. "Let's toast to Ellie's memory and to what we are building on the ashes of her destroyed life."

We all clink glasses, even Scarlett. She's very quiet as we put our drinks down and I can't help wondering what story she has that she ain't ready to tell yet.

I look around the table, thinking about Ellie, and Meghan, and Sarah, and all the other unnamed women that Armstrong messed with over the years, grateful they're finally getting justice and the chance to tell the world the truth about what happened to them.

I can't wait for my new podcast to begin.

Thanks for reading! I hope you enjoyed *Censored Truths* and maybe even solved the mystery before CJ did.

Censored Truths is the first mystery in the **Cedarwood Justice** series, which began with *Reinventing Hannah*. This series is about young adults bravely standing up for the truth despite the potential consequences. Most of the books can be read as stand-alones (although I am planning a sequel *to Censored Truths* soon!), but they're all connected by themes like the price of standing up for yourself and others, healing from past trauma, and powering through fear to be the bold survivor you long to become.

If you liked this book, check out:

⊚ *Reinventing Hannah* — After an unspeakable assault, Hannah Kollmann is done being quiet. But reclaiming her voice doesn't just mean standing up to bullies — she also faces pressure from her old friends to go back to being the quiet, shy girl they thought they knew.

⊚ *Poison in the System* — Brianna Hunter was caught with someone else's drugs, but the law said she was guilty. Keeping her head down and trying to survive life in a group home won't work, not after someone is poisoned and the adults in charge only care about protecting the program, not the girls in it. Brianna's search for the truth could force her to lose everything: her second chance, the little bit of freedom she has, even her life.

Coming soon:

My next release is *Her Sacred Oath*, the first book in **Behind Closed Doors**, a new thriller series for adults about professional women who must choose between their safety and doing what's right.

And later, look for more from **Cedarwood Justice** in *Shattered Illusions*, as Dani tries to leave her past behind—but when another girl turns up dead, she's the prime suspect.

To stay in the loop about new releases and exclusive behind-the-scenes content, **hop aboard the Enigma Express**, my weekly newsletter for readers and trauma-informed storytellers:

https://authorjackori.com/enigma-express

Or follow me on the Cedarwood Justice substack:

https://cedarwoodjustice.substack.com

acknowledgments

So many people helped make this book possible, including some who don't even know how they helped shape it.

The idea for *Censored Truths* began with me trying to follow the writing advice In James Frey's excellent *How to Write a Damn Good Thriller.* Later I realized I was actually writing a mystery and read *How to Write a Damn Good Mystery* instead. Both those books helped shape my approach to this story (so did whoever wrote the Sleuth's Journey template for Plottr, which seriously changed how I approach mystery writing.)

Dr. Armstrong's misbehavior and the school's insistence on covering it up came from an anonymous entry on a listicle about things people know but don't talk about, so thank you to whoever put that out there. I'm sorry this kind of crap happens in real life and hope this story makes a difference.

I also wouldn't have a book that's half as strong as it is without the help of my developmental editor, Annie Mydia of Winning Writers. I'm so glad I took a chance and paid for a developmental critique when I thought I was a lot closer to the finish line than I was!

I also appreciate all the people who follow me on Facebook, Instagram, and Threads who make a point of liking and favoriting every post about *Censored Truths* or writing in general. Your excitement and support helped me keep going until the book was done. I also wouldn't have got the legal and police aspects of the story right without the help of the people on the **Cops & Writers** and **Legal Fiction** groups on Facebook.

Special thanks to my friend Alexis, who always cheered me on even while going through stuff of her own, and to my friend Anne for reading an early draft and being so excited about it that I decided to write a sequel when *Censored Truths* was done.

And finally, I'm grateful to every reader who picked up this book and joined CJ and their friends on this journey. My favorite part of being a writer is impacting readers' lives with my stories, whether or not we will ever cross paths otherwise.

about the author

Jack A. Ori is a transgender and autistic author who writes emotionally charged amateur sleuth mysteries and contemporary young adult stories about trauma, justice, and reclaiming your voice. He is the author of *Reinventing Hannah*, *Censored Truths* (formerly published as *Open Secrets)*, and *Poison in the System*, and the creator of the *Cedarwood Justice* series.

Jack is also a Senior Staff Writer for TV Fanatic, where he reviews television dramas through a trauma-informed and LGBTQ+ lens.

facebook.com/LGBTAuthorJackOri

x.com/authorjackori

instagram.com/authorjackori

other books by jack ori

CEDARWOOD JUSTICE

Reinventing Hannah

Poison In The System

Shattered Illusions (coming soon)

The Night Quinn Disappeared (coming soon)

BEHIND CLOSED DOORS

Her Sacred Oath